Deep River

ALSO BY SHUSAKU ENDO

The Final Martyrs
The Girl I Left Behind
The Samurai
The Sea and Poison
Stained Glass Elegies

SHUSAKU ENDO

Deep River

TRANSLATED BY VAN C. GESSEL

A NEW DIRECTIONS BOOK

Manufactured in the United States of America
New Directions Books are printed on acid-free paper
First published clothbound by New Directions in 1994 and as NDP820 in 1996.
Published by arrangement with Peter Owen Publishers, London

Library of Congress Cataloging-in-Publication Data

Endō, Shūsaku, 1923–
    [Dīpu ribā. English]
    Deep river / Shusaku Endo ; translated by Van C. Gessel.
        p.   cm.
    ISBN 978-0-8112-1320-2
    I. Gessel, Van C.   II.   Title
PL849.N4D5613   1995
895.6'35—dc20   94–38913
                                                                  CIP

Celebrating 60 years of publishing for James Laughlin
by New Directions Publishing Corporation
80 Eighth Avenue, New York 10011

15 14 13 12

CONTENTS

ONE The Case of Isobe   7

TWO The Informational Meeting   28

THREE The Case of Mitsuko   34

FOUR The Case of Numada   69

FIVE The Case of Kiguchi   84

SIX The City by the River   104

SEVEN Goddesses   127

EIGHT In Search of What Was Lost   148

NINE The River   169

TEN The Case of Ōtsu   182

ELEVEN Surely He Hath Borne Our Griefs   190

TWELVE Rebirth   194

THIRTEEN He Hath No Form Nor Comeliness   205

Deep River

Deep river, Lord:
I want to cross over
into campground

Negro spiritual

ONE

The Case of Isobe

Yaki imo-o. Yaki imo. Piping hot yaki imo-o.

Whenever Isobe reflected back on the moment when the doctor informed him that his wife had incurable cancer, the voice of a street vendor peddling roasted sweet potatoes below the window of the examination-room came back to his ears like a sneering mockery of his dismay.

A man's dull, happy-go-lucky crooning voice.

Yaki imo-o-o. Yaki imo. Piping hot yaki imo-o-o.

'This is the cancer right here. It has metastasized over here as well.' The doctor's finger crawled slowly across the X-ray, almost in rhythm to the potato vendor's voice. 'Surgery will be difficult, I'm afraid,' he explained in a monotone voice. 'We'll try chemotherapy and radiation, but…'

Isobe swallowed hard and asked, 'How much longer will she live?'

'Maybe three months.' The doctor averted his eyes. 'Four at best.'

'Will she be in much pain?'

'We can alleviate a certain amount of the physical pain with morphine.'

The two men were silent for a few moments. Then Isobe asked, 'Would it be all right to use the Maruyama vaccine and some other herbal medicines?'

'Of course. Go ahead and use any folk remedies you want.'

The doctor's uncomplicated approval suggested that there was no longer anything he could do for Isobe's wife.

Once again they lapsed into silence. Unable to bear it, Isobe rose to his feet, and the doctor shifted back towards the X-ray, but the sickening creak of his revolving chair sounded to Isobe like a declaration of his wife's impending death.

I must be ... dreaming.

It still seemed unreal to him as he walked to the elevator. The idea that his wife might actually die had never entered his thoughts. He felt as though he were watching a movie when suddenly a completely different film was projected on to the screen.

He peered vacantly at the sky, a gloomy colour that winter's evening. He could still hear the voice of the potato vendor outside. *Piping hot yaki imo.* He scanned his brain for the most convincing lie to tell his wife. She would surely see through the workings of his mind with the keen sensitivity of the afflicted. He sat in a chair beside the elevator doors. Two nurses walked past, chatting cheerfully together. Though they worked in a hospital, they were filled with a vigour and a youthfulness foreign to illness and sorrow.

He inhaled deeply and gripped the doorknob of her room tightly. She was sleeping with one arm resting across her chest.

He sat down on the single stool and mulled over the lie he was cooking up in his head. His wife languidly opened her eyes and, seeing her husband, smiled feebly.

'Did you talk to the doctor?'

'Um-hm.'

'What ... did he say?'

'You're going to have to stay in the hospital for three or four months. But he said you'd be a lot better after four months. So you've just got to tough it out a bit longer.'

Aware of the clumsiness of his lie, he felt a faint layer of perspiration beading on his forehead.

'Then I'll be making your life difficult for another four months.'

'Don't talk nonsense. You're no trouble at all.'

She smiled; he had never spoken so gently to her before. It was a smile all her own. When they were first married and Isobe came home from work exhausted from all the intricacies of human associations, she had been there as he opened the door to welcome him with this enfolding sort of smile.

'When you leave the hospital and have a chance to rest up and get much better . . .' – Isobe compounded his lie to cover the guilt he felt for his lifelong neglect of this woman – ' . . . we'll go to a hot springs resort.'

'You needn't spend so much money on me.'

'You needn't' – the words reverberated with the same subtle loneliness and sorrow as the voice of the potato vendor far off in the distance. Could it be that she knows everything?

Unexpectedly, as if muttering to herself, she announced, 'I've been looking at that tree for some time now.'

As she gazed through the window of her room, her eyes were directed far away towards a giant ginkgo tree that spread its many branches as though in an embrace.

'How long do you think that tree has been alive?'

'Maybe two hundred years, I'd guess. I imagine it must be the oldest tree around here.'

'The tree spoke. It said that life never ends.'

Even when she had been healthy, his wife had been in the habit every day of speaking like a little girl to each of her pots of flowers as she watered them on the veranda.

'Send me up some beautiful flowers.' 'Thank you for the beautiful flowers.' She had learned to conduct such conversations from her flower-loving mother, and she unashamedly continued the practice even after they were married. But the striking up of a conversation with the ancient ginkgo tree must mean that she had instinctively discerned the shadow veiling her own life.

'So now you're talking to trees?' He laughed at her to shield his own uneasiness. 'Well, why not? We've got some sense now of what's going to happen about your illness, so you can go ahead and have your chats every day with the ginkgo.'

'That's right,' she answered lifelessly. Then, as if sensing her own lack of enthusiasm, she stroked her haggard cheeks with her fingers.

A chime sounded. This signal announced the end of visiting hours. Carrying a paper sack filled with her dirty clothes in his hand, he rose from his chair.

'Well, I suppose I must be going.' He gave a deliberate yawn. Then, extending one hand, he gripped his wife's hand in his. Never once had he done anything so embarrassing before she entered the hospital. Like most Japanese husbands, he was ashamed to present any outward display of his love to his wife. Her wrist had grown decidedly thinner, providing evidence that death was subtly spreading through her body. She responded with her characteristic smile and said, 'You're getting enough to eat, aren't you? Take your laundry over to my mother's.'

'Right.'

He went out into the corridor. He felt as though chunks of lead had been jammed into his chest.

In one corner of the room a television with the volume turned down was broadcasting a vapid game show. Four young married couples were each tossing enormous pairs of dice; if their rolls totalled ten, they would win a three-day, two-night vacation to Hawaii.

Seated beside his sleeping wife, he peered absent-mindedly at the screen. A couple who had rolled a ten joyfully clutched each other's hands. Tiny scraps of confetti floated down from above their heads.

Somewhere in the room Isobe heard someone give a derisive laugh. He had the feeling that 'someone' was purposely parading a happy couple before him on the television just to intensify his agony.

Over many long years, Isobe had often been perplexed and confused by his work and by the interplay of human relations, but the situation in which he had now been placed was in a completely separate realm from that string of daily setbacks. Within three or four months, the wife sleeping before his eyes would most surely be dead. It was an eventuality that a man like Isobe had never considered. His heart felt heavy. He had no faith in any religion, but if there were any gods or buddhas to be contacted, he wanted to cry out to them: 'Why are you bringing this misery upon her? My wife's just an ordinary woman of goodness and gentleness. Please save her. I beg you.'

At the nurses' station Tanaka, the head nurse whose face was familiar to Isobe, was writing something on a chart. She glanced up and nodded towards him, her eyes brimming with compassion.

When he returned to his home in Ogikubo, his wife's mother, who lived nearby, was just putting his dinner into the refrigerator. He reported on his wife's condition, but he left the doctor's diagnosis nebulous. He lost courage when he reflected on the shock his mother-in-law would receive if he told her the truth.

'Dad'll be home early today, so I'd better get back.'

'Thanks for everything.'

'With her in the hospital, this house suddenly seems very large.'

'That's because she's so cheerful by nature.' Inwardly, he repeated his appeal to the gods. *She's plain, but she's a good woman. Please, you must save her.*

When his mother-in-law left, he was struck, just as she had observed, by the emptiness of his house, an emptiness he had not noticed before. It was because his wife wasn't there. Until a month earlier, it had seemed only natural to Isobe that his wife would be at home, and he had neither been particularly conscious of her presence nor even initiated a conversation with her unless there was something he wanted. They had not been able to have children of their own, so they had tried adopting a girl. She had not taken to them, and ultimately they felt as though they had failed. If there was some blame to be placed, it was on the taciturn Isobe, who found it difficult to speak kindly to his wife and daughter and to express his own feelings. His wife was the one who led conversations at the dinner-table, with his responses limited to an occasional 'Uh-huh' or 'That's fine.' Often she would sigh at him and complain, 'Can't you talk to her a little more?'

He began actually talking to his wife after she entered the hospital.

The doctor's prognosis was cruelly precise: less than a month after Isobe was given the news, she developed a fever and began to complain of internal pain. Still she struggled to smile, so as not to cause her husband any anguish, but her hair began to fall out after the radiation treatments, and she moaned faintly, evidently stricken with fierce, lightning-like pain whenever she shifted her body even slightly. Thanks to the chemotherapy, she immediately vomited up anything she ate.

Tormented to see her like this, Isobe entreated the doctor, 'Could you possibly give her morphine?'

'Yes, but if we don't time its use properly, it will simply hasten her demise.'

The doctor had contradicted his earlier comment. The policy at Japanese hospitals, where the goal of practising medicine is to prolong human life, is to draw out the patient's life for every possible day. Although Isobe realized that in the long run his wife could not be saved by such treatment, in his heart lurked the wish for her to live one extra hour, even one extra minute. Yet, when he thought of Keiko gritting her teeth to stop showing her pain, concerned no doubt for the effect her cries would have on her husband, he felt like saying, 'No more! Don't fight it any more.'

One day on his way home from work, when he opened the door to her room for the hundredth time, he was surprised to find her smiling at him.

'You wouldn't believe how relaxed I feel today. They gave me some special IV,' she reported in a spirited voice. 'It's like a miracle. I wonder what kind of medicine it is?'

'Maybe some new antibiotic.' *So they've started the morphine.*

'If this medicine works, I'll be able to leave the hospital sooner. And we can't afford this private room.'

'Don't worry about it. We can handle a month or two of private room bills.'

He had, however, already used up the money she had put into savings so they could take a trip to Spain and Portugal after his retirement. She considered this trip a substitute for the honeymoon they had not been able to take, and she had spread open a map and marked the unseen cities of Lisbon and Coimbra with red circles, which stood out like imprints of happiness. She had even asked Isobe, who had spent nearly two years at his company's American office, to teach her some simple English conversation phrases.

> Not telling the truth
> again today I went out
> of the hospital

> With a shudder, I
> open my eyes and think of
> life without my wife

Recently Isobe had written this wretched doggerel in his appointment book while waiting on a platform bench for his train to arrive. Since he didn't bet on horses or play mah-jong, his only meagre pleasures were drinking *sake*, composing miserable haiku, and playing *go*. He had never shown his poems to his wife. He was the kind of man who was embarrassed to reveal his own feelings openly in words or on his face, the kind of husband who hoped for a relationship in which his wife would understand him even if he did not utter a word.

> So slender it is,
> this outstretched arm of hers with
> its protruding veins

One Saturday evening when he arrived at the hospital earlier than usual after work, he discovered in his wife's room a woman with a broad forehead and large-pupilled eyes wearing a triangular cap on her head.

'She's a volunteer.' Cheerful because the morphine took away her pain, his wife Keiko introduced the woman to her husband. 'This is the first time I've seen a volunteer since I came here.'

'Is that so?' the woman asked as she stared at Isobe. 'The head nurse, Miss Tanaka, asked me to look after your wife. My name is Naruse.'

'Are you ... a housewife?'

'No, I was divorced when I was young. During the week I do something that passes for a real job, but on Saturday afternoons I'm part of the volunteer group here at the hospital.'

Isobe nodded as though interested in her explanation, but inwardly he was troubled. He was afraid that this amateur helper might inadvertently let slip to his wife the true name of her affliction.

'She knows all about how to take care of a patient. She was just helping me eat my supper.'

'Well, we'll put our trust in you.' Isobe bowed his head, putting emphasis on the word 'trust'.

'I'll leave you alone, then, now that your husband's here.'

Naruse Mitsuko nodded her head politely, picked up the tray with half the food still remaining, and left the room. From the way she spoke and the quiet way she closed the door, Isobe decided that she was a volunteer he could rely upon.

'She's good, isn't she?' Keiko sounded as though finding this woman had been her own doing. 'She graduated from the same university as you.'

'Why do you suppose someone like her ... does volunteer work here?'

'Because she's someone like her, silly. She knows all sorts of things.' With a woman's frank curiosity, she mused, 'I wonder why she got divorced?'

'How would I know? You shouldn't nose around in other people's business.' His voice sounded angry; inside, he was worried that the easy familiarity that can develop between women might prompt this volunteer to divulge Keiko's illness to her.

'The strangest thing happened.' Keiko seemed as though she were peering far off into the distance as she spoke to her husband. 'I fell asleep after my IV, and in my dreams I saw the living-room in our house, and I was looking at you from behind. After you'd boiled some water in the kitchen, you started getting ready for bed without turning off the gas to the stove. I yelled as loud as I could to warn you that if you left the teapot there and all the water boiled away, you could start a fire. . . . But you had this indifferent look on your face. I shouted to you over and over again. But then you turned out the bedroom light. . . .'

Isobe stared fixedly at the opening and closing of his wife's lips as she spoke. Everything she described in her dream had actually happened. The night before, after he turned out the bedroom light and fell asleep, he awoke to an indescribable apprehension in his heart. At that moment, he realized that he had left the gas on in the kitchen, and he sprang to his feet. When he scrambled into the kitchen, the teapot was glowing as red as a cherry.

'Really?'

'Yes. Why?'

Keiko listened with a nervous face as he explained what he had done. Then, with the look of one who has just awakened from a dream, she said, 'Well, perhaps I'm still good for something. They say that dreams can come true, and I suppose sometimes they do.'

Isobe worried that his wife talking to trees and having odd dreams might be an indication of how close death was approaching. When he was a child, his grandmother had told him that people who were about to die could see things that healthy people couldn't.

Her pain was abated with the morphine, but the debilitation of her body was so pronounced that Isobe recognized it even though he came to see her every day. But the morphine left her mind alert.

'Miss Naruse told me something interesting today. She said that scholars have acknowledged that dreams have various profound meanings. What did she say it was called? Oh, dream therapy. She told me that through my dreams I could understand what was in my unconscious mind. But that's all she'd tell me.'

Listening to her story, Isobe for some reason felt uneasy about the large-eyed Miss Naruse. There was something about her that made it seem as though she could see through to the very workings of Keiko's mind.

Once the vitality that the morphine provided suddenly drained away, like the evening glow on a summer's day that flares up for just an instant before darkness takes over, Keiko had to wear an oxygen mask constantly, and her breathing was agitated as she slept. One Saturday evening when he noiselessly opened the door, she lay with her eyes clamped painfully shut, an intravenous needle stabbing into her arm, while beside her the woman volunteer was rubbing her legs. When Keiko heard her husband come in she opened her eyes lethargically, but she no longer flashed her trade-mark smile. In a wispy voice she mumbled, 'I feel like I'm falling . . . to the bottom of the earth.' Then she went back to sleep. There was no change in the volunteer's expression as she looked at the patient. He felt as though that icy gaze were saying 'There's no more hope', and an inexpressible pain seized him.

'How has she been today?'

'She was able to talk a little.'

'She doesn't know what's happening.' He lowered his voice to a whisper. 'I haven't said anything to her. I'd appreciate your co-operation.'

'I understand. But . . .' Mitsuko said softly, 'your wife may already know. Patients with terminal cancer are far more aware of their approaching death than people around them imagine.'

'She's never said a word to suggest anything like that,' he protested, making sure that his wife was still sound asleep.

Mitsuko's voice continued to run cold as she said, 'That's just out of her consideration for you.'

'You have some cruel things to say, don't you?'

'I'm sorry. But, as a volunteer, I've seen many similar cases.'

'What did my wife talk to you about today?'

'She was worried about how helpless you'd be without her.'

'She was?'

'And she said something peculiar. She said her conscious mind had slipped out of her body and was looking down from the ceiling at the shell of her body lying on the bed.'

'Do you think that's the side-effects of her medicine?'

'It could be. But once in a while patients in the final stages of their cancer have the same experience. None of the doctors or nurses believe them, of course.'

This phenomenon struck Isobe as a portent of his wife's death. Again today the sky was dark grey beyond the window, and he could hear the dull-witted voice of the potato vendor outside the hospital. The pedlar could have no idea what impact his torpid voice had on those who heard it. A scene from Lisbon, with pots of thriving flowers in every window. The shores of the sea at Nazareth, with women in black

15

robes mending their nets on the pure-white beach. If his wife were
going to see apparitions, he would rather she saw these kinds of scenes
instead of her own corporeal shell stretched out upon the bed.

This incident of the mind fleeing the body was, after all, an omen
that the end was near.

The doctor called him over to the nurses' station. 'I think we've got
another four or five days. If you're going to send for any relatives . . .'

'Four or five days?'

Behind his glasses, the doctor lowered his eyes. The pocket of his
soiled examination coat was crammed with ballpoint pens, thermo-
meters and the like. At times such as this, he had no desire to see the
expressions on the faces of his patients' families.

'So soon?' Isobe spoke the meaningless words with lingering hope,
though he had not forgotten for a single day that the doctor had ini-
tially predicted she would live only three or four months.

'Will she remain conscious until the end?'

'That's hard to say. Very likely she'll go into a coma two or three
days beforehand.'

'She won't die in pain, will she?'

'We'll do everything we can to relieve her suffering.'

Finally that day had come pressing in before his eyes. 'Desolation'
would not be the proper word to describe his feelings now; it was
more the sense of emptiness he imagined he might feel standing all
alone on the surface of the moon. Bearing up against that hollow feeling, he quietly gripped the doorknob of her room. Nurse Tanaka and
a young assistant were constructing an oxygen tent.

'Ah, your husband's here.' The veteran nurse spoke encouragingly.

'Darling.' With a flutter of her hand she summoned her husband to
her bedside, then pointed to the table next to her pillow. 'When it's
over . . . look through the diary in here.'

'I will.'

The two nurses knew enough to leave the room, after which Keiko
said, 'Thank you for these many years. . . .'

'Don't talk nonsense.' Isobe turned his head away. 'You silly woman,
you talk as though you're near death or something.'

'I'm sorry. But I know what's happening. By tomorrow, I may not
be able to talk at all.'

There was no more time for shame or embarrassment. Tomorrow
the partner he had lived with for thirty-five years could well be leaving this world.

16

He sat in the chair next to her bed and stared silently at his wife's face. He was weary, but a far deeper exhaustion clouded her face. Sluggishly she opened her eyes a crack and looked at her husband, but it seemed even that caused her pain, and once again she closed them.

Nurse Tanaka came back into the room and placed a new oxygen mask on her face.

'If this bothers you, you can take it off. But this one will be more comfortable for you.'

Keiko did not respond. With her eyes still closed, she continued to breathe, her shoulders heaving.

She slipped into a coma that night. From time to time she would mutter something deliriously. Isobe could do nothing but sit beside her and clutch her hand. Doctors and nurses in endless succession tested her blood pressure, gave her injections, checked her pulse. Isobe contacted her father, mother and younger brother who all lived in Tokyo.

As he hung up the pay-phone and was about to return to her room, a young nurse came running down the hallway towards him. 'Sir, she's calling you. Please hurry.'

When he entered the room, Nurse Tanaka opened the oxygen tent and said in an agitated voice, 'She's trying to say something. Put your ear right up to her mouth.'

'It's me. Me! Do you understand?'

Isobe placed his ear directly by her mouth. In a gasping voice, she was desperately struggling to say something in fits and starts.

'I . . . I know for sure . . . I'll be reborn somewhere in this world. Look for me . . . find me . . . promise . . . promise!'

She spoke the words 'promise . . . promise!' more forcefully than the others, as though these final words were her last desperate plea.

Several days passed as if in a dream. Despite his every effort, he could not convince himself that his wife was actually dead. Over and over again he told himself, *She's gone off on a trip with a friend, she'll be back soon.* Three days later, when the swarm of black automobiles came to a halt in front of the crematorium near the Kōshū highway and the clusters of survivors were swallowed into the building as though on a conveyor belt, and even when they sat waiting their turn for the ceremonies, the same sorts of thoughts filled Isobe's mind. Through the window of the waiting-room he could see the plume of smoke rising from the crematorium's tall chimney, but it reminded him of nothing more than the overcast skies he had often seen from her hospital window. *She's off on a trip,* he mumbled in the general direction of the smoke. *When she gets back from her trip, life will all return to normal.* Disconnected from his thoughts, his lips formed words of appreciation to speak to the assembled mourners.

An attendant came in to announce the beginning of the cremation. Before long, a middle-aged man dressed in a uniform and cap stood in front of Isobe and flipped the switch to the furnace, and a sound like the bullet train rumbling across a steel bridge filled the room. *What is happening? What are they doing?* Even at this point the dumbfounded Isobe had no idea. 'Now if you'll please use these chopsticks to collect the bones and place them in this urn,' the uniformed man declared without expression, sliding out a large black box. Isobe could not bring himself to believe that the strangely pallid fragments of bone strewn in the box were those of his wife. *What the hell is this? What are we doing?* He mumbled to himself as he stood beside his weeping mother-in-law and several other female relatives. *This isn't her.*

The funeral urn was wrapped in a white cloth and, holding it in his arms, Isobe returned to his house with the family members and the Buddhist priest. When he entered the house, the furniture they had sat on together, and the favourite household items she had often used, were arranged just where she had placed them when she was alive. The women in the family began serving plates and bowls of food and glasses of beer to the guests.

'After we hold the seventh-day memorial service,' one relative, the foam from his beer still frothing on his face, observed, 'the next will be the forty-ninth day observance, won't it?' Since this fellow had taken charge of all the arrangements for the funeral, his mind seemed to be full of nothing but the remaining obligations.

'What day next month will the forty-ninth day fall on?'

'It's a Wednesday.'

'I know you're all very busy, so please leave everything to me. We'll handle it with the utmost circumspection.'

'But, Your Reverence,' another man questioned the priest, 'why is it that this gathering is held on the forty-ninth day in Buddhism?'

'Let me explain.' Fingering the rosary beads on his lap, the bald-headed priest had a look of pride as he offered his response. 'In Buddhist teachings, when an individual dies, their spirit goes into a state of limbo. Limbo means that they have not yet been reincarnated, and they wander uneasily about this world of men. Then, after seven days, they slip into the conjoined bodies of a man and a woman and are reborn as a new existence. That is why we have the observance on the seventh day after death.'

'I see.' Hearing this explanation for the first time, the men sat staring at the priest, clutching their glasses of beer.

'So it's every seven days, is it?'

'That's right. And no matter how slow the person is in getting reincarnated, by the forty-ninth day they invariably attain new life by being reborn as someone's child. . . .'

'Hmm.' As one, the group emitted what was either a sigh of curiosity or of relief, but not one of them really believed anything the priest was saying.

'I see. So that's why at Buddhist temples after a funeral they're always talking about the forty-ninth day this, the forty-ninth day that,' one of the group volunteered, but inwardly they all regarded this as a simple money-making measure on the part of the temples.

His wife's delirious ravings echoed in Isobe's ears: 'I know for sure . . . I'll be reborn somewhere in this world. Look for me . . . find me. . . .'

As Isobe sat lost in recollection of those words, the gentle priest came up to him, and with a bow of his head said, 'I have finished my duties, so I'll be leaving now.'

When everyone had finally gone, Isobe opened up the two travelling bags he had brought back from the hospital. They contained the items his wife had used while she was there. A dressing-gown, a négligé, underwear, a towel, her toiletries, a clock – and included among all these, the diary she had written in the hospital. It was a small notebook covered in black leather that M. Bank handed out for publicity to all its customers at the year's end. He felt a clutching in his chest as he opened the first page.

> Your kimonos and winter clothing: in the paulownia wood box marked A in the closet.
>
> Your spring and autumn kimonos, summer wear, and formal kimonos: in the paulownia box marked B.
>
> Be sure to brush your kimonos and have them cleaned at the end of each season.
>
> Your sweaters and cardigans are in paulownia box C.
>
> I've explained all of this to my mother.

Our savings passbook and personal seal are in a box at the bank, along with our stock certificates and real estate title papers.
If you have any questions, talk to the branch manager, Mr Inoue, at M. Bank, or to our attorney, Mr Sugimoto.

His eyes clouded over, and Isobe hesitated turning the page. On every page his wife had noted down, one after the other, all the daily instructions her husband would need in order to avoid problems after she was dead. *Be sure to turn off the gas before you go to bed; here's how to clean the bath-tub* – these were all tasks that he had left to his wife until now. She had explained each of them in simple detail.

'Do you think I'll be able to do this?' he bellowed towards the memorial tablet and photograph of his wife hanging in the living-room. 'You can't just leave the house like this.... Come back... at once!'

Some twenty days before she died, she had made the following notation, almost like a memo to herself rather than a journal entry:

22 January
Cloudy. Another IV today. The veins in my arms have pretty much collapsed by now, and my arms are covered with blackish bruises from the haemorrhaging. I've been talking to the ginkgo tree outside my window.

'Mr Ginkgo, I'll be dying soon. I envy you. You've been alive for over two hundred years now.'

'I wither too, when winter comes. Then in spring, I come back to life.'

'But what about people?'

'People are just like us. Though you die once, you return to life again.'

'Return to life? But how?'

'Eventually you'll understand,' the tree replied.

25 January
When I think of my clumsy husband, who won't have anyone to look after him when I'm gone... I'm filled with concern.

27 January
In a lot of pain until evening. I can handle the physical pain with the medication, but my mind... my mind grows weary from the fear of death.

30 January
Miss Naruse came as a volunteer today. She always seems so

serene and so much in control that I end up telling her all the
worries and secrets I can't convey to my husband.

'I realize that I'm probably going to die. I haven't said
anything to my husband, but...'

She had the good grace to smile in response. It was just like her
not to offer any empty words of denial or consolation.

'Miss Naruse, do you believe in rebirth?'

'Rebirth?'

'Do you think it's true that, once a person dies, she can be born
again into this world?'

She stared straight at me for a moment, but she did not nod her
head.

'I can't get rid of the feeling that I'm going to be reborn and
meet up with my husband again.'

Miss Naruse turned her eyes towards the window. To the scene
I had grown accustomed to seeing day after day after day. The
giant ginkgo tree.

'I have no idea,' Miss Naruse muttered. She picked up my
dinner-tray and left the room. From behind, she looked hard and
cold.

The empty days continued in procession. He stayed late at work,
delaying the time of his return home, in an effort to fill the hollow
cavity in his heart. He managed somehow to bandage his melancholy
by taking his late-working chums at the office out for dinner and
drinks. But it pained him to have to return home and look at the items
his wife had used. Her slippers, her teacup, her chopsticks, the family
budget book, her brief scribblings in the phone book. Every time his
eyes rested on these mementoes, a pain like a stab from an awl punctured his chest.

Sometimes he would wake up in the middle of the night. There in
the darkness he would try to persuade himself that his wife was sleeping
in the next bed.

'Hey. Hey!' he would call out. 'Hey, are you asleep?'

The only response, finally, was black silence, black emptiness, black
loneliness.

'When are you coming back from your trip? How long do you plan
to desert this house?'

In the darkness he would close his eyes and project images of his
wife's face on to the backs of his eyelids. *Where are you, you idiot?*

What are you doing, abandoning your husband like this ...?
'I know for sure ... I'll be reborn somewhere in this world. Look for me ... find me.' Her final ravings continued to ring in the depths of his ears, like a distinct echo.

But Isobe could not bring himself to believe that something so outlandish could happen. Because he lacked any religious conviction, like most Japanese, death to him meant the extinction of everything. The only part of her that was still enduring was the daily items in the house that she had used while she was alive.

When you were still here, Isobe thought, *death seemed so far removed from me. It was as though you stood with both arms outstretched, keeping death from me. But now that you're gone, suddenly it seems right here in front of me.*

The only course left him was to go once every other week to the cemetery at Aoyama, where he would splash water on the Isobe family grave-marker, change the flowers and press his hands together in prayer. This was the only response he could offer to his wife's plea to 'look for me, find me'.

December came. He could not bear spending the holidays in an empty house that was on the brink of disarray, precisely because his late wife had been so fond of the decorations and the special delicacies of the New Year. To his great relief, a niece who was living in Washington DC wrote and invited him to spend his holiday period in the United States. Isobe accepted the invitation, hoping to find some relief from the loneliness that persisted, no matter how busy he kept himself.

He had lived for a time in Washington when he was still single. He drove around the city in his niece's car, but little seemed to have changed. His niece's husband, a researcher at the Georgetown University medical centre, took Isobe to his office on the campus, which reminded him of an old European university, and he walked through the college town, which felt like walking back into the nineteenth century. One evening he found a book on the kitchen counter at his niece's: it was a best-seller written by the famous film star Shirley MacLaine, complete with a photograph of the author on the cover.

'This is Shirley MacLaine, is it?' Isobe asked. 'I really liked her in the early days. I understand she's quite taken with Japan.'

'This is a very popular book right now,' his niece replied.

'What's it about?'

'She writes about her quest for her previous lives.'

22

'This niece of yours believes in all that nonsense.' Her husband smiled sarcastically. 'Her bookshelf is filled with this kind of stuff – books on New Age science and the like.' With the logic of a doctor, he explained that in America a wave of exaggerated interest in the paranormal and in near-death experiences had recently turned into something of a social craze.

'The good doctor here can only think rationally about everything.' Her cheeks puffed out in displeasure. 'There's all kinds of things in the world you can't explain away with rational argument.'

'That's only because they can't be explained yet. Some day science will decipher them all.'

'But,' Isobe, who had been listening quietly, interjected, 'this book by Shirley MacLaine – well, frankly, I have to admit I don't believe in a previous life or anything – why has it become a best-seller? I'm more interested in the answer to that.'

'There, you see?' Isobe's niece seemed to mistake his curiosity for support of her views. 'I hear that research into these kinds of things has been conducted in all seriousness at American universities ever since the Vietnam War.'

'Only by psychologists who know nothing about science, and some New Age philosophers,' her husband sneered. 'I'm told that there are some people studying this business of previous lives at the University of Virginia.'

'There certainly are. A book by a scholar named Stevenson at the University of Virginia is number three on the best-seller list at our local bookstore.'

'Who's this Stevenson fellow?'

'I haven't read his book yet, but apparently this professor and his staff are collecting data on children from all over the world who claim to have memories of their previous lives, and they're doing a full-scale study of them.'

Sipping the mixed drink she had fixed for him, her husband shrugged his shoulders. This is just too stupid even to talk about, he seemed to be signalling.

Isobe twirled his glass with one hand, once again hearing his wife's final words.

Had she seriously believed in a former life, or in a life to come? A part of her had been naïve enough to carry on conversations with trees and flowers, and to believe in prescient dreams, and Isobe was inclined to think that her rambling comments had been nothing more than the product of an earnest yearning.

But that notion made him realize, with an attendant clutching pain in his chest, how important he had been to his wife throughout her life.

He had not the slightest feelings of endorsement for anything like an afterlife or reincarnation. Like his niece's husband, he had smiled and nodded when she got worked up over her description of the MacLaine book, but he had not meant any of it.

With a yawn, his niece's husband tried to bring the conversation to an end. 'Why do women like to talk about such things?'

'Well, my dead wife also...' Isobe started to say, but he stopped himself. Although he did not believe in them, his wife's last words remained a meaningful secret he did not want to reveal to anyone else. They were like a precious memento his wife had bequeathed to him.

While he was killing time in the gift shop at the Washington airport on the day of his departure, he discovered both Shirley MacLaine's *Out on a Limb* and Professor Stevenson's *Children Who Remember Previous Lives* propped in a corner of the display window, labelled as best-sellers. This seemed less like a coincidence than the workings of some invisible power, and though he still did not believe the preposterous things his niece had talked about, he couldn't stifle the feeling that his dead wife had been pushing him from behind, directing him towards the display window. Without even thinking, he bought the books.

He began reading on the plane. A Pan Am stewardess who brought him a drink glanced at the cover of the MacLaine book and said, 'That's a really interesting book. I was fascinated by it.' His niece's claims had been right on target.

Isobe, however, was more impressed with the results of Professor Stevenson's research. The professor reported on a variety of field studies, and there was something trustworthy in the way that he judiciously and objectively noted that 'While these phenomena have unquestionably occurred, we cannot conclude on the basis of these experiences that individuals have had a previous life.' Reading this persuasive study, Isobe began to feel just a glimmer of faith in his wife's last words.

Dear Mr Osamu Isobe
Thank you for your letter of 25 May. I'll try to respond to the questions you raised.

Here at the University of Virginia, we have been conducting studies on life after death under the guidance of Professor Ian Stevenson since 1962. At Professor Stevenson's direction, we have searched out children under the age of three from many nations who claim to have recollections of a previous existence, and we have been collecting testimonials from these children, as well as objective statements from their parents and siblings, and even information regarding their physical characteristics. Our studies form just a part of the research that has been done since the Vietnam War to cast light on near-death or out-of-body experiences, paranormal powers, and other areas of investigation that have borne fruit in the United States.

At the present time, the conditions we place upon instances of 'reincarnation' that have become the objects of our study are as follows:

(1) instances for which a considerable amount of evidence supporting the veracity of the claims exists, which cannot be explained away as clairvoyance, telepathy, or subconscious memory;

(2) instances in which the subject possesses a sophisticated talent (such as speaking a foreign language or playing a musical instrument) which they clearly could not have learned in their present life;

(3) instances in which the subject has markings in the same location as wounds which they received in the previous life they are remembering;

(4) instances in which those experiences labeled as memories display no significant reduction in clarity as the subject ages, and which do not have to be induced through hypnotic trance;

(5) instances in which a large number of the survivors and friends from the subject's past life confirm the person's reincarnation over a long period of time;

(6) instances in which the identification between the subject and the past personality cannot be explained through the influence of parents or other individuals (the reason we put greatest emphasis upon children under the age of three is that at later ages there is an increased possibility that children will confuse and hallucinate random conversations between adults with their own memories).

We insist upon these rigorous conditions because our research has nothing to do with the occult, with obscure religious movements, or with clairvoyants, but is first and foremost an objective, scholarly study.

I should add that in no sense have we concluded at the present time that human beings are in fact 'reincarnated'. We have simply reported the fact that phenomena suggesting the possibility of 'reincarnation' have been isolated in many nations of the world.

We have collected over 1600 cases of 'reincarnation', but, unfortunately, we have only one case in which the subject claimed that her previous life was spent as a Japanese. The details of the case are as follows.

A girl by the name of Ma Tin Aung Myo, who was born in the village of Nathul in Burma in December of 1953, began to talk incessantly about her previous life from the time she was about four years old. One day while she was out walking with her father, she saw an airplane flying overhead and began to wail and shout, displaying evident terror. Thereafter she showed extreme fear whenever she saw an airplane, and when her father questioned her about it, she said it was because she knew she would be shot at. Then she became downcast and began to plead, 'I want to go to Japan.'

With the passage of time she began to reveal that she had been born in the northern part of Japan, that she was married and had children (the number would sometimes vary with the telling), that she was drafted into the army, and while stationed in Nathul, when she was preparing to cook a meal beside a pile of firewood, an enemy plane appeared overhead. She – that is, the Japanese soldier – was standing there in a pair of shorts with a waist-band wrapped around her stomach, when the enemy plane suddenly did a steep dive and began strafing the ground with machine-gun fire. She ran and hid behind the pile of firewood, but a bullet struck her in the groin and she died instantly.

That is the story told by Ma Tin Aung Myo. She later claimed she has the feeling that she ran a small shop in Japan before she was drafted, and that in the army she had cook's duty, and that the Japanese troops were in the process of withdrawing from Burma when she was killed.

Her story does not include the name of the Japanese soldier, or any of the names of his family or the places where he lived. She does, however, dislike Burmese food, and prefers sweet foods and a curry derived from very sugary coconuts. She says over and over that she wants to go back to Japan where her children are, or that she wants to go to Japan when she grows up. Her family reports that Ma Tin Aung Myo mutters to herself in a language they cannot comprehend, but we don't know whether it is Japanese or just some infantile babblings. Strangely enough, she has a scar in the groin area, in exactly the same location where she claims she was shot in her previous life. For more details on this case, I would encourage you to read Professor Stevenson's research report.

I will, of course, be happy to contact you should we come across any more cases in our research in which the subject claims to have been Japanese in a previous existence.

Sincerely,

John Osis

Human Personality Research Division
Department of Psychology
University of Virginia School of Medicine

TWO

The Informational Meeting

'The sacred river Ganges purifies the heart as it wanders through the maze-like market-places where men and animals clamour. India, where in ancient days civilization flowered on the banks of the Indus.'

Video images were projected one after another on to the screen: the Taj Mahal, looking like a white teacup turned upside-down; an old Brahmin monk with red markings on his forehead; an Indian dance with erotic hand movements. The elderly composed well over half of the twenty or so men and women gathered to hear a description of the tour of Buddhist holy sites on which they would be embarking in another two weeks.

To the accompaniment of coughs and quietly shifting bodies, slides depicting scenery that all looked very much the same, and Hindu temples that all looked very much alike, flashed on the screen. Broad streets in Bombay and Calcutta, almost reeking of the smells of sweat and body odours of the masses; Buddhist holy spots such as Lumbini, Kapilavastu, Buddh-Gaya and Sarnath. It seemed strange to Mitsuko to think that, though it was now autumn in Japan, in less than three weeks she would be walking this land beneath the hot light of the sun.

The lights came on. Mitsuko, sensing the smells of the other people's breathing mingled with the air of the auditorium, pulled a handkerchief from her purse. A man seated in front of her turned round when he smelled the cologne that scented her handkerchief. A look of surprise appeared on his face.

'Now your tour guide, Mr Enami, will discuss some items you should be aware of to enjoy your trip. Please refer to the handout we've given you.'

A man who looked to be thirty-four or -five, wearing round-rimmed glasses, stood in front of the screen and introduced himself. 'My name is Enami, and I'll be your guide. I was a student in India for about four years. During that time, I was able to lead tours for this same Cosmos Tours company, and from my experience there are three things I'd like to bring to your attention. The first is the water. When we get to India, please be sure not to drink any unboiled water. I would encourage you either to drink water that has been boiled, or to drink cola or juice. Some of our customers have ordered iced water or a whisky on the rocks at the hotel and ended up with terrible stomach problems because of the ice.'

He went on to describe the unique ways of using a toilet in India and explained that the left hand was considered unclean. He cautioned against patting children on the head with the left hand, and added that they did not need to tip for services unless they made special requests for assistance. Following precisely the items printed on the handout, he explained how to look out for thieves.

'In India there is a religious system of social ranking known as the caste system. They call it *varna jati*. It is very complex, and I can't explain it in simple terms. But it would probably be useful for you to know that there is a group of people who do not fit into even the lowest varna. These people are known as outcasts or as untouchables. Today the untouchables are called Harijans, a perfunctory title that means "children of God", but in reality they are a people who have been subjected to bigotry from early times. As you witness this discrimination on your trip, it may be disturbing to you, but please bear in mind that there is a long religious and historical background to this situation.'

When he had finished giving various suggestions for the trip, he encouraged questions from the group.

'Excuse me, but so that we can get to know each other better, when you ask a question, could you please state your name?'

Two or three people raised their hands.

'My name is Numada. I would very much like to visit a wild bird sanctuary. Is there a chance I could spend a little extra time in Agra or Bharatpur?'

'This tour is of the holy Buddhist sites, but you are all free if you want to stay over in a particular town and then rejoin the group later. You're fond of animals, are you?'

'Yes.'

'India itself is like a great natural animal sanctuary. Everywhere you look there are monkeys and mongooses and tigers. And let's not forget the cobras.' Everyone laughed. 'If you do decide to remain in a particular place, however, we would ask that you stay in a hotel that we designate. If you eat elsewhere, you'll be charged an extra fee.'

'I understand.'

After a woman asked about the climate and the appropriate clothing for this season in India, an elderly man raised his hand.

'Is it possible to request a memorial service at one of the temples in India?'

'When you say temple, I assume you're talking not about a Hindu temple but a Buddhist temple? I'm sorry, but your name is . . . ?'

'Kiguchi.'

'Mr Kiguchi, is there any particular type of memorial service you are interested in?'

'No, but I lost a lot of friends during the war in the fighting in Burma, and I fought against some Indian soldiers myself, so I thought maybe I could request a memorial service on behalf of comrade and foe alike. . . .'

The group was silenced for a few moments.

'I can't promise anything, but generally I think those can be arranged. I should add one thing. In India today, adherents of the Hindu religion make up an overwhelming majority, followed by Muslims, while Buddhism has all but disappeared. Nominally the number of Buddhists is said to be around three million, but in reality a large number of the Buddhist devout are to be found among the untouchable class. To put it another way, the people at the lowest level of society, those who do not fit into any of the social classifications, have sought salvation in Buddhism, which teaches the equality of all mankind. The caste system has, in any case, been a pillar that has supported Hinduism and supported Indian society, and as a result Buddhism has weakened there.'

This came as a surprise to the group. Their main purpose in travelling to India was to visit famous locales associated with Buddhism, and the impression was strong in their minds that India was the land of the Buddha, the land of Sakyamuni.

'What is it then that the Hindus believe?' a guileless elderly woman asked. She was setting out on this Buddhist pilgrimage with her husband.

'Your name, please?'

'It's Okubo.'

'Thank you. Hinduism is very complex, and I can't explain it in simple terms. I think the best way is to have you look at the images of their gods after we actually arrive there. They believe in many different gods, and let me show you a few slides right now.'

A peculiar female image was projected on to the screen. With one foot she trampled on the corpse of a man, and her neck was adorned not with a necklace but with severed human heads that she had flung over her shoulder with one of her four arms.

'This is a representation of the goddess Kālī, which often adorns temples and homes in India. The holy mother Mary in Christianity is a symbol of tender maternal love, but the goddesses of India are for the most part called earth-mother goddesses, and while they are gentle deities at times, they are also fearsome beings. There is one goddess in particular, Chāmundā, who has taken upon herself all of the sufferings of the people of India. I want to be sure to take all of you to see her image.'

When the lights came on, Mrs Okubo exclaimed, 'Whoo, that was scary!', making everyone chuckle.

'Well, we've run past our allotted time, so we'll close this meeting. Thank you all for your patience.' Enami pushed his thick glasses up his nose and again bowed awkwardly.

When Mitsuko stood up and was about to start out of the auditorium with the rest of the group, the man who had been sitting in front of her called out, 'Aren't you Miss Naruse?'

'Yes.'

'Don't you remember me? My name's Isobe – you took care of my wife in hospital.'

The serene woman with terminal cancer and the husband who visited her nearly every day surfaced from the depths of Naruse Mitsuko's memory.

'You did a great deal for her then. But I never thought I'd run into you again in a place like this.'

Isobe peered at Mitsuko as though he were searching her for some memory of his wife, and she found his gaze stifling.

'It looks like we'll be travelling to India together. What a coincidence.'

It was clear that she was trying to change the subject, so Isobe said, 'I had no idea you were interested in visiting Buddhist holy sites.'

'I don't have any particular interest in Buddhism.' She smiled non-committally. Images of the goddesses who sought after human sacrifices and blood were still etched upon her eyelids. She herself had no real sense of what she wanted to see in India. Perhaps she wanted to superimpose upon herself images of goddesses who combined good and evil, brutality and love. No. That wasn't all. There was one more thing she sought.

'I thought your interest was in France, Miss Naruse.'

'Why did you think that?'

'I remember my wife saying something of the sort.'

'I did go to France once, but I don't like the place much.'

Mitsuko's unembellished response deflated Isobe, and he said nothing for a moment. She realized the severity in her tone and said, 'I'm sorry, I shouldn't be so impudent. Are you just going to India as a tourist, Mr Isobe?'

'Well, that's part of it.' He looked perplexed. 'I'm going in search of something. It's really a sort of treasure-hunt.'

'Everyone seems to be going to India with different feelings. There was that fellow who's interested in animals, and the man who wants a memorial service for his war comrades.'

The pavement was strewn with dirty brown leaves that had fallen from the roadside trees. A line of taxis was parked in front of the door, and an American woman curiously examined a toy at an open-air shop. Mitsuko felt burdened by Isobe, who still seemed to want to talk, so she said, 'I must be going. I'll see you again at Narita Airport.'

'We're supposed to be there by ten-thirty, wasn't it?'

'Yes, two hours before departure.'

She bowed and climbed into one of the waiting taxis. Through the window Isobe's solitary figure retreated into the distance. The way he carried his shoulders and slouched his back were the very image of a lonely man who has lost his wife.

The taxi raced past the university that Mitsuko had attended, heading towards the intersection at Yotsuya. The leaves of the phoenix trees were a wilted yellow. When they stopped for the signal, she could see the snack-bar called Allo-Allo she had frequented in her college days, unchanged from those times. For a moment she was drawn into her memories of those easy-going days when she had first come to Tokyo from her home in the Kansai. In those days her friends had all called her Moïra. In this snack-bar she had tossed back glass after glass of *sake* with her boy-friends. She had been a foolish student then, imagining that these days spent with her classmates constituted some sort of 'youth'. Even at that time, unlike her school-friends who thought only of the commonplace lives they would be leading in the years ahead, she had wanted to live fully. But at a point in time when she had not yet realized the difference between the two, that pierrot had appeared before her. That fellow Ōtsu she had trifled with....

THREE
The Case of Mitsuko

When she was a student in the French literature department of her university, all of her friends called her Moïra. Half in jest, they had taken the nickname from the heroine in Julien Green's novel, *Moïra*, which they were using as a text in their French language class.

Partly for the fun of it, the young woman Moïra seduces the puritanical student Joseph, who is renting a room in her family's house. Because the university Mitsuko attended was operated by a male Catholic order, a few of the students had received Christian baptism. There was something about these Christian students that made the other male students at the university look down on them as unapproachable, impossible to get along with, and boorish. They were not actually discriminated against, but most of them were regarded as somehow undesirable companions.

At a party one evening, a couple of younger men tried to spur Mitsuko into action.

'Hey, I know something that'd be fun. Why don't you come on to that fellow Ōtsu?'

'What department is he in?'

'He's in philosophy. He's the sort of fellow you feel like playing a joke on just by looking at him. The kind who can't bring himself to talk to a woman. I'm willing to bet he's a virgin.'

'Is he that timid?'

'That's why you'd be just the person to sweeten him up, Miss Naruse.'

'But what for?'

'He's always got a big grin on his face, trying to get everybody to like him. One look at him, and I'm positive you'll want to torment him, Miss Naruse. You know what I'm talking about, don't you?'

At that particular time, the student movement that momentarily rocked the university had finally petered out, and a feeling of emptiness had settled over a majority of the student body. Mitsuko herself was at the age where she wanted to stretch her wings. Motivated by an inferiority complex for having come to Tokyo from a small town, she prevailed upon her father, who blinked at his daughter's self-indulgence, and thanks to him she was able to rent an apartment that was luxurious for a student. She gathered a group of friends around her, and together they went out drinking brandy, which most of the rest could not afford, and drove around in her sports car. Yet there was always a hollowness in her heart. Whenever the young men told her she held her liquor well, or that her car was flashy, a feeling something like anger or desolation directed towards herself but inexpressible in words issued forth from the depths of her heart.

'Well, I might, if I feel like it.'

'So seduce him the way Moïra seduced Joseph. Using a key or something. . . .'

There is a scene in *Moïra* in which the heroine deliberately places the key to Joseph's room between her breasts. To retrieve his key, Joseph has no choice but to touch Moïra's breasts. The young men jokingly suggested a similar ploy to Miss Naruse.

That was one of the many irresponsible conversations she enjoyed during her second year in college. Among university students in Tokyo, it was commonplace for young women to drink *sake*, to smoke cigarettes and to engage in such banter.

But that was all there was to it, and she gave no more thought to Ōtsu. To her, a joke exchanged at a party was forgotten when the party ended, and it evaporated from her mind like the candy-floss she had bought at festivals as a child.

A couple of weeks passed. In a chair near the centre of the library Mitsuko was thumbing through a dictionary, wrestling with the final scene of *Moïra* which she had to translate in class the following day. Suddenly someone poked her in the back. When she turned round, two lower classmen brought their faces close to hers, as though they were about to reveal some vital secret.

'There's Ōtsu.'

'Ōtsu? Who? Oh, him?'

'Over there next to that pillar, can you see the fellow writing something down with a dead-serious look on his face? That's him.'

Even now, after many long years had passed, Mitsuko could still remember the profiled face of Ōtsu she had seen that day. By their day most university students had stopped wearing uniforms, but the chubby Ōtsu had removed only the stiff-collared, rustic jacket of his student uniform and sat in his chair with the sleeves of his white shirt rolled up. He looked for all the world like a steadfast bank employee perched at his desk, counting each precious banknote one by one.

'So I'm supposed to get something going with that sweat-hog?'

'You can understand why we want to goad him on, can't you?'

It was true: there was always a male student or two at the university who provoked in a woman the urge to torment him. Ōtsu's bumpkin look roused just that sort of feeling in the women at this university.

'You haven't forgotten what you promised us at the party, have you? Every night you can find him in the chapel, saying his prayers.'

'And I'm supposed to drag him down the path of degradation, right? I'll think it over.'

Suddenly she took a dislike to having these lower classmen jabbing her casually in the back, and she coldly dismissed them. Mitsuko still had no desire to approach Ōtsu as a joke.

Her classmates, however, had one more plan for toying with Ōtsu.

When it reached closing-time, Mitsuko got up and started down the stairs. Ōtsu was standing in the doorway, clutching to his chest a soiled collection of books wrapped in a *furoshiki*.

'Excuse me.... My name is Ōtsu,' he called to her in a craven voice.

'What?'

'Kondō said you wanted to talk to me about something.'

Kondō, of course, was the student who had pointed out Ōtsu's seat to Mitsuko.

'I have nothing to say to you,' she replied callously. 'They're all just playing a trick on you.'

'On me? Kondō and his friends?' Ōtsu nodded. 'So that's it.'

'You aren't angry?'

'I'm used to it, ever since I was a child. Being made fun of.' An affable smile, like a full moon rising, crested on his spherical cheeks.

'It's because you're too serious about everything.'

'It is? I just think of myself as a plain old ordinary person.'

'They say you're a square.' As she peered searchingly into his face, Mitsuko was suddenly gripped by a perverse desire. She could understand clearly why Moïra had wanted to torment the puritanical student Joseph. 'Everyone says that about you.'

'They do?'

'Yes. For starters, don't you think it's a little strange these days to be wearing that uniform in the middle of summer?'

'Sorry. It's just what I'm used to. I don't really do it on purpose.'

'Are you a Christian?'

'Ummhmm. My family are believers, and I've been one since I was a child.'

'Do you really believe in it?' The question sprang to her lips unbidden. Even though she attended this Christian university, Mitsuko had never considered believing in any of its teachings, and she hated even having to listen to the sermons.

'Sorry,' Ōtsu answered like a child who has done something wrong, 'but I do.'

'Well, I just don't get any of it. You're a strange one.'

She turned away and, ignoring Ōtsu, went down the stairs. No matter from which angle you studied him, Ōtsu was not the kind of man to stimulate the curiosity or interest of a young woman. Even today, Mitsuko found it beyond belief that she had ever become entangled with him. If anything, the whole thing had started from the rather childish desire to make fun not of Ōtsu, but of the God in whom he believed.

Several days after their meeting in the library, on a hot day just before the summer vacation, Mitsuko had come out of classroom number 109 and was sitting on a shaded bench with another young woman from the French department drinking cola from a paper cup. Ōtsu stood out among the swarms of students passing in front of them because he was the only one wearing a stiflingly hot black uniform jacket as he walked along.

Mitsuko turned to her friend. 'That one's really a yokel, isn't he?'

'Him? He always dresses like that,' her friend answered. 'But he's really quite good on the flute.'

'He plays the flute?'

'A while back, he played a Mozart piece at a university concert. It was the first time anyone had ever heard him play, and we were all surprised.'

'I can't believe it.'

'His grandfather was an important political figure.'

'Why does he wear that silly uniform?'

'You'll have to ask him.'

That was the first budding of curiosity Mitsuko felt about Ōtsu, who previously had interested her not in the slightest. The malicious element in the French department wanted to unnerve Ōtsu for reasons different from Mitsuko's, however.

'Did you guys know that he's supposed to be very good on the flute?'

Kondō and his crowd laughed when Mitsuko took them to task.

'Of course we did. That's what's so weird about him. We want you to have some fun with him because he's weird.'

'Cut it out. I'm not interested.'

'I hear that every day after class he goes to the Kultur Heim.'

'The Kultur Heim?'

'Yeah, that old chapel at the other end of campus where the priests all hang out.'

'What does he do there?'

'I suppose he says his prayers.'

So that was the kind of fellow he was. A man who resided in a world towards which Mitsuko felt an instinctive revulsion.

'Miss Naruse, do you like that sort of fellow? Or do you hate them?'

'I hate them.'

Having lost track of the sorts of goals that had stirred up the generation of student rebels four or five years earlier, these young men filled their hollow lives with mildly inflammatory incidents. And yet they knew all along that their actions merely piled emptiness upon emptiness.

When Mitsuko declared her hatred for that kind of man, she was half telling the truth and half lying. In a nebulous sort of way, she sensed that Ōtsu led a life different from that of the ordinary student, but at the same time she sniffed the aroma of hypocrisy so common in such men, and that had led her to say 'I hate them.'

To find out whether the rumours were true, Mitsuko half-jestingly proposed to the young men that after class she go to have a look around the Kultur Heim, which was near the building where the priests working at the university lived.

The Kultur Heim was one of the oldest, most serene buildings on the campus. Ivy covered half its walls, there were several meeting-rooms on the first floor, and on the second floor was a chapel. She still remembered that one of the steps on the way up creaked as she mounted them. When she first enrolled at the school, she had come once with some friends to look at the building, and that creaking stair had left an impression on her mind. On that occasion, a foreign priest had been kneeling in the chapel and praying, supporting his forehead with one arm.

After classes, the chapel was baking in the intense sunlight that poured in from the thickly growing summer garden. The silent chapel was empty, and the only sound was the chime of a clock somewhere in the distance. Its echoes somehow made her think of the university in the southern United States that appears in *Moïra*.

'He's not here.' Mitsuko scowled at her comrades. 'Why do you tell me such nonsense?'

'We're just passing along what everyone says about him. . . . This really upsets you, doesn't it, Miss Naruse?'

Kondō and his chums understood Mitsuko's personality, but they flinched at the harsh tone in her voice. Mitsuko herself was bewildered by her own eagerness over something indefinable.

'It makes me sick to think of a man coming to a place like this and dropping to his knees to pray.' The words spewed from her mouth. The others were silent, trying to gauge the fluctuations in Mitsuko's emotions.

Five or six minutes had passed when they heard footsteps and a creaking sound. They knew intuitively that the footsteps belonged to Ōtsu. Before long he stood in the doorway, all eyes on him as though he were some sort of ghost who had materialized, wrapped in a corona of light.

'Oh!' His eyes rounded in surprise, but he soon flashed a clumsy smile. 'What are you doing here?'

'Mr Ōtsu.' In stark contrast to a few moments earlier, Mitsuko's voice was tender. 'Is it true that you come here every day to pray?'

'Sorry, but it's true. But what are you . . .?'

'We came to invite you to a party. You know the Allo-Allo near the intersection at Yotsuya?'

'Behind the Chūō Publishing Company on the corner?'

'That's the one. Wouldn't you like to join us?'

'But wouldn't I just be in the way?' he asked in confusion. 'I don't have much experience at having a good time.'

'There's nothing to be so nervous about. Are you coming or not?'

'Sorry. I'll come.'

As Mitsuko led the group out of the chapel, the clock at the bottom of the stairs chimed five. The group of students began to jabber about this unexpected development.

'Do you think he'll really come?'

'He will. Now, you fellows mustn't make fun of him. But I want you to get him drunk.'

'We hear and we obey.'

The Allo-Allo, where Mitsuko and her group often hung out, stayed open late, and to the great delight of Kondō and his chums, Mitsuko always picked up half the tab.

But a half-hour, then an hour passed, and still Ōtsu had not appeared.

'He's given us the slip.' From time to time they glanced regretfully towards the door.

'No, he'll come.' For some reason Mitsuko declared this with confidence. She remembered the look on Ōtsu's face when he responded to her invitation with an amiable smile and a promise to come. She was convinced that, like Joseph, it was his *moïra*, his fate, to fall into her trap.

No sooner had she proclaimed her faith in Ōtsu than the door to the snack-bar gave the same creak as the stairs at the Kultur Heim. And Ōtsu, carrying a school bag in one hand, entered timidly through the door, his face the picture of virtue.

'A drink to make up for your tardiness. Drink up!' Kondō picked up a glass and held it out to Ōtsu.

'I'm afraid I'm not much of a drinker.'

'But you must!'

While the company chanted 'Drink up! Drink up!' Ōtsu gaspingly drained the glass of its amber liquid. The other students stared at one another dumbfounded at the way he tossed back his drink.

'Miss Naruse, won't you have a drink in return?' Ōtsu cordially held his glass out to her. 'We can make it just half a glass since you're a woman.'

'Why? Because I'm a woman? Fill 'er to the brim.' Her pride wounded, Mitsuko thrust the glass forward for filling, then poured the stinging liquid down her throat as the group again shouted 'Drink up! Drink up!' A bone-chilling sense of emptiness suddenly sickened her. *What the hell am I searching for, doing these ridiculous things? Letting these*

men goad me on, making fun of Ōtsu – is this what my life is all about?
To quell her cheerless thoughts, Mitsuko emptied her glass and challenged Ōtsu to another round.

Ōtsu shook his head. 'That's enough. Sorry. I shouldn't have done that.'

'Why not? You haven't done anything wrong,' she retorted. 'You say the strangest things.'

'I give up. Sorry.'

'"Sorry, sorry" – you're going to depress all of us.'

Mitsuko's anger was directed towards herself. Towards the hollowness within herself. Ōtsu had probably never felt like this.

'Mr Ōtsu, do you really go to Kultur Heim and pray every day?'

'Sorry, I . . .' he prevaricated.

'Are you really doing so sincerely?'

'Sorry.' Ōtsu surprised them by continuing, 'I'm not sure whether I believe in it or not.'

'Well, you certainly spend a lot of time on your knees for not being sure.'

'I don't know if it's just force of habit I've got into over the years, or inertia. All my family were Christians, and my dead mother was a firm believer, so maybe just out of my attachment to her I . . . I can't explain it very well.'

'If it's just inertia, you should dump the whole nonsense.'

Ōtsu did not reply.

Mitsuko stared beguilingly at Ōtsu. 'I'll help you get rid of it.'

Someone in Kondō's group muttered, 'Moïra has finally showed up.'

Along with Moïra, she thought of Eve, the same Eve who seduced Adam and caused the eternal banishment of mankind from the garden. Within each woman lurked the impulsive drive to destroy herself.

'Have another drink.'

'All right.' Ōtsu's answer was compliant, and he brought the glass to his lips. Mitsuko could tell he was doing his best to be docile and keep the mood of the party from souring. That realization made her even more furious.

'You really must forsake this God of yours. We're going to keep pouring liquor down you until you promise us you'll forsake him. If you'll dump him, we won't make you drink any more.'

For these students, this was no more than idle fun. Only Mitsuko was instinctively aware how heavily the words she spoke in jest weighed on Ōtsu's heart.

'So which will it be? Are you going to drink, or are you going to jilt him?'

'I'll drink.' Ōtsu's face was flushed all the way to his ears. He was clearly the sort who suffered considerably when he drank *sake*. For no reason Mitsuko recalled hearing about the officers in the age of Christian persecution in Japan who had forced the believers to trample upon the *fumie*. What exhilaration those officers must have felt as they made another person betray the God in whom he believed.

His shoulders heaving as he panted for breath, Ōtsu drank down a third of the glass that had been set in front of him. Then suddenly he leaped to his feet and staggered towards the bathroom.

'That's enough.' Weary of the game, one of the students implored Mitsuko. 'He's going to throw up. If you make him drink any more, he'll pass out.'

'No.' Mitsuko shook her head perversely. 'He's going to drink until he promises.'

'You're vicious.'

'Aren't you the ones who told me I had to play the role of Moïra?'

'Well, yes, but . . . there are limits.'

Eventually a pale-faced Ōtsu, wiping his mouth with a cheap white handkerchief, came back, supporting himself with one hand against the wall. 'Could I have some water, please?' he begged. 'I vomited.'

'No water. Have some more *sake*. Otherwise, you must keep your promise.'

Ōtsu tossed a rueful look at Mitsuko, who was leaning back against a pillar with folded arms. Like a dog pleading for mercy. The look further stimulated her enmity. 'But,' he begged.

'But what?'

'Even if I try to abandon God . . . God won't abandon me.'

Mitsuko gaped in disbelief at the man's face, which appeared ready to break into tears at any moment. Ōtsu covered his mouth again and tottered towards the bathroom.

'There, you see? He wasn't able to hold his drink after all,' Kondō mumbled, placating his own conscience.

Despite Ōtsu's efforts, a pall settled over the group, and Mitsuko stood up. 'I'm going home. This is a bore.' All she knew for certain was that the clumsy man who had scurried to the toilet was unlike anyone she had ever met.

Much later, when Mitsuko thought back on how she had behaved in those days, she had to lower her eyes in embarrassment. She was overcome with self-loathing. A country girl enjoying her first year of college in Tokyo had been nearly desperate to open herself to experience. Along with her revulsion, she sensed the existence of some inexplicable thread, something invisible to the eye that had bound her to Ōtsu. Though there was no reason for such a thing to be possible.

Mitsuko and her friends had left the snack-bar, discarding Ōtsu, who was still vomiting in the bathroom, like an old rag. The following day she was not the least bit conscious of his existence until she went to school and saw him sitting dejected on a bench beside the student activity building. Only then did she recall her coldness of the previous night.

'Mr Ōtsu.'

Once again he looked up at her with remorse, like a mongrel that had fallen into a ditch. A slender pinpoint of contrition pricked at her heart.

'I'm sorry about yesterday. I didn't think you'd be such a poor drinker.'

'Sorry. After you were so kind to invite me along. . . .' To her surprise, Ōtsu lowered his head. 'I'm always like this. I try my hardest to fit in with the group, but I end up failing and spoiling everybody's fun.'

Feeling both pity and scorn for Ōtsu's good-naturedness, she sat down beside him. She peered into his eyes, drew her face near his and whispered, 'There is a way to make friends, you know.'

'Yes?'

'It's simple. Stop wearing that serge uniform. And stop going to Kultur Heim in the evening and kneeling down to pray. Your mother may have believed it, but you don't have to believe that kind of stuff.'

'That kind of stuff . . .'

'I'm just a stupid young woman, but even I know what Marx had to say about religion. And I know that Western Christianity plundered many lands and killed many people in the name of spreading their gospel. When you get caught up in that kind of stuff, it spoils all the other students' fun. For one thing, you're not really sure you believe it, are you?'

'I'm not. But I haven't the courage to decide everything on the basis of logic like you do. I was brought up in that environment ever since I was a child, and. . . .'

Suddenly Mitsuko was bored. Why in the world was she sitting on this bench fraternizing with this tiresome man? Beside a man who held no interest for her?

'You must stop going to that Kultur Heim, starting today. If you do, I'll let you be one of my boy-friends.'

To dispel her ennui, Mitsuko voiced a notion that floated up in her mind like a bubble. Even as she spoke the words, she wondered if Moïra had seduced the solid student Joseph in an attempt to escape the same hollowness she now felt.

'Now listen to me.' She pressed her thigh as though accidentally against his trousers. 'You mustn't go there to pray any more.'

The thrill of snatching away from a man something he believes in. The pleasure of deforming a man's life. She pressed more firmly against his thigh and watched with satisfaction as Ōtsu's expression clouded over.

With that, she raced off to class.

Throughout her morning and afternoon classes, she savoured her achievement and chuckled to herself. Listening to the gruff voice of the French priest who taught seventeenth-century literature beneath the hot afternoon sun, she initiated a conversation with the God in whom she had no faith. The way a child makes up an imaginary friend and talks to it.

'Well, God, what would you think if I stole this fellow away from you?'

The thought rescued Mitsuko from the tedium of the lecture. When the white-haired priest finally collected his books and left the classroom, she set out for the Kultur Heim with a mixture of anticipation and curiosity rattling about in her head.

In the old building covered with tangled vines the smells of dampness and plaster faintly mingled. When she climbed the worn steps, one of them creaked as it had on her previous visit.

The chapel was deserted. She sat in the seat furthest to the back, out of view of the doorway, and decided to remain there for no more than twenty minutes. She knew that the solemn chimes of the large clock at the bottom of the stairs would announce the time every fifteen minutes.

Well-used hymnals, prayer-books and Bibles were scattered amongst the pews. With a yawn, she flipped open the large Bible that rested in the pew in front of her and began to read.

... he hath no form nor comeliness; and when we shall see him, there is no beauty that we should desire him.

He is despised and rejected of men; a man of sorrows, and
acquainted with grief: and we hid as it were our faces from
him. . . .
Surely he hath borne our griefs, and carried our sorrows.

Mitsuko put her hand to her mouth and yawned again. These words
had no reality for her. How was Ōtsu able to read and believe these
lifeless phrases? She recalled the self-loathing words Ōtsu had uttered:
'I'm always like this. I try my hardest to fit in with the group, but I
end up failing and spoiling everybody's fun.' She wondered if Ōtsu
had read this page in the Bible.

As if that thought were some sort of signal, a stair creaked. It was
not Ōtsu who appeared, however, but a priest who laboured at the
university, dressed in his white summer robes. Unaware of Mitsuko's
presence, he knelt near the altar and clasped his fingers together. She
watched him from behind for a time, feeling as though she were looking at some bizarre extraterrestrial, but finally she tired of that and
began speaking to the scrawny, naked man on the cross hanging to
the right of the altar.

'He's not going to come, you know. He's dumped you.' She ad-
dressed the ugly man she did not believe in, then heard the clock at
the foot of the stairs announce the passage of fifteen minutes.

She stood up and left the chapel. When she opened the door of the
Kultur Heim, which had seemed almost like the incarnation of tranquillity, her ears were suddenly flooded with the sounds of the student
band practising their music and the young men in the sports teams shouting
to one another. There on the bench where she had earlier sat she found
Ōtsu, perched glumly with a bundle of books on his lap.

'Mr Ōtsu!' Mitsuko called out in an excited voice, like a woman
who has discovered her lover at their chosen rendezvous. 'You kept
your promise to me, didn't you?'

'Yes.' Ōtsu lifted his head and forced a painful smile. 'But . . .'

'I'll keep my promise too. I'll let you be one of my boy-friends.
Let's go.'

'Go . . . where?'

'To my room.' Mitsuko sadistically surveyed her prey. A man who
listens to anything I tell him, a man who will abandon even God for
me – a man like that I want to torture even more. She snatched up a
book from the pile on Ōtsu's lap and found it was a work by Nakamura
Hajime.

'Wow, so you read stuff like this, do you?'

Ōtsu sluggishly rose from the bench and followed hesitatingly behind her.

'Can't you walk any faster? So you're interested in Buddhism, huh?'

'Not really. Professor Bell in the philosophy department is making us write a report on this book.'

'Professor Bell — isn't he that Catholic priest who does Zen meditation? But in his heart of hearts he's still a European, isn't he? That foreigner teaches you about this kind of stuff?'

'Yes.'

'I hate that. The priests here all talk like they know everything there is to know about Buddhism and Shinto, but in their hearts they think that European Christianity is the only true religion.' Mitsuko repeated the speech she had delivered numerous times since her arrival at the university to even the most marginally honest of students. By 'even the most marginally honest of students' Mitsuko and her friends meant those who had enrolled at this Christian university but refused to be baptized.

'Is that so? Maybe that's true.' Ōtsu gave a vague, faint-hearted reply, looking back over his shoulder from time to time. Mitsuko realized what he was unconsciously searching for.

'Am I the only one' — hesitation appeared in his eyes — 'coming to your room?'

'Yes, just you. Nobody else is around today — not Kondō, not Tanabe, or anyone.' She started to say 'Now you've become my boy-friend', but she deposited the words away in the strong-box of her heart. It was a savings account she could draw upon later to taunt this young man. *You are prey that has already fallen into my trap.*

She unlocked the door at her Kōjimachi 2-chōme apartment.

'Here we are,' she said, urging him on. 'What are you waiting for? Take off your shoes.' She gently nudged Ōtsu's shoulder.

'Sorry,' Ōtsu said, his voice almost a gasp.

'You're just like Joseph.'

'Who's he?'

'A student in the novel *Moïra* by Julien Green. He's a country boy just like you, a student who shakes whenever he's near a girl.'

'I am frightened. I've never done this before.'

'In the end, though, Joseph succumbs to Moïra's seduction.'

Ōtsu was speechless. He squinted at Mitsuko. The expression was so different from his usual attempt to force a smile that he seemed almost like a separate person.

'And,' he swallowed hard, 'what happened to this Joseph?'

'Joseph?' For the first time, Mitsuko had a vivid recollection of the novel's ending. 'Joseph ends up murdering the temptress Moïra.' She knew, of course, that Ōtsu lacked such courage. Her pleasure was rooted in that knowledge.

For a time nothing was said.

'Is that really what happens?' He looked up at her inquisitively.

Why were men all the same in the end? She realized that she had hoped to find something in Ōtsu that was different from the other students. Something the other men lacked. A dream of trees, a dream of water, a dream of fire, a dream of the desert.

She took a can of beer from the refrigerator and handed it to Ōtsu. As she reached towards him, she purposely staggered against him to provide him with a pretext for action. But he steadied her and tried nothing else. Only when she said 'A coward, aren't you?' did the lust that had been pent up for many years suddenly burst open, and he pounced on her body. His breath smelled of the curry he must have eaten in the student cafeteria. Mitsuko was gripped by the urge to tear herself apart.

'Wait.' She pushed him away with both hands. 'Let me at least take a shower.'

The pleasure of sullying herself was blended with abhorrence at her motivation. The sweaty smell of his body, the curried stench of his breath, the clumsy, bumbling touch of his hands as he stroked a young woman's breasts for the first time. Mitsuko, who had been intimate with several young men since entering college, coolly observed his movements, as she always did.

'You really don't know anything, do you?' she remarked as she watched Ōtsu's head move up and down above her chest.

'Sorry.'

His answer irritated her, but she was aware of how clear her thoughts were in the innermost part of her brain. Unlike other young women, she was unable to give herself over to ecstasy no matter who the man might be.

From somewhere in the apartment building she could hear a baseball game being broadcast on television. She allowed Ōtsu to fondle her, but she would not permit him to kiss her or engage in intercourse. And in the midst of it all, she made sure to ask: 'Are you going to go to church next Sunday?'

He said nothing.

'You're not going?'

'No.'

She closed her eyes and endured Ōtsu's lips snailing across her chest. Her feelings were tinged with an emptiness like a sudden chill wind that scatters cherry blossom. The ugly, naked figure of the man she had seen beside the altar in the Kultur Heim came back to life at the back of her tightly clenched eyes.

'So, what do you think?' she said to the scrawny man. 'You're completely powerless. I win. I think he's pretty much jilted you. He's dumped you and come to my room.'

He's jilted you. . . . As she formed the words in her mind, Mitsuko suddenly thought of the day to come when she would cast Ōtsu off.

By now she had already come to understand. The pleasure she took from Ōtsu derived not from anything even remotely carnal, but from Ōtsu's rejection of that man.

The sensations of pleasure, which ultimately receded like an ebb tide. In the instant that her prey gave his last dying pant, Mitsuko's joy of the hunt summarily faded and died.

I wonder how I should appease him when it's all over?

She could almost see Ōtsu's face clouded with surprise and entreaty. Because he was so inexperienced and sombre, and particularly because this was his first encounter with passion, he probably would not consider this just a college fling, like the other male students did. In *Moïra*, Joseph in a fit of rage put his hands around the throat of the woman who had enticed him into evil and choked her to death.

'That's enough. I'm tired of it.'

That evening, finally bored, she pushed Ōtsu, who was nestled up against her, aside. The sun had set, and the blare of motor-cycle engines and other noises she had been able to hear throughout most of the day had finally given way to silence. Beneath her window, a young woman was singing.

> 'We'll shake, we'll shake the tree of dreams,
> That solitary tree of dreams
> In the centre of the verdant field.'

As she listened to the song, Mitsuko suddenly recalled the days of her youth, lost so long ago.

'Go home.'

'Have I . . . done something to make you angry?'

'Yes. I'm tired of you.'

Ōtsu would not think of protesting. She watched as he turned his back and dejectedly began to dress.

'Have you decided what you're going to write your thesis on?' She couldn't help feeling sorry for him, and dutifully asked the question.

'Yes, scholasticism in the modern age.'

'What in the world does that mean?' It was all she could do to keep from laughing at the pompous topic that emerged from the mouth of this man, who just minutes before had been gorging himself like a child on her breasts. 'Is that something Professor Bell told you to do?'

'Sorry. Professor Bell says if you don't know something about scholasticism, you really can't understand Europe.'

'It's nothing more than a relic of the past, isn't it? It's just a weapon the priests use to defend their own stale religion. I don't know much about it, but there can't be anybody in Japan doing such outdated research.'

'Professor Bell says it has to be done because there are so few Japanese who really understand Europe.'

'Strange, isn't it – telling a man who can come to a woman's room to write about Christian philosophy?'

Three Sundays that stank like rotted figs passed. As she watched Ōtsu's head sway above her, Mitsuko thought of other things. Ōtsu was all alone in his ecstasy, the only one absorbed in what he was doing; Mitsuko stared vacantly at the calendar hanging on her wall. *I want to go somewhere, go somewhere in search of something. Something real, something enduring. I want to seize hold of life. . . .* Before she was even aware, the pages of the calendar, with its photographs of landscapes from all over Japan, had flipped over to a snowy December scene in the north-east.

'During the winter vacation, I think maybe I'll go to Bangkok.' She was speaking not to Ōtsu, whose face was buried between her bare breasts, but to herself.

'What?' Ōtsu lifted his head. The sweat that beaded his forehead and the spittle that stained his mouth were disgusting.

'Where are you going to spend winter break?'

'Me?' A smile of undiluted goodness flashed in his bloodshot eyes. 'I'm staying in Tokyo. My family's here.'

'Don't you want to go skiing or something?'

49

'I'm kind of uncoordinated, so I'm not really good at skiing. What about you?'

'I'd like to go to Bangkok, or maybe Guam.'

'By yourself?'

'Don't be silly. Kondō and some of the other fellows said they'd come too.'

'Kondō?'

It pleased Mitsuko to see Ōtsu's face contort in agony. Just like the evening when she first brought him to her room, a young girl was singing beneath her window. As she listened to the song, she concluded that the time had come to dump Ōtsu.

'Is there some reason I can't go with Kondō?'

'Do you love me?'

'I don't belong to anyone. Not to Kondō, not to you.'

'Have you been to bed with Kondō?'

'Of course,' she answered defiantly. 'We're not at high school, you know.'

'Then,' he asked fearfully, 'you don't love me?'

'Don't talk like a child. You've had more than your share of fun. It's about time to finish up here anyway.'

Ōtsu sat up and searched Mitsuko's face, humiliation brimming in his eyes.

'I was planning to . . . to introduce you to my father and brother one of these days.'

'Your family? Ah, I guess you're a Christian after all, hmm?'

'He's a very good father to me. I think he'll understand how I feel about you.'

'Ōtsu, I have no intention of marrying you.' She sat up and candidly declared, 'Not you, or anybody else I'm seeing just now.'

'But you said I was your boy-friend. . . .'

'I did. But you can't marry every single boy-friend that comes along.'

'You're horrible,' Ōtsu said loudly. It was a voice filled with an anger unusual for him. 'You're awful. I could kill you.'

'Why don't you?'

Joseph had surrendered to his rage and strangled Moïra. But Mitsuko had seen that Ōtsu lacked that same courage.

'Go home,' she said coldly. 'I'm sick of you.'

Ōtsu's head drooped, and he said nothing.

'We'll shake, we'll shake the tree of dreams,
That solitary tree of dreams
In the centre of the verdant field.'

The girl below the window was singing the same nursery song as before.

'Get out.'

Ōtsu's round, honest face twisted. Then he turned away, noisily put on his shoes, noisily opened the door, and disappeared.

Several days later, a pleading letter arrived from Ōtsu. Mitsuko read quickly through it and tossed it into the waste-paper basket. He also telephoned, but as soon as she heard his voice, she hung up without a word. When he laid in wait for her at school, she spoke as though nothing had happened. 'Hello, how are you?,' she would call to him, and then hurry away, surrounded by her friends.

The man Mitsuko married was so plain and proper that her old school chums were startled.

She had got into the habit of saying, 'Playing around and getting married are two different things.' But when her college friends came to the reception at the Hotel Ōkura and saw her standing and bowing to guests in front of a gold screen with her new husband, her parents and the go-between, they whispered to one another: 'She's a shrewd one, that bitch. That poor sap of a groom probably thinks she's a virgin.'

The husband, chosen through a series of arranged interviews, was the son of a contractor who was erecting a series of high-rise buildings in Tokyo, and though he was still only twenty-eight, he had been given an executive position with the company. When the reception concluded, another party was held in the hotel bar, attended by the sons of equally famous businessmen and politicians, and their topics of conversation ranged from golf to their new sports cars to recent happenings at the young men's association meeting. Mingling with his peers, Mitsuko's husband conversed with such enthusiasm he seemed a completely different person from the man she had got to know during their brief engagement. Mitsuko was the one who ended up standing to the side, smiling and pretending to be listening.

Shortly after they became engaged, Mitsuko realized how different were her own sensibilities from those of the man who would become her husband. In the early stages of the relationship she invited him along to an exhibition of Roualt prints and to a concert by the Vienna

Chamber Orchestra, but she soon realized that he was going simply out of duty.

'I can't help it. I just don't know anything about paintings.'

She was chilled by his faint snores as he leaned against her and dozed when they went to see Morishita Yōko's ballet corps, but the frankness of his admission that he did not understand such things reminded her of Ōtsu. *I'm marrying this man,* she honestly felt at the time, *so that I can overcome my selfish impulses.*

Once she became a member of normal society, she started to understand how foolish had been the urge to corrupt herself that had raged through her body during her college years. Something destructive lurked within the depths of her heart. Mitsuko wanted to wipe out every mark of its existence, the way an eraser removes every trace of writing on a blackboard, before it assumed tangible form. She wanted to marry a man who had no interest in and no understanding of any of the things that stimulated the destructive force within her – Wagner's operas, Redon's paintings – and she wished earnestly, whole-heartedly to become a commonplace housewife and to bury herself like a corpse amongst men and women who were replicas of her husband.

'Yat-chan, you simply must trade in that Benz of yours,' one of her husband's friends demanded at the party after the reception. 'The only people who drive Benzes these days are gangsters. There are plenty of nice new models made right here at home.' This friend, who worked for an automobile company, turned his glance towards Mitsuko. 'One day soon you should test drive one of our cars, Mitsuko.'

'I'm afraid I don't know anything about cars.'

'Well, whatever the case' – he appeared suddenly to recall something – 'do you happen to know a man named Ōtsu?'

'Yes, there was a fellow named Ōtsu at my university,' she answered without changing expression. 'If that's the Ōtsu you mean...'

'My elder sister married his brother. Her brother-in-law told her he'd had a terrible crush on a coed named Naruse.'

'Really? He was in a different department altogether.' Without the least hesitation in her voice, she elicited a laugh from the group by saying: 'I had no idea. If I'd known that, I wouldn't have married this Yano fellow.'

Her husband gave an acrid smile for the benefit of his friends, but his face was puffed with pride.

'Too late, I'm afraid,' the friend responded. 'This Ōtsu has gone into a seminary in Lyon. He's going to become a Catholic priest.'

'A priest – doesn't that mean that he can never associate with women?' someone interjected. 'So he'll have to stay a virgin his whole life?'

Her eyes on the table, Mitsuko picked up her champagne glass and brought it to her lips. So Ōtsu had entered a seminary. He would become a priest. The man who had clung to her breasts like an infant, his head rising and falling above her. She drained her glass, just as she had one night many years before.

'You're quite a drinker, aren't you, Mitsuko?' Yano's friend remarked with surprise.

'She is, she is,' her husband beamed. 'Even I can't keep up with her. She can drink four dry martinis and act like it's nothing at all.'

'My father was a heavy drinker.' Trying her hardest to shift the conversation away from Ōtsu, she thought of an afternoon in the Kultur Heim. The chapel where the foreign priest in his white robes had been praying. The chiming of the clock at the bottom of the staircase. The words she had defiantly hurled towards the cross at the altar: 'What would you think if I stole this fellow away from you?'

But the scrawny, powerless man with his arms outstretched on the cross had at some point reclaimed Ōtsu. *Still, that doesn't change the fact that I won. With startling rapacity God had merely picked up a man I discarded.*

Her husband, having no inkling what was going through her mind, was listening with relish to his friend talk about the sports car he owned. Scanning his profile, Mitsuko fashioned an image of the life she would spend with this man. *This is fine. All I have to do is bury myself in this happy, simple face.*

It was Mitsuko's idea to limit their honeymoon trip to France. Yano had wanted to go to the west coast of the United States, which he had visited many times, but she was able to get her way.

'You just want to go to France?' he asked, deflated. 'Don't you want to go to London and Rome and Switzerland too?'

'I want to take my time seeing France. That's what I've always wanted to do.'

Their hotel in Paris near the Seine was an American-style intercontinental facility she knew her husband would like. She herself would have preferred a smaller, more old-fashioned French *pension*, but on this point she compromised.

From their hotel near the place de la Concorde they were able to walk to the Church of La Madeleine, the Impressionists' museum and the Louvre.

Yet, though she had anticipated that such a thing might happen, her disappointment began the day after they arrived in Paris.

'This square is one of the sites of the Revolution. At the time of the uprising, Marie Antoinette and Louis XVI were both beheaded by the guillotine here,' she had said with excitement.

But her husband gave only a dutiful nod, 'Oh?' It was clear he had no interest in the French Revolution or in Marie Antoinette. Before their departure, the only tourist information with which his friends had provided him involved the taking in of Lido shows, the purchase of Sulka neckties, the climbing of the Eiffel Tower and the visiting of *chanson* bars in Montmartre.

At the Louvre he spread open the Paris tour book he had bought in Japan, and he scurried around the museum looking only at the must-see paintings. 'So this is the *Mona Lisa*. How about that?' He nodded in satisfaction.

As she watched his behaviour, Mitsuko remembered a scene exactly like this in the novel she had analysed in her senior thesis for the French literature department. This was *Thérèse Desqueyroux*, by the Nobel Prize author François Mauriac. The protagonist, Thérèse, is the daughter of a provincial landowner from Landes, near Bordeaux, and she marries Bernard, the son of another landowner from the same region. Remarkably for a young man of this area, Bernard had graduated from the department of law at a university in Paris. Like her family, he was a Catholic, and he was a prime catch for people of their status.

Following a grand, countrified wedding ceremony they set off to Paris on their honeymoon, but it was not long before she, like Mitsuko, began to weary of her husband.

Thérèse's husband was by no means a bad man. His way of thinking was doggedly conventional, and admittedly he was an excessively plain man of good common sense. He was one of those men who sought never to stray from the accepted standards of public morality and practical wisdom, and more than anything feared veering from the beaten track; his fondest desire was to lead an uneventful life. It was his very effort to give no offence that made Thérèse feel an inexplicable weariness whenever she was by his side.

Mauriac, whose depiction of these traits of Bernard is so nonchalant as to be almost brutal, sketches out a scene in which Thérèse and her husband visit the Louvre on their honeymoon. There Bernard opened up his Michelin guide and raced from room to room, looking only at the 'famous paintings that must be seen'. The *Mona Lisa* had been one such painting.

'This place is too big. I'm exhausted. I just don't know anything about paintings.' Yano abandoned his attempt half-way and told his wife he would wait for her at the coffee shop in the museum.

Left to herself, Mitsuko felt a sense of liberated pleasure. Without even thinking of doing so, she began to compare Bernard and her husband, and Thérèse to herself. Pondering why she had chosen *Thérèse Desqueyroux* instead of *Moïra* for her senior thesis, Mitsuko even began to sense a frightening premonition in her selection.

That day, in a bookstore on the Palais-Royal near their hotel, she bought the familiar old Grasset edition of *Thérèse Desqueyroux*. She recalled the days she had spent at the university reading this novel in the original, referring frequently to her dictionary to help her though a more perplexing use of the French language than she had encountered in Julien Green. It was about the time, after dumping Ōtsu, that she had realized her own folly and began to throw herself into her studies.

Looking at her husband asleep beside her, she reread the portion of the novel describing Thérèse's wedding night. Bernard sought out Thérèse's body like a pig rooting in its sty. Mitsuko's husband and, many years earlier, Ōtsu, had behaved in exactly the same way.

'Are you still awake?' Yano turned over and looked sleepily at her. 'Put your book down and go to sleep.'

'Uh-huh.'

So Ōtsu was going to become a priest. And he was now here in France, in Lyon. That scrawny man had picked up what she had cast away. Like a young child who rescues a filthy, wailing puppy that has fallen into a ditch.

'I've had enough of Paris,' her husband all but shrieked as they ate breakfast in the hotel the following morning. 'Nothing but museums and plays day after day.'

'I'll bet you'd rather see the shows at the Lido or in Montmartre.'

'I suppose so. I'd like to see them just so I'd have something to talk about after coming all this way to Paris.'

'Well, that does create a problem. As a woman I'm not interested in places like that. I wonder if there's anyone who could take you to the kinds of places you'd enjoy.'

'There is. One of my company's clients has a branch office here in Paris.'

'Then why don't you have someone from there show you around? It doesn't make any difference to me.' She put down her coffee-cup. 'Right, I think I'll take a little trip out of Paris by myself and come back in four or five days. While I'm gone, you can have your fill of fun wherever you'd like.'

'By yourself? Where would you go "out of Paris"?'

'There's a place I've always wanted to visit. You know that novel I've been reading in bed since we arrived? It's the book I wrote my graduation thesis on. And now I've finally come to France. I want to see the area where the novel takes place. It's near Bordeaux.'

'Doesn't it seem a little strange to go off in different directions for four or five days on our honeymoon?'

'That's what's fun about it!' She opened her eyes wide, relishing her own suggestion. 'Let's each of us enjoy this trip. You can stay here in Paris eating delicious food and seeing your amusing shows. . . .'

'When you say "near Bordeaux", just where do you mean?' Yano still seemed unpersuaded.

'A region called Les Landes. It's a wilderness, with sand and pine groves stretching as far as the eye can see. I really want to see what it looks like.'

Yano was reluctant for a time to let his wife go off by herself, but ultimately his new bride won the day. When they finally reached that conclusion, Mitsuko felt, just as she had in the Louvre, a sense of emancipation, this time greater than the first, spread through her breast.

Look at yourself. Mitsuko took herself to task. *You still haven't abandoned your true feelings. Weren't you planning to bury yourself in your husband?*

She averted her eyes from him as he munched on his breakfast and muttered within her heart: *This will be my final selfish act. Just one last time. After that, I'll become a humdrum housewife.*

The day she left Paris was slightly overcast. She shared her compartment on the train for Bordeaux with an old woman knitting, a middle-aged father and his young daughter. The girl stared into Mitsuko's face and demanded 'Est-ce que Madame est Chinoise?' Her father reproved her for her rudeness, but his smug gaze shifted ceaselessly back and forth from the gully between Mitsuko's knees to the copy of *Thérèse Desqueyroux* that rested on her lap.

She had forgotten some of the vocabulary, but since she had already hammered the general outline of the story into her head, she was able to flip through the pages with minimal difficulty. Bernard had not been a bad husband in any sense that the world would acknowledge. Never missing a Sunday mass, it would never have occurred to him to do anything to deceive his wife. He had been brought up as a bourgeois in a tiny village in the Landes region, and he had never done anything to invite gossip from the people of his village. In that French country town, where nothing was more important than reputation, Bernard had been a model husband.

Yet, when Thérèse was with her husband, she felt listless. The exhaustion she had felt while still on their honeymoon turned into an imperceptible dust that piled up in her heart when they returned and settled into their new life together in the village of St Clair. Especially when the first signs that she was pregnant appeared – partly, perhaps, because it was the hottest time of the summer – she felt heavy, as though chunks of lead had been hung on her body.

When Mitsuko had read as far as that and raised her head, the father sitting opposite her quickly shifted his gaze. Outside the window cracks of blue sky had finally appeared, and the brown roofs of farmhouses, pastures where cattle grazed and villages with church buildings passed one after another before her eyes.

Suddenly she wondered what her husband was doing at that moment in Paris. But she felt no longing for him. Mitsuko stared at her own rather grim face reflected in the window glass and at her large eyes, and could feel almost painfully how Thérèse had felt. *In the past I was Moïra; now I am Thérèse.* In the innermost part of her brain, someone's voice – the voices of her past boy-friends – sang that refrain. Mitsuko felt that, unlike other women, she was unable truly to love another person. A dried-out woman, as arid as the sands. A woman in whom the flames of love had been extinguished.

Just what is it you want? Mitsuko inwardly flung the question at the girl in the same compartment who continued to stare quizzically at her. But it was also the question Mitsuko was posing at herself. *Just what is it you're searching for?*

One night's stay in Bordeaux. The next morning she had the hotel make her a sandwich, and following the directions given her by the assistant at the reception desk, she boarded the bus for Langon. She took the bus because she had learned, by leafing through the pamphlet provided her by the hotel employee, that the train mentioned in the novel that had run to the village of St Symphorien where Thérèse lived had long ago been done away with, and that a bus now covered the route.

Langon, where the midday sun shone down on the deserted roadway.
'So there's no longer a train?' she tried asking a middle-aged woman
waiting for the bus.

'A train?' The woman shrugged her shoulders. 'Many years ago
there was a rail line for goods trains loaded with pine timber, but it
never carried any passengers.'

Mitsuko realized that the train in the novel that had transported Thérèse into the forest of darkness had been Mauriac's
invention. If that were the case, then Thérèse had not passed
through an actual forest in the dark, but had in fact travelled
through the darkness in the depths of the human heart. So that
was it.

So that was it! At this realization, Mitsuko knew that she had left
her husband in Paris and come to this rustic area in order to search
out the darkness in her own heart.

The bus continued to speed down the road surrounded by a dense
pine forest. In the forest giant ferns spread out everywhere like um-
brellas, and pines queued up like people in a crowd.

Sometimes in summer when cloudless days proceeded one after
another without a break in this forest, parched branches would rub
against one another and start a mountain fire, the smoke from
which would smudge the white disc of the sun. The occasional
ramshackle huts in the forest were the spots where men who had
come to hunt turtle-doves would spend the night. Even though this
was the first time Mitsuko had laid eyes on the scenery in the Landes
region, she knew all about such things from her reading of *Thérèse
Desqueyroux*.

In the village square at St Symphorien, which was as barren as a
desert, Mitsuko got off the bus with several other people. When she
walked into the combination restaurant-hotel in the square, the young
people who had been playing a game in the lobby stared at this Japanese woman with timorous eyes. It was only a rare Asian who came
to visit their village, which had nothing to recommend it to the tourist.
She ordered a meal and reserved a room.

'You're Japanese, are you?' the aproned woman who owned the hotel
asked as she studied Mitsuko's passport. 'We had a young Japanese
staying here five years ago. Yes, I remember him well. He said he was
a student in Lyon.'

At the mention of Lyon, the name of Ōtsu surfaced in her consciousness. As she fitted her room key into the lock and opened the

door, she had the impish thought that perhaps she should go on to Lyon before returning to Paris.

She broke into a sweat as she walked around the village in the still-hot evening sun. Thérèse and Bernard, their arms linked like the most genteel of engaged couples, had passed through this square, and in the church near the square they had been married. A life filled with resignation and weariness. Her upright husband, whose very existence had enervated her. From society's perspective, there was no point on which this man could be criticized. Because he was blameless, Thérèse grew irritated both with him and with herself. This irritation collected below the level of her conscious mind, waiting quietly for the moment when it would finally burst into flames like the forest of umbrella pines.

That night, after the occasional sounds of motor-cycle engines had faded away, came the night in St Symphorien which the author had described as like 'the silence at the ends of the earth'. Lying on the bed in her dimly lit room, Mitsuko opened her eyes wide and stared at the ceiling, asking herself: *What do you really want? Why have you come by yourself to such a place?*

She reached for the telephone and dialled the hotel in Paris. Not that she had suddenly wanted to hear Yano's voice. But because in the darkness of Landes she had suddenly become frightened that her thoughts were becoming too much like those of Thérèse. Hadn't she married Yano in order to fill the emptiness within herself? Hadn't it been so she could bury herself in some human-like life among his friends who could talk of nothing but their work and their golf? They had tried several times at the hotel to put the call through, but there was no answer. Evidently her husband had not yet returned from his explorations of Paris.

Thérèse boarded a train that did not exist in reality and entered into the darkness of her own heart. Mitsuko, too, concluded her pointless journey to Landes, where she had been unable to discover anything, and headed for Lyon.

She arrived at Lyon at 2 p.m. and took a room in a hotel facing the place Bellecour. She had an assistant at the reception desk check to see if the religious order that had run their university operated a religious congregation in Lyon. It was almost disappointing how easily the address and telephone number were located. The moustached assistant pointed at a map of the city and showed her a section called

Fourvière in the oldest part of Lyon. Mitsuko knew at once that this was the novitiate she wanted, since it belonged to the same religious order.

When she dialled the telephone number, a man's voice kept repeating, 'Ōtsu? Ōtsu?' When he finally caught on, he raised his voice and said, 'Oh, you mean Augustine Ōtsu.' She was kept waiting a long while, until finally the unforgettably forlorn voice of Ōtsu came through the receiver. The moment she heard his voice, she remembered his round face and his breath that smelled of curry.

'It's me. Na-ru-se.' She purposely kept a cheerful tone in her voice, but Ōtsu said nothing for a few moments.

'Mr Ōtsu, I'm in France. With my husband. And I've just arrived here in Lyon by myself. I'm at the Hôtel Bellecour.'

'Really?'

'Really. I heard a rumour that you were in Lyon, so I thought I'd try to ring you, and it's turned out to be true. I hope I'm not bothering you?'

'No.'

'I understand you're going to become a priest.'

Silence again. He was lost for an answer. She could almost see the jittery look on his face, and Mitsuko purposely poured sweetness into her voice.

'I suppose that means you couldn't see a woman like me?'

'No, that's not the case.'

'I'm thinking of going back to Paris tomorrow. What about tonight?'

'Sorry. I can't at night. But tomorrow morning I'm going to the Catholic university on the rue du Plat. The class finishes at eleven, and then I'll come to your hotel.'

'Do you know it?'

'Yes. It's a famous hotel in Lyon.'

After she had hung up, Mitsuko took a walk along the River Saône, guidebook in hand. The waters of the river were black, and waterfowl soared above the cargo-laden boats. Next, she went to see the ancient Roman theatre that had been restored on a hill in Fourvière. Perhaps because the bluff at Fourvière was the oldest part of Lyon, houses with peeling walls stood here and there like mouths plagued with cavities. Atop the hill she stood on a set of stone steps that afforded a panorama of the city. She had a panoramic view of the grey city of Lyon, which squatted like a cloudy sky. Although she had had no plans to come here, now that she suddenly found herself in Lyon, it seemed to her a pitiful city, lacking any of the vitality of Paris.

She climbed down the stairs and went in search of the novitiate where Ōtsu lived. The building, like all the houses in Fourvière, was old, shadowy and blotched by the winds and snows. As she stood examining the building two or three seminarians, sporting berets and the kinds of gowns that high-school students had worn before the war, came out of the doorway and walked down the hill. To her, they looked like members of some incomprehensible alien race, and Ōtsu was now living among those aliens.

The following morning at around eleven-thirty Ōtsu called at her hotel as he had promised. When the reception desk contacted her and she went down to the lobby, Mitsuko discovered Ōtsu, standing apart from the well-dressed gentlemen and ladies, wearing a beret like the two seminarians the previous night, and draped in a black, tattered monk's robe. Looking as always like a stray dog that has just crawled from a ditch, Ōtsu seemed out of place in the hotel lobby.

'It's been a long time,' Mitsuko said in greeting.

Ōtsu managed a timid grin and uttered his trade mark, 'Sorry.'

'The way you're dressed . . . you've really changed.'

'You too, Miss Naruse. . . . Sorry, your name is different now, isn't it?'

'It's Yano now, but that sort of thing doesn't matter. Can we go outside? Or are you theology students prohibited from walking with women?'

'It's fine. I explained the situation to the rector.'

They cut across the place Bellecour and walked along the banks of the dark, stagnant Saône. Again today the river was gloomy, and a cargo ship slowly chugged towards the north.

'I shouldn't say this, but Lyon certainly seems lifeless compared with Paris.'

'That's what all the Parisians say. They claim we're old-fashioned.'

'Will you be staying here for a long while?'

'I have two more years until I graduate. But being the kind of person I am, I don't know whether I'll even be able to finish.'

They leaned against a fence on the river bank and watched the cargo ships and waterfowl. Both Mitsuko and Ōtsu avoided mentioning their past association. Ōtsu, looking like a pitiful soldier beneath his stained beret. Many years before, this face had sought her breasts like an infant.

61

'Back in our school-days we once forced you to drink a lot of *sake*, didn't we?'

Ōtsu said nothing.

'Didn't you ... abandon your God then?' She thrust her fingers into Ōtsu's old wound. Her maliciousness ignited on contact with Ōtsu's cowardly face. 'So why is it that you became a student at the seminary?'

Blinking, Ōtsu looked down into the black current of the River Saône. On the surface of the water soap-like bubbles had formed and flowed along.

'I don't know. It just happened.'

'I want to know the reason.'

'After you snubbed me ... I began to understand ... just a little the sufferings of that man who was rejected by all men.'

'Now hold on.... Don't just gloss over this whole thing.' Mitsuko was hurt. But that only strengthened her desire to drive Ōtsu into a corner.

'Sorry. But that's really how it was. It was because of something I heard. After you broke up with me, I fell to pieces.... I didn't know where to go or what to do. I couldn't think of anything else, so I went back to the Kultur Heim again, and as I was kneeling there, I heard it.'

'Heard it? Heard what?'

'A voice, saying "Come to me. Come. I was rejected as you have been. So I will never abandon you." That's what the voice said.'

'Who was it?'

'I don't know. But I do know for certain that the voice told me to come.'

'And what did you do?'

'I answered, "I come."'

She recalled the Kultur Heim that afternoon as the sun streamed through the window. At the foot of the stairs the chimes of the clock rang out. There had been that scrawny man hanging beside the deserted altar, and the words printed on the page of the Bible someone had left at the pew. The words that had said, 'he hath no form nor comeliness; and when we shall see him, there is no beauty that we should desire him'.

'Well then, Mr Ōtsu, I suppose that means that it's thanks to me that you've become a seminarian.'

Mitsuko smiled. But she sensed something squirming within her forced smile.

'That's true.' A delighted smile illuminated Ōtsu's cheeks for the first time. 'After everything that happened to me, I began to think that God, like a magician, can turn any situation to the best advantage. Even our weaknesses and our sins. Yes, that's how it is. A magician puts a wretched sparrow in a box, closes the lid, and then with a wave of his hands opens the lid again. The sparrow in the box has been changed into a pure-white dove and comes flying out.'

'And you're that wretched sparrow.'

'Yes. I who was once so pitiful.... If you hadn't dumped me ... I ... would not be living this kind of life.'

'How you exaggerate things. You try to come up with such profound meaning when all that happened is that you were jilted by a woman.'

'Sorry. But in my case, that's what actually occurred.'

Ōtsu's face in profile was turned towards the brown-chimneyed old roofs. From among the clusters of houses the black steeple of the Church of St-Jean-Apôtre, one of Lyon's famous attractions, towered like a giant. She couldn't bring herself to think that Ōtsu was rationalizing for his past just because he was a sore loser. But since she did not believe in this God of his, she had to conclude that his reminiscences were nothing more than a desperate attempt to make some sense of his experience. All that she was able to understand was that this miserable fellow had entered a realm completely alien to the world in which she, her friends from the past, and her husband and his associates now lived.

'You really are a strange one, aren't you?'

'Maybe I am. But ... I didn't change myself. I was transformed by the conjurings of God.'

'Listen, could you please stop using that word "God"? It makes me nervous, I can't relate to it, and it doesn't mean anything to me. Ever since I was in college, I've felt distant from that word "God" which the foreign priests used.'

'Sorry. If you don't like that word, we can change it to another name. We can call him Tomato, or even Onion if you prefer.'

'All right, then, just what is this Onion to you? You said at school that you really didn't understand him very well. When someone asked you whether God existed.'

'Sorry. To be honest, at that time I really didn't know. But now in my own way I do.'

'Tell me.'

'God is not so much an existence as a force. This Onion is an entity that performs the labours of love.'

'That's even more repulsive. How can you use such unsettling words as "love" with a straight face? And what do you mean by "labours"?'

'Well, for instance, the Onion found me abandoned in one place, and at some time he gave me life in a completely different location.'

Mitsuko chortled. 'That hasn't got anything to do with the power of your Onion. Your feelings just sent you off in that direction.'

'No, that's not true. It was the work of the Onion transcending my own will.' For the first time Ōtsu spoke decisively, and he lifted his eyes to look her directly in the face. He was different from the somehow ineffectual fellow she had known, whose only redeeming feature was his goodness.

Mitsuko changed the subject. 'How long do you plan to keep me standing here? It's already well past noon. Since I made this trip all the way to Lyon, let's have lunch somewhere.'

'Sorry. Since I study at the seminary, I don't know any good places.'

'I know that. I'll treat you. And I won't make you guzzle alcohol this time.'

A look of innocent delight crossed his face, like that of a dog being led out for a walk.

They returned to the place Bellecour, where Mitsuko had noticed from her hotel window a convenient restaurant on a corner of the square marked by a statue of Louis XIV. Their table was surrounded by mirrored walls of vermilion colour, and the table-napkins had been arranged like tiny pyramids. The waiters looked on from a distance in bewilderment as the Japanese seminarian dressed in a stained robe seated himself.

Dotting his threadbare robe with drops of soup as he ate, Ōtsu heaved a sigh. 'This is delicious. How many years has it been since I've eaten something as good as this?'

'You would've been better off not choosing your present way of life. There are any number of restaurants in Tokyo now that serve food as good as this. Excuse me for asking, but is it the work of that Onion of yours that drove you into this kind of life?'

Ōtsu gripped his spoon like a child and grinned.

'You're a strange man. You're Japanese, aren't you? It makes my teeth stand on edge just to think of you as a Japanese believing in this European Christianity nonsense.'

'You haven't changed at all, have you, Miss Naruse?'

'I haven't, but I'm serious.'

'I don't believe in European Christianity. I....' Another drop of soup spattered his frock. Clutching his spoon, Ōtsu pleaded with Mitsuko like a little child. 'Miss Naruse, now that you've come to France ... haven't you felt any sense of friction?'

'Friction? I've only been here ten days, you know.'

'I've been here three years. For three years I've lived here, and I've tired of the way people here think. The ways of thinking that they've kneaded with their own hands and fashioned to meet the workings of their hearts ... they're ponderous to an Asian like me. I can't blend in with them. And so ... every day is hell for me. When I try to tell some of my French classmates or teachers how I feel, they admonish me and say that the truth knows no distinction between Europe and Asia. They say it's all because of my neurosis or my complex or whatever. My views about the Onion, too....'

'You're as uncouth as ever. Here you are having a lovely meal with a beautiful woman, and you can't talk about anything less tedious?'

'Sorry. But ... I haven't seen you in so long.... It's like I want to tell you all the feelings that have been pent up inside me for three years.'

'Then go ahead and talk. Tell me all you want about your Onion.'

'I can't make the clear distinction that these people make between good and evil. I think that evil lurks within good, and that good things can lie hidden within evil as well. That's the very reason God can wield his magic. He made use even of my sins and turned me towards salvation.'

Clenching his knife and fork with both hands, Ōtsu jabbered as though possessed. The look on his face was the same as those on the faces of the young people who had participated in the student riots, conducting pointless debates in the local taverns. How foolish Mitsuko and her friends had thought those students were in their school-days.

'But my way of thinking is considered heretical in the Church. I've been reprimanded. You don't make distinctions between anything, they insist. You don't discriminate clearly. That's not how God is. That's not what your Onion is like, they tell me.'

'Then why don't you just chuck the whole bothersome business?'

'It's not that simple.'

'You've got to do something besides just talk: You must also eat. The waiter's having fits because he can't bring the next course.'

'Sorry.' Ōtsu obediently chewed away, grinning childishly back at Mitsuko, who studied him closely.

'This onion soup . . . it's delicious!'

She wondered if she would have been happy married to this man, or if she would be more bored than she was with Yano.

'Another thing is, I trust my Onion. It's more than just faith.'

'Are you sure . . . you're not going to get excommunicated?' she teased. 'They still excommunicate people, don't they?'

'My priesthood order says I have some heretical tendencies, but they haven't kicked me out yet. But I can't lie to myself, and when I finally go back to Japan . . .' – he sucked the spoon into his mouth as though he were going to swallow it – '. . . I want to think about a form of Christianity that suits the Japanese mind.'

'I understand. But please hurry up and finish your meal.'

Actually, Mitsuko was fed up with his endless oration. It was like being forced to listen to a parochial piece of music. This man, who was throwing his life away for a useless hallucination. A world too distant from her own. What Mitsuko did understand was the ineffable weariness and muted hatred that the wife in *Thérèse Desqueyroux* had felt towards her estimable husband. She would tuck that weariness and hatred in the deepest part of her heart and carry on her life at Yano's side, though he reminded her so much of Bernard.

When they left the restaurant, she followed the French custom and shook Ōtsu's hand. 'Goodbye. I hope I'll see you again in Japan.'

'Thank you for the delicious meal.' Ōtsu nodded. 'And sorry.'

'Don't get yourself excommunicated, Mr Ōtsu,' Mitsuko joked. 'Do your best to get a little more adept at living.'

When she arrived in Paris that evening, Mitsuko hopped into a taxi at the railway station and gave the driver the name of her hotel, feeling as though she had returned home from a long journey. It seemed as though she had spent many years familiarizing herself with the banks of the Seine, where the street lights blurred over; with the Cathedral of Notre-Dame that soared up in its own illumination; with the black, gloomy Conciergerie.

'Now that you've come to France . . . haven't you felt any sense of friction?' Ōtsu's complaint was suddenly rekindled in her mind, but the reply she now mumbled to herself – 'I don't feel any friction at all. I wish I didn't have to go back to Japan' – was so loud that the taxi-driver, who clenched the butt of a cigarette in his mouth, turned round and looked at her.

She returned to the hotel, but Yano, as she had expected, was out. She bathed and did her make-up, waiting for his return. She climbed into bed and began watching television, but at some point the weariness of her solitary journey caught up with her and she fell asleep.

She awoke at the sound of the door opening. Yano came in smelling of alcohol.

'You're back? I would have been here if you'd let me know when you were coming back.'

'I'm sorry. You'll have to forgive me for being so self-indulgent on our honeymoon.'

'Did you have a good time?'

'Yes. I went across to Lyon after Bordeaux. The Church of St-Jean-Apôtre in Lyon and the ancient Roman theatre were splendid.' One after another she purposely listed places she knew would not arouse her husband's interest. 'I was able to see Les Landes. There's nothing but a pine forest and a pathetic village, so I know you wouldn't have wanted to spend more than an hour there. And how about you?'

'Mr Takabayashi from M. Limited showed me around.'

'"Paris for Men Only"?'

'I don't know about that. Montmartre and the Lido ... well, they weren't as interesting as I'd imagined. Takabayashi had a good laugh at our expense. He said he didn't know too many other newly-weds who behaved like us.'

Despite his remark, Yano didn't seem particularly displeased. Rather than being dragged by his wife to museums he was unprepared for, or to concerts he couldn't appreciate, this simple-minded man had had a far better time enjoying 'Paris for Men Only' with other Japanese.

Even so, that night he devoured Mitsuko's body like a pig wallowing in the food in its sty. The expression on a man's face when he is making love to a woman – from Mitsuko's experience – looks exactly the same from one man to the next. The bloodshot eyes and heavy panting. Only Mitsuko kept her wits about her. Unable to give herself over to the intoxication of passion, she wondered if she were a woman intrinsically incapable of loving another person. But what was love? Ōtsu had said that his Onion was an entity of unbounded gentleness and love, but....

Strangely, the image that was awakened in her mind at this moment was Ōtsu, walking across the place Bellecour in his seedy robe and huge lace-up boots. Ōtsu, oblivious to her feelings, blabbering on about his Onion. He was as tedious as her husband, who could talk of nothing but golf and new car models, but he was the complete antithesis of Yano and her friends from college.

Just what the hell is it I want? It was the only thought that filled her mind throughout her honeymoon.

FOUR

The Case of Numada

The sale of duty-free items began on the JAL flight bound for Delhi, and the stewardesses, whose faces until then had been those of prim *demoiselles*, suddenly took on the look of department-store assistants as they began selling liquor and tobacco from their carts. Numada thought he might buy some perfume for the wife he had left at home, but having no idea what kind she might prefer, he turned to Isobe in the neighbouring seat.

'Do you know anything about perfume?'

'Perfume?' Isobe grimaced. 'I'm afraid I don't.'

'I've left my wife at home, and I'm off to see India all by myself. . . . I thought I'd spend a little conscience money on her.'

'Oh, so it's a gift for your wife? That's very nice. Maybe if you asked the stewardess.'

'Are you going to buy something for your wife, Mr Isobe?'

'My wife is dead.'

'I'm sorry. I didn't realize.'

The stewardess asked how old Numada's wife was, then recommended a product called Ambassador. With a businesslike smile she asked, 'Will you be paying in yen or in dollars?'

Feeling diffident towards Isobe, Numada quietly placed the bottle

of perfume in his carrier-bag. Isobe had closed his eyes and was doz-
ing. In the seats behind them a honeymoon couple, the Sanjōs, were
snatching up items on offer in voices that betrayed their indifference
to those around them.

'You're buying two bottles of brandy?'

'They said it was hard to get liquor in India.'

'Then I'm throwing in some perfume, too.'

A stewardess spoke to Numada. 'Might you, by any chance, be the
Mr Numada who writes children's stories?'

Numada nodded in silent embarrassment.

'I studied children's literature in college. I read several of your
stories.'

'What I write ... it's actually not children's fiction. It's really stories
with dogs and birds as the main characters.'

'I just love cats.'

Isobe listened to this conversation with his eyes closed. If his wife
were still alive, he thought, he would certainly not be going to somewhere like India.

Numada spent the days of his youth in Dalian, Manchuria, which
at that time had been colonized by the Japanese. The Dalian he remembered was filled with the smells of the Russians who had occupied the land before Japan. The streets were lined with brick homes
and buildings, which were rare in Japan, and the roadways radiated
from their centre in the city square. Acacia and poplar trees, found in
Japan only in Hokkaidō, lined the streets, and the Japanese, brimming
with the vulgarity and the high-handedness of the parvenu, strolled
these streets disdainful of the Chinese who had lived here for countless years.

Even to the eyes of a child like Numada, the district where the Chinese lived seemed squalid and pitiful. When his father and mother
took him to the Chinese market-place, it reeked of the distinctive odour
of garlic, and pigs' heads and plucked chickens hung in many a shop.

Most mornings, Chinese women and children carrying baskets would
come peddling to the homes of the Japanese. Quail squawked and
scratched around inside some of their baskets, while others held brightly
hued melons or water-melons. Women and children hauled these heavy
panniers from door to door, the poles biting into their shoulders. Japanese housewives haggled and bartered as though it were expected,
then finally made their purchases.

Numada's mother hired one of those Chinese children as a house-boy. The Japanese in Dalian lived in Russian-style houses with chimneys, and on occasion they would take in Chinese children to help with housework and errands.

The boy hired in the Numada house was a fifteen-year-old youth named Li. He spoke broken Japanese, and with clumsy hands he helped Numada's mother in the kitchen, and in late autumn he began stoking the stove with coal. He had a gentle personality, and he would do his best to protect Numada, six years his junior, whenever his parents scolded him, and if Numada was late coming home from school, he would worry about him and come half-way to meet him.

One day on his way home from school, Numada picked up a stray dog that was covered with mud and had dried mucus clogging the corners of its eyes. It was a Manchurian hound with jet-black hair and a purple tongue, but it was so filthy his mother ordered him to get rid of it. 'Just one day!' Numada pleaded, almost in tears, and after he had Li wash the dog, he placed a wooden box filled with straw in a corner of the recessed dirt floor of the kitchen.

Lonely that night, the puppy wailed incessantly. When Numada went into the kitchen to pat its head, his father came out in his nightdress and roared: 'I can't stand this noise! Get rid of him tomorrow!'

The next day, all Numada could think about during school was the puppy. When classes were finished, he raced home. Li was chopping firewood in the garden, and when he saw Numada, he put his finger to his lips and motioned for Numada to come with him.

Numada followed Li to the coal-shed beside the fence. When the puppy, which was tied up behind the blackly glistening heap of coal, saw Numada, he frantically wagged his little tail and peed everywhere.

'Master, not tell Mother this,' Li instructed Numada, his smile a blend of shrewdness and gentleness.

'Only Master and Li know.'

'All right.'

From that day, the coal-shed became the two boys' secret hideaway. When he returned home from school, Numada would stealthily take the leftovers Li had put into a can and deliver them to the dog. They named him Blackie, and after his eyes healed and he learned to go quietly to sleep, Li brought Blackie back to the yard and said to Numada's mother, 'Madam, this dog come back. He not cry any more. He OK.'

She seemed aware of Li's fib, but she finally gave in to her son's entreaties and let him keep the dog.

About a month later, they fired Li. The padlock to the coal-shed had been opened and over half their supply of coal had disappeared. A Japanese policeman called, and he suspected Li of the theft. Someone reported that they had seen Li talking with other young Chinese boys near the shed.

'In any case, ma'am, he's the only one who had free access to the key.' The policeman noisily sipped a cup of tea at the doorway. 'You can't trust them. No matter how docile they look, you never know quite what plots are going through their minds.'

When Numada's father interrogated Li, the boy continued to shake his head in denial. Numada listened from behind the door to his father's angry accusations, and he felt as though his throat were going to close up on him as he stole glances at Li, who was making incoherent excuses.

The upshot was that Li was kicked out of the Numada house. There were any number of houseboys or amahs to be found in Dalian to take his place.

On the day he left, Li carried with him only a pathetically tiny, soiled bundle of possessions.

'Master, sayonara. Master, sayonara.' Li opened the kitchen door and repeated over and over, 'Master, sayonara. Master, sayonara.'

Many years later, Numada could still remember Li's acquiescent smile.

Blackie grew larger. He wagged his tail so vigorously it seemed as though it would twist right off. He changed from a puppy into a plump adult Manchu hound. While Numada was off playing with his friends, the dog would wait glumly beneath an acacia tree for them to finish. When Numada set off for school or returned home, the dog would follow sluggishly behind him. If Numada said anything to him – 'I hate studying. I wish they'd just get rid of all the schools' – Blackie would peer into his face as though he were staring at something far off in the distance.

In the autumn of Numada's third year in primary school, the relationship between his parents soured and there was talk of divorce. This was completely unexpected, unimaginable to Numada. He had never even considered the possibility that he and his father and mother might end up living apart from each other.

At night when his father came home drunk, he would argue for long hours with his wife in the living-room. From time to time he could hear his father's shouts and his mother's weeping voice, and he would pull the covers up over his head to block them out, sometimes even stuffing his fingers in his ears so he could get to sleep.

He hated coming home from school. At home he would have to look at his once cheerful mother, who now sat by herself in the dark, chilly room and stared out of the window lost in thought. Even though it was not a great distance from school to his home, Numada would take his time along the road, walking slowly, stopping to stare at the remains of autumn cicadas dangling from the tangled threads of spiders' webs, or delaying his return home by even one more minute by scribbling graffiti on a red brick fence with chalk. At a crossroads he would hear a Chinese vendor selling roasted chestnuts, and carriage mules waiting for customers along the roadside flicked their tails and ears to chase away swarming flies. While Numada's attention was caught up in these activities, Blackie would come to a halt and scratch his head with his leg and sniff around the wall while he waited for his master.

'I don't want to go home.' Numada could talk only to Blackie. The pain from home engorging his heart that he could not discuss with his teachers or schoolmates he conveyed only to Blackie.

'I hate it! I hate it when night comes. I'm sick of hearing Dad and Mother argue.'

Blackie stared at Numada's face, and feebly wagged his tale in bewilderment.

Can't be helped. That's what life's all about, Blackie would answer. When Numada himself grew older and thought back on those days, he was certain that Blackie had spoken to him.

'Dad says he's going to live away from Mother. What am I going to do?'

Can't be helped.

'If I live with Dad, that would hurt Mother, and if I live with Mother, that would be a bad thing to do to Dad.'

Can't be helped. That's what life's all about.

Blackie had been the one who understood his sorrow in those days, the only living thing who would listen to his complaints: his companion.

Autumn came to an end, winter passed, and a late spring finally came to Dalian in May. It was decided then that his mother would return to Japan and take Numada with her. White buds the size of young girls' earrings dangled between the leaves of the acacia trees that lined the streets. Next to the pavement a carriage waited to take mother and son to Dalian harbour. His father withdrew in silence to an inner room and did not come out to see them off. Only Blackie loitered in front of the mule that swished at horseflies with its tail.

When the carriage lurched forward, Numada turned round and watched as Blackie chased after them. His eyes grew moist even though he struggled not to cry, and he turned his face away so that his mother wouldn't notice. Even after they turned a corner, Blackie continued in pursuit. He seemed almost to know that this was the last time he would see Numada. Eventually Blackie tired and came to a stop, growing smaller in the distance while he watched with resignation in his eyes as Numada left him. Numada as an adult had still not forgotten those eyes of Blackie's. It was thanks to Li and to this dog that he had first come to know the meaning of separation.

If I hadn't had Blackie with me then, Numada thought in later years, *I doubt I ever would have written a children's story.*

Blackie was the first dog to teach him that animals can converse with humans. Not just conversing – he had also learned they can be companions who understand your sorrows. Numada, realizing that the only way to achieve such a thing in our present day and age was through *Märchen*, had chosen the writing of children's stories as his life's work while he was in college. He took great pleasure writing in his books about dogs and goats and ponies, and, yes, birds too, who understood the sorrows of children – because the various sorrows associated with human life have already been generated in childhood.

Once after he had become a children's writer, Numada owned a peculiar bird known as a hornbill. It would be closer to the truth to say that he had had the bird forced on him by an old man at the local department store who ran the pet department where freshwater fish and songbirds were sold.

This old man was a strange one himself, with a face like a bird, who warmed up suddenly to Numada when he discovered he was a writer of children's stories, and he took it upon himself to provide Numada with a complete tank unit filled with guppies, and turned up uninvited to give impassioned lectures on the proper care of songbirds.

One day he popped up on Numada's doorstep, accompanied by a

young man in working clothes, carrying a large *furoshiki*-wrapped parcel. 'This fellow's a friend of mine. He has a shop at Shibuya where he sells little birds and animals. He's just recently got his hands on a hornbill. And here's what I said to him. "I know a man like Mr Numada would want a bird like this."'

Numada couldn't fathom why he had been chosen to be the owner of this hornbill, but the old man, oblivious to his opinions, untied the knot to the *furoshiki*.

Inside the wire cage, a black bird perhaps five or six centimetres tall clung to its perch. It had a large beak, and there was a massive protuberance on its upper beak that resembled a rhinoceros horn. It looked for all the world like a large-nosed pierrot.

'It was captured in Africa.' The old man nudged his friend, 'That's right, isn't it?'

'Yes, this is a bird that lives only in the tropics. He has a very interesting face.'

'You can use this bird in your stories, sir. Because of his freakish face.'

Why had the old man supposed that a bird as queer as this could become the hero of one of his stories? The characters that appeared in his little collections of tales were all everyday dogs and cats and rabbits and pigs that children could feel close to.

'Well, why not, after all? I'll leave it here for a week, so you can have a go at taking care of it.' Ignoring Numada's hesitancy, the old man and his chum left the birdcage in Numada's office and vanished.

Once they had gone, the room occupied only by Numada and the hornbill suddenly grew silent. In that quiet space, the bird with the pierrot face balanced on its perch and stared at a single space in the void. Its face was so comical it seemed all the more doleful.

'Now, where did you come from?' Numada asked. 'Are you really from Africa?'

Numada had never been to Africa. It was a world far too removed, far too inaccessible in comparison with America or England, which he had visited. Had this pierrot, born in the dense jungles of Africa, ever imagined that he would be brought to an unfamiliar land like Japan? Even birds, like people, had their various fates determined for them.

Numada's wife was not happy that her husband had taken in this troublesome bird, but his children were delighted. They named the hornbill Pierrot-chan, and every day they ogled him in his cage, but in less than two weeks they tired of this and kept their distance. The hornbill didn't sing in a charming voice like a canary, and moved around very little in his cage. And the odour wafting from the cage was overpowering.

'Pierrot,' Numada called to him. 'You're not getting a very warm reception here, you know. Would you like to go back to the pet store?'

Pierrot gave no response at all, but stared like a stuffed bird at a single point in the air, shifting his body only slightly to change position.

One day Numada opened the door to the cage and let Pierrot loose, hoping to grant a small measure of freedom to this bird from the distant jungles of Africa. But Pierrot took a few hesitant steps, evidently at a loss, and came to a stop beside the glass door. There he stared fixedly out of the window.

Numada set about his work. Noiselessly, the hornbill continued to stare outside. As dusk approached, the sunlight on the window began to fade. The only sound to be heard was the dry scratching of Numada's pen as he wrote his manuscript.

It was then he heard the unbearably plaintive cry. It was a painful wail filled with sorrow, and it faded away like a candle-flame that sputters and dies. The hornbill had sung out. It seemed to Numada that Pierrot had channelled his flood of emotions into a single cry of 'I'm lonely!' For the first time, he felt a sense of affinity with this comical Pierrot.

A new bond between Numada and Pierrot was forged that day. During the day, Numada would cut apples into tiny pieces, and when he tired of his work he would toss a slice to Pierrot, who perched beside the window. Pierrot would stretch out his neck and skilfully snatch the slice up with his large beak. This amusement frequently brought comfort to Numada as he wrote, and it seemed almost like a game played between congenial brothers.

At night, after his family had all gone to sleep, while Numada worked at his desk, Pierrot would discourteously spread his wings without any warning and fly up to the bookshelf near Numada. From the shelf he would look down at Numada while he worked.

'So, what are you doing there, old fellow?' Pierrot asked.

'I'm writing a children's story.'

'What kind of story?'

'Sort of a free rendition of dreams I had when I was a child. In my stories human children can talk to dogs and even to birds like you.

The dog in this one's named Blackie, and Blackie and the young hero...'

'Boring. Those are just dreams made up to please yourself, aren't they? Take a look at me. I've been brought from the distant forests where my friends reside to this alien land so that I can be a source of comfort to you.'

'Maybe that's true. But you have no idea how much comfort birds like you and dogs have brought me since I was a child. Even tonight... having you here in the room with me... it helps.'

Numada didn't know how to explain his yearning for a connection with every living thing. The seed that Blackie had planted inside Numada in his childhood had slowly sprouted to create an idealized world that he could describe only in his children's stories. In his stories, a young man could understand the whisperings of flowers, the conversations exchanged between trees, and could even decode the signals that bees and ants sent to their respective fellow-insects. A solitary dog and a single hornbill had a share in the loneliness that he as an adult could not dispel on his own. . . .

But Pierrot, as if in disregard of his sentimentality, flapped his wings on the shelf and headed off for another corner of the room. When Numada got around to looking in his direction, Pierrot was sleeping with one leg lifted and the feathers on his head pricked up.

'I can't stand the way it messes up your room. And it does its business right on the floor.' Numada's wife frequently complained about the way Numada let the hornbill have free run of his study. Most of their marital tiffs centred on the bird. Just as his wife said, even though Numada opened the window often, his room still smelled of the peculiar odour of a bird, and the black carpet was dotted here and there with Pierrot's white droppings. There was no question that this bird with the odd face was as big an annoyance and nuisance to Numada's wife, who had to tend to the house, as Jesus had been to the rabbis of his day.

It is a strange metaphor to compare such a bird with Jesus, but Numada had his reasons for doing so. Numada had taken a liking to Rouault's paintings, and there was something about the many Pierrot faces he portrayed in his works that resembled this hornbill. He knew that for Rouault clowns were a symbol of Christ. There was no reason to expect that his wife could understand the spiritual exchanges that took place between Numada, as he worked late into the night, and this bird, which studied his every move. Over the course of his marriage, Numada had realized that in every companionship there remains a mutually insoluble loneliness. But in the stillness of night, his own loneliness and the loneliness of the bird came into contact with one another.

Two months passed. The old man from the pet store who brought the bird over never appeared again. Maybe he and his friend had imported the bird and then ran into problems when they couldn't sell it. If that were the case, something in Numada's feelings drew him towards the bird for that reason, also.

Numada started to complain of low-grade fevers in the afternoons, and he began to feel an indescribable heaviness in his body. The doctor in the neighbourhood who examined him said he could hear a rustle in Numada's chest, and while he was taking him over to the X-ray room, he asked in a roundabout way, 'I don't suppose you've ever had any problems with tuberculosis?' The results of the X-rays were bleak, as the doctor had suspected. At the university hospital, where his publisher arranged for Numada to undergo further tests, he was immediately ordered in for a year of treatment.

Numada and his wife were confused and perplexed at this unexpected calamity. He had in fact contracted tuberculosis as a young man, and at the time had received pneumothorax treatment, which was the only available therapy, but the pulmonary cavities that he had thought were healed had at some point suffered a relapse.

His wife began making various preparations before his hospitalization, and said to him with a sober look: 'Listen . . . what are we going to do about that bird after you go into the hospital? There's no way I can take care of it myself. Please have the pet-store owner take it back.'

What she said made sense. 'All right, I will,' he said, nodding.

He went back into his study and let Pierrot out of his cage. As always, Pierrot walked over to the window and stared at the Tanzawa mountain range, bathed the colour of wine in the evening sun.

'Sayonara.' His hands thrust into his pockets, Numada looked down at the bird and muttered. Suddenly he thought of the day in his youth when he had said 'Sayonara' to Blackie. Then, too, incontestable circumstances had forced him and Blackie apart. And now once again an unforeseen situation was obliging him to part with Pierrot, who had brought such consolation to his nights.

Numada ended up spending not just one year but two in the hospital. During that time recently developed antibiotics had some effect, and he went under the surgeon's knife. The two operations failed, however, because the pleurae that had undergone pneumothorax treatment many years before had fused together, and he ended up with pneumonia and pleural effusion. Neither the physician in charge, who made his regular rounds, nor the professors at the university hospital, who turned up once a week with young interns in tow, said anything to Numada. But he could tell from the expressions on their faces that they were at a loss how to treat him.

To Numada, it was distasteful to consider staying alive another ten or fifteen years bereft of the ability to do anything. Numada and the other patients on his floor knew of a patient down the hall with pleural effusion upon whom surgery had failed, rendering him a living corpse.

'I'd like you to go ahead and operate,' Numada pleaded with the attending physician, but the cloudy reply was 'Well, we're considering that, but. . . .' If they stripped the pleurae that had fused together even more after his two most recent operations, the doctors feared that Numada might run the risk of massive haemorrhaging.

While these deliberations were going on, Numada would often climb by himself to the roof of the hospital and stare at the sun setting in the west. He realized as he stood there that he had adopted the same pose as the hornbill. When he was released from his cage, the bird would peer from the study window at the wine-coloured Tanzawa range and the sun setting on Mount Ōyama. Numada had come to understand to a painful degree just how Pierrot had felt.

He wondered how the bird was doing. He wished he could have spent his nights in his hospital room with the bird. He was tired of feigning vitality in the presence of the doctors and nurses and his wife, and as in the past it was the bird, and not another human being, that he craved for a companion with whom he could share his feelings. He wanted the kind of miserable, foolish Pierrot that Rouault had drawn. . . .

But he couldn't bring himself to express these feelings to his wife. He couldn't heap an additional burden on her, for she came to visit him between taking care of the children and looking after the house.

Then one day while he was reading the newspaper, he showed a photograph of some migratory birds to her and casually muttered, 'I wonder where my hornbill is these days?'

She said nothing at the time, but three or four days later she appeared in his room carrying a large *furoshiki* parcel.

'Here, this is for you.' There was affected enthusiasm in her voice as her husband stared curiously at the parcel. 'Please open it up.'

He untied the knot, and under the cloth wrapping found a square wooden cage with a myna bird as black as lacquer frantically flapping its wings inside.

'Dear.' Numada was moved by his wife's thoughtfulness.

'You haven't got your hornbill any more, so try to keep going with this myna.'

'I didn't mean you to do something like this when I made that remark.'

'It's all right. You wanted it, didn't you? I could tell as much.'

Numada felt guilty towards his wife. Ever since he was a child, he had confessed the secrets of his heart to dogs and birds instead of to other humans. This time, his wife had managed to discern somewhere in his heart the desire to confess his despondency over the string of failed operations to a bird like the hornbill.

At the same time, he felt that it was better like this. Even if he did tell his wife of his inconsolable suffering, all it would do would be to cause her distress. It would bring her pain to no purpose, and serve merely to heap more burdens upon her. But if he told all to a bird . . . it would silently take it all in.

'Are you feeling a little cheerier now?' his wife asked exultantly. 'This is the first time in a long while I've seen a happy look on your face.'

The chime signalling the end of visiting hours rang, and as she picked up her bag and started out of the room she winked at him.

Inside its cage, the myna bird leaped back and forth between its two perches without showing any signs of boredom, but it never once sang. It seemed as though the bird-store owner had not yet taught it to say even 'good morning' or 'hello'.

But after he had finished supper and it was almost time to go to sleep, Numada heard a strange voice call 'Ha ha!' from inside the birdcage. It was the bird's first song.

'Ha ha!' was not this bird's native song. After he thought about it for a moment, Numada realized it was the sound of laughter.

Had it been placed next to another myna that spoke in human vocabulary, but picked up only the laughing voices of the store-owners?

When Numada woke up in the middle of the night, he would quietly lift the *furoshiki* from the cage that hung above his bed. The myna sat with both legs poised on its perch and stared back at Numada. Its eyes were just like those of the hornbill that had balanced on his bookcase and watched the movements of his pen.

'I wonder if I'm going to get better? My pleurae are fused together, and if I have another operation. . . .' Numada spoke to the bird the words he could not say to his wife. 'If I have another operation, I'm sure to haemorrhage a lot. The doctors are afraid of that. But I can't stand the thought of spending the rest of my life in bed. I want to have that operation, no matter what. You understand how I feel, don't you?'

The myna cocked its head a bit and leaped from perch to perch. And then, mimicking a human voice, it laughed, 'Ha ha!'

Each evening, he divulged his agony and his regrets to the bird. Just as he had complained of his loneliness as a child to Blackie.

'I don't want to cause my wife any more distress. You're the only one I can talk to this way. . . . I'm scared of dying. I want to live and write even better stories. I'm worried, if I die, how my wife and children will live. . . . What should I do?'

'What should I do?' – the echo of those words seemed so theatrical that Numada was embarrassed. But that was how he honestly felt.

'Ha ha! Ha ha!' The myna chortled. The laugh seemed at once to mock his cowardice and to offer encouragement.

Numada turned out the light in his room and felt that the only real conversations he had had in his life had been with dogs and birds. He didn't know anything about God, but if God was someone humans could talk to from the heart, then for him that was, by turns, Blackie, the hornbill and this myna.

His third operation, a gamble of sorts, was performed in December. On a morning when the steam heat in his room spewed out louder than usual, Numada was given an anaesthetic and a nurse wheeled his stretcher down the long corridor towards the operating-theatre. *When they bring me back down here*, Numada thought as he stared at the astral lamps on the ceiling, *will I still be alive?*

He was brought back to his room after four hours of surgery, but it wasn't until the following morning that he awoke from the anaesthetic. A rubber tube had been stuck into his nose and an IV needle had been inserted into his arm. From time to time a nurse came in to test the half-conscious man's blood pressure and give him a shot of morphine. Everything was as it had been after his second operation.

Several days later, when he finally regained consciousness, he asked his wife, who had remained at his side, 'How's the myna?'

She was at a loss for an answer. 'I was so busy taking care of you, I left it on the roof of the hospital and forgot all about it. By the time I realized and went up to look ... it was dead.'

There was no point in blaming his wife. She couldn't have been expected to look after the myna on the roof when she had to devote all her attention to caring for her husband, who hovered between life and death.

'I'm sorry.'

Numada nodded, but he wanted at least to see the cage.

'The cage.' He tried to sound unconcerned to avoid hurting her feelings. 'The nurses might get upset if you just left it sitting up there.'

'I'll throw it away tonight.'

'It'd be a shame to throw it away. I like that cage. Once I get better, maybe I'll get a sparrow or something.'

To continue the conversation was too suffocating for him, and the wound on his punctured chest was aching. He said no more.

That evening, his wife went up to the roof and brought the birdcage to his room.

'Put it there.'

'It's filthy. Let me wrap it in something.'

'No. Leave it like that.'

His wife went to the nurses' station. Left alone in his room, Numada was able to study the cage carefully. The myna's brownish-white droppings had encrusted the perches and the floor of the cage. Two black feathers had stuck to the droppings. As he looked at the feathers, he was struck forcefully with the realization that the bird that had listened each night to his grumblings and his pain had died. Suddenly Numada remembered crying to the myna, 'What should I do?'

I wonder if it died in place of me?

A feeling very close to certainty boiled up like hot water from his lacerated chest. He realized how much of a support dogs and birds and other living creatures had been to him throughout his life.

Numada's recovery after surgery, the source of such profound concern to his doctors, was nearly miraculous. When he passed the test for pleural effusion, the doctor in charge shook Numada's hand and said, 'You're a lucky man. I'm very relieved. I can tell you this now, but. ...'

'I know,' Numada nodded. 'It was a fifty-fifty gamble, wasn't it? The potential for danger was very high, and you and the other doctors weren't sure what to do.'

'To tell you the truth ... while you were on the operating-table ... your heart stopped for a time.'

Projected against Numada's eyelids at that moment were a myna bird laughing 'Ha ha!' and a hornbill peering down at him from the bookshelf with a mocking glare.

FIVE

The Case of Kiguchi

Kiguchi was impressed that their guide, Enami, who sat in the seat beside him, was able to fall asleep as soon as the plane lifted off from Narita Airport, and with the way he dived into his meal the moment it was brought round. Enami put his fork down and looked over at Kiguchi.

'You don't eat meat, eh?'

'It must be my age. I can't bite it with my dentures. That's probably why I've ended up liking fish better.'

Kiguchi turned his eyes away from his plate and looked out of the window. He could, of course, see nothing, but he wondered if the land below was covered with jungle.

'Is that a jungle down there?'

'Let's see.' Enami glanced at his wrist-watch. 'Judging from the time, we could be flying over Thailand now, so there's a possibility that it's jungle. Are you interested in jungles?'

'I fought in the Burma jungle during the war.'

'Really? I'm afraid that's something my generation doesn't know much about, but I understand the fighting was fierce in Burma.'

Fierce – Kiguchi smirked at the word. The retreat, the starvation, the daily torrents of rain, their despair and exhaustion – these were things that Enami's generation could never begin to understand. Kiguchi had no desire to talk of them. All he could do was grimace when he was asked about them.

The sea of trees pounded by the rain. Their retreat through those trees. Malaria. Starvation. Despair.

We trudged through there like sleep-walkers heading for death.

He had heard that India also had a rainy season, but he had no sense of what it was like. But Japanese soldiers such as himself had experienced the rainy season in Burma, to the east of India, down to the marrow in their bones. The rainy season had arrived while his unit was on the retreat from Mount Popa to Sinzwe, pursued by British and Indian troops.

Suddenly – and 'suddenly' was the only way to describe it – one morning in May, the temperature had dropped precipitously. Humidity choked the air. The sky, which had been clear the previous day, was covered with steel-grey clouds. The rainy season had begun. Thereafter, rain fell each day, the initial drizzle turning into a downpour.

The downpour was quite unlike the rainy season in Japan. The bonnet of bluish-black leaves from the sea of trees echoed with a deafening crash, and water poured between them like a waterfall.

The unit to which Kiguchi and Tsukada belonged walked from the east side of the Pegu Yoma towards the west. No; they hadn't walked. They had desperately dragged their legs along from a determination to stay alive.

By then every member of the unit was suffering from malnutrition. Over half the men had contracted malaria. Their doctor, Ōhashi, had warned the men not to drink the water, since cholera had reached epidemic stages in the flatlands, but many of the soldiers consistently found blood in their stools, whether from dysentery or malaria they couldn't tell.

It had been three days since they had put anything resembling food into their mouths, and that had been some mangoes from a grove they stumbled across on the outskirts of a tiny village. They skinned the hard, green mangoes and sliced the white fruit into tiny pieces and salted them before they ate them. The taste reminded the soldiers of the pickled vegetables they had eaten almost daily in Japan. Dr Ōhashi made the rounds of the men, who moved their hands and mouths like ravenous demons, and warned them, 'There may be cyanide in them. Be careful!' Even so, they gobbled the fruit down.

As a result, many of the soldiers developed stomach-aches. One, then another would peel off from the unit and disappear into the sea of trees to cope with their diarrhoea. Their stools were black in colour and smelled dreadful. Some fell over where they had crouched to relieve themselves, unable to move any more. When the senior soldiers barked at them, in lifeless voices they pleaded, 'I can't walk. Please let me die here.' Eventually these pleading voices could be heard throughout the jungle.

Occasionally the rain would stop. And for a brief time the clouds would clear away. Tiny birds would begin to sing here and there. Between their cheerful, chirping voices, human moans of 'Let me die here' echoed to the right and the left.

The columns of Japanese soldiers seemed less like a retreating force of fighting men than the night-time rout of a detachment of phantoms. Even when they encountered an officer hobbling along with a cane hand-made from a pine branch as he struggled to keep up with his unit, the soldiers would pass him with empty eyes, pretending they could not even see him. Their weapons, presented to them on behalf of the Emperor as objects more precious than their own lives, were discarded along with their swords, and many of the men carried nothing more than mess-kits and hand-grenades at their waists. The mess-kits contained the 'Firefly Gruel' they would sip that day, a kind of porridge made from jungle weeds with a few grains of rice floating in it. Hand-grenades were their ultimate weapons, to be used to take their own lives when they no longer had the strength to move. In fact, from time to time the jungle ahead of and behind them shook from the sudden roar of an exploding grenade. These were the sounds of men taking their own lives. Even at those sounds the surviving soldiers, who walked like somnambulists dressed in tatters, registered no change in the expressions on their faces.

After Kiguchi was repatriated to Japan, he never wanted to remember that hell again. He didn't want to talk to anyone about it. Even had he chosen to discuss it, there was no reason why the women and children who had remained in Japan could comprehend it. Those who were drafted and indolently welcomed the conclusion of the war at bases far from harm's way could not begin to grasp it. The only ones who could truly understand what they had been through were their comrades who had passed through the sea of trees and hobbled with them along the road that the soldiers would later call the 'Highway of Death'. Tsukada was the valued war comrade who had journeyed through that inferno with Kiguchi.

As they dragged their legs along in utter exhaustion, they lost track of whether they were dreaming or awake. Kiguchi had seen an exact replica of himself walking alongside him.

'Walk! You must keep walking!' His double, or perhaps the Kiguchi who was about to collapse physically, had bellowed at him. 'Walk! Keep walking!'

Even after he returned home alive, Kiguchi could not bring himself to believe that this had been an apparition. He was certain that his exact duplicate had stood at his side, berating him.

When they entered the Highway of Death, Kiguchi and Tsukada had their first glimpse of a terrifying spectacle. The corpses of Japanese soldiers lay piled in heaps on both sides of the road. Maggots swarmed around the noses and lips of the dead, and even of the soldiers who were still faintly breathing, and from the right they heard some men cry 'Kill me!' The same voices echoed from the left. All called out 'Kill me', as though they were a chorus singing *sotto voce*. But none would come to their aid. In spite of the grisly scene, when the rains stopped, the birds chirped happily away. All Kiguchi and his comrades could do was avert their eyes and mutter 'Sorry, sorry' to themselves.

Then suddenly a soldier, his ribs poking through his skin, sat up and shouted, as though it were his final howl, 'That bastard Mutaguchi!' Mutaguchi was the commanding officer of the Japanese Army in Burma, the man who had ordered every division to participate in this reckless operation. He was the officer who had sent notice to each soldier declaring: 'This battle is the ultimate duty of our soldiers. Every one of you is to believe firmly in inevitable victory, and you are to attack the enemy with all your might, even if you are the last soldier left alive.'

They finally made their way to the slope of a valley where they found three or four houses, but the residents had all fled. The soldiers desperately searched the houses one by one for food, but could find nothing to put into their mouths. The units that had already passed this way had rummaged through everything.

In a small hut a sick soldier abandoned by his unit waited, barely breathing, for death. The blanket coiled around his body hinted at the feverish chills of malaria that tormented him. He leaned against the wall of the hut, peering languidly at Kiguchi and Tsukada, then closed his eyes. He no longer had the energy to speak.

'Did they leave you here?' Kiguchi approached the man and asked.

The soldier nodded almost imperceptibly. But he seemed to have resigned himself to everything – even to death – and sought no assistance. No doubt he would use up the last reserves of energy in his body tonight or tomorrow and breathe his last.

In the end ... this is what'll happen to me. Kiguchi was thinking more of his own pathetic situation than expressing his pity for this soldier. Such feelings rallied what remained of his own energy.

'You've got to hold on. I'm sure help will come.' Tsukada spoke the conscience-salving words and fled from the hut with Kiguchi. It was pitch-black on the other side of the doorway, and they could hear no response from the ailing soldier.

It was the following day that Kiguchi was besieged by what he had feared when he saw that dying soldier in the hut.

That evening, Kiguchi felt indescribable waves of chills wash over his spine. Soon every one of his joints felt as though they had come unhinged, and he could no longer keep up with the ranks of companies that continued to stream past.

'Tsukada.' With no shame or self-respect left to him, Kiguchi called feebly to the comrade who had come to his side. 'I've got malaria. I can't walk. You go on.'

Tsukada said something, but Kiguchi could not make it out. *I'm going to die like this*, he thought, his conscious mind blurring as he lay on the ground. Later, drops of rain began to fall on his cheeks through gaps in the tree leaves, and when he opened his eyes at the sensation, what he saw was the grizzled, sunken-cheeked face of Tsukada, his neck gaunt and his Adam's apple protruding.

'You stayed here with me?' Kiguchi asked as his voice choked with tears. He and Tsukada had been comrades in arms since the machine-gun corps had been organized at Akyab a year before.

'Yeah.'

'And our company?'

'They've gone on ahead. The orders from the company commander are for us to meet them at the River Kun as soon as you're able to walk.'

'I ... I can't do it.'

'Eat this.' His mess-kit contained the paltry mixture of rice and weeds they called 'Firefly Gruel'.

'Where did this rice come from?'

'A fallen soldier had it,' Tsukada answered. 'This is the last of it.'

'You're not giving it to the owner?'

'I don't think he has the energy to eat. Don't think about it. You sleep, and eat what I find for you.'

Kiguchi nodded and closed his eyes, which were clogged with tears and dried mucus. During this retreat, in which every one of the Japanese soldiers suffered from hunger and disease and weariness, there was nothing unusual about a soldier abandoning a debilitated comrade, even if it was his friend. If he did not abandon the other, there was no guarantee for his own life. But Tsukada did not abandon his friend Kiguchi.

In his ebbing consciousness, Kiguchi heard faint explosions from British reconnaissance planes and the massive pounding of the Japanese 92-mm heavy artillery guns. He had the impression that the fighting was continuing somewhere in the distance, but perhaps his ears were playing tricks on him.

When birds began shrieking in the trees near dawn, Kiguchi awoke trembling throughout his body from fever. Tsukada was nowhere to be seen.

So he's left me, has he?

Later, when he reflected on it, it seemed strange to him, but his mind at that time was oddly at peace, and he felt neither resentment nor anger, since abandonment was a law of nature in these circumstances. Just as a wounded bird or insect would die quietly in this jungle, he too would expire here, and disintegrate and return to the earth: that was how he felt.

The cry of a bird, overflowing with life. As he listened to it, he closed his eyes. This was how everything would come to an end. He heard the sound of footsteps crunching dry leaves, then approaching him. It was Tsukada.

'Ah!' Kiguchi began to weep. 'I thought you'd . . . gone to join the company.'

'Eat this.' Tsukada took a chunk of something black from his mess-kit and brought it to Kiguchi's lips with a pair of chopsticks. 'It's meat.'

'Meat? You found some meat?'

'Last night I went down from this valley and found a village. It was deserted, but there was one dead cow. We can still eat. I cooked it, so there's nothing to worry about.'

'Thank you.' But Kiguchi was so weak that, even though the 'Firefly Gruel' would slip down his throat, he was unable to swallow the decaying meat.

'If you don't eat . . . you'll die!' Tsukada snarled, forcing the tiny morsel into his mouth. 'You must make yourself eat.' But Kiguchi, unable to bear the smell, coughed it up again.

Even now Kiguchi didn't like to think back on that ghastly rout. After his repatriation, he almost never spoke to anyone about his war experiences.

Once back in Japan, however, after resuming his life with his wife and children, every now and then he would be driven to distraction by the emotions that came flooding back. His parents' house in a hot-springs resort area near Nagano City had been fortunate enough to escape the air raids, and his family had been evacuated there, but when his children complained that all they had to eat then was rice mixed with other grains, or that they hadn't been able to get any sweet meats, he responded with violence excessive for a father. His wife, who knew only the gentle man he had once been, could merely look on with stupefaction at the change in him. When this happened, being the sort of man he was, he would go back to his room, pull the covers over his head, and moan and weep. He could see before his eyes the Highway of Death piled deep with corpses, and the still-living soldiers with maggots swarming over their noses and mouths. From the very depths of his heart he abhorred the 'Democracy' and 'Peace Movements' in post-war Japan that passed judgement on everything without regard for any of that suffering.

Three years after the defeat, Kiguchi finally returned to Tokyo. He started up a small freight company, and business progressed smoothly thanks to the boom in the munitions industry during the Korean war.

Around the time Tokyo began to look like a real city again, Kiguchi noticed one day that a man on the subway platform was staring curiously at him. It was his friend Tsukada. When they recognized each other, they cried out like animals and rushed towards one another.

That night, Kiguchi made the rounds of the bars with Tsukada. At a grilled chicken shop Tsukada related, in the southern dialect he had picked up somewhere along the way, that he had moved in with his wife's family in Uto in Kyushu and now worked for the national railways, and that he had come up to Tokyo on business. The two men talked about all manner of things, but they never mentioned the Highway of Death. Kiguchi was painfully aware of the feelings that led Tsukada to avoid the topic.

'Are you sure you can handle all this liquor?' Kiguchi began to feel a little uneasy at the way Tsukada gulped down his *sake*. As he continued to drink, the light in his eyes gradually darkened and he lapsed into silence. He poured one glass of liquor after another down his throat, as though he were trying to force something back. Kiguchi felt he could understand what his friend was going through.

'Would you like me to help you home?' he asked, but Tsukada shook his head, and after they left the shop, he disappeared into the nearly deserted Shibuya Station.

That was their first meeting since the war, and several more years passed. Some ten years later, Tsukada wrote to Kiguchi to ask if he could find him a job in Tokyo. In the latter he wrote: 'I'm asking you to help me, as one who shared the pleasures and pains of that Highway with you in the past.' Those words made Kiguchi a bit uneasy, for he sensed in them Tsukada's attempt to remind him of how he had fed the stricken Kiguchi 'Firefly Gruel' and brought him meat. But he put in a word with an acquaintance, and secured Tsukada a position as the manager of an apartment building.

Tsukada came to Tokyo with his wife, and Kiguchi went to meet them on the platform at Tokyo Station. Tsukada's wife stood behind her husband and bowed over and over again to Kiguchi.

'Listen,' Tsukada explained to his wife, 'I was a seasoned soldier – I'd joined up six months before Kiguchi here. In the army, there's a difference in status between a trained soldier and a new recruit, even if in age they're only a month apart.' Kiguchi could sense the feelings of inferiority that drove Tsukada to speak with such deliberate haughtiness, and he courteously told her, 'Your husband ... did a lot for me on the battlefield.' She continued to display her gratitude with incessant bowing.

Since Tsukada was the kind of man who performed his assigned duties faithfully, just as he had while on military service, Kiguchi was given no reason to be ashamed for having introduced him to the friend who owned the building.

'The only problem,' Kiguchi's friend said, smiling sardonically, 'is that he gets a bit carried away bellowing at deliverymen who don't obey the parking rules, and at pushy salesmen.'

Kiguchi apologized, acknowledging that this had been Tsukada's nature ever since he had known him in the army.

'He takes things too seriously,' his friend replied, smiling. 'Men who are too serious are the first to break.'

Men who are too serious are the first to break. A year after moving to Tokyo, Tsukada vomited blood.

'I'm so sorry. He had too much to drink again last night.' Tsukada's wife, who telephoned Kiguchi with the news, apologized falteringly. 'He told me I wasn't to let you know ... but they took him to the hospital in an ambulance.'

'The hospital? Which hospital?'

Kiguchi had invited Tsukada out for drinks a couple of times since his arrival in Tokyo. Both times he had spoken some words of caution to Tsukada for his somehow maniacal way of drinking, but Tsukada had said: 'Since the war, I haven't been able to make my way around the world like you have. If I don't drink, I can't stay in good spirits. You understand, don't you?' With an answer like that, Kiguchi could say nothing, having shared that grotesque hell with his friend.

He raced over to the hospital, where Tsukada's wife was waiting for him by the elevator. Her husband, she reported, had been placed in the intensive care unit and was now sleeping. He had vomited up a tremendous amount of blood and fainted in their bathroom.

She seemed to fear stomach cancer more than anything, so Kiguchi consoled her, 'It's blood that he's coughed up from his stomach. With cancer, you don't bring up so much blood.' He then went to talk to the middle-aged doctor who was handling Tsukada's case.

In a corner of the hallway, the doctor reported in a soft voice: 'He's not in any condition for us to run any tests yet. But in the digital examination we found a lump on the right side of his abdomen. It may be the oesophageal varices that accompany cirrhosis. His wife says he's been drinking a lot of *sake*.'

'Yes.' Kiguchi decided to divulge everything to this homely fellow. 'He seems to be drinking like an alcoholic.'

'Is there any sort of psychological reason why he feels he has to drink?'

'Psychological?'

'Well, for instance....' The doctor looked at the chart in his hands. 'Any contention at home, or problems at work?'

'I don't think there's anything like that.'

'If his drinking has any psychological foundation, then to cure him of his dependency, I think we ought to have him talk to a psychologist at the same time we work on his physical condition.'

'Would you like me to talk to him about it? We were the best of friends during the war.'

'Ah, wartime friends, were you?'

As he walked back down the corridor, Kiguchi concluded that the impressions he had vaguely felt were true after all. But he had no idea what it was that was clouding Tsukada's eyes and making him drown in alcohol. As he started towards the intensive care ward to talk to Tsukada's wife, he passed a short young foreigner wearing glasses who was pushing an old man in a wheelchair towards the elevator. The young foreigner's abominable Japanese was making the old man laugh. His face was as long as that of a horse, and he reminded Kiguchi of the silent film comedian he had seen as a young man – the actor named Fernandel.

When Kiguchi visited the hospital again five days later, Tsukada had just been moved from intensive care to a regular ward. He was lying in a bed beside a sunny window in the large ward and had opened his threadbare pyjama top so his wife could wipe his back. His collar-bone poked out, and Kiguchi thought he had lost a lot of weight. What he had heard was true: a person with cirrhosis seems to lose weight right before your eyes.

'Kiguchi. I'm sorry. I'm very sorry.' As he sat cross-legged, Tsukada put his hands on his knees and bowed his head again and again. 'To think I'd turn out like this after all you've done for me. . . . But, hell, after a month in the hospital, I'll be all right. The doctor said my liver's not too good, but I feel fine, just fine.'

'You've got to stop drinking once you're out of here,' Kiguchi said with a stern face. 'Your illness is the result of too much drink. You can't have even one more drop.'

'I can't give it up. If you take my liquor away from me, my life won't be worth living.'

'You heard what the doctor told you. If you keep on drinking, it'll kill you.'

It was evident that Tsukada's mood was souring even as they spoke. He crossly pushed away his wife's hands as she wiped his shoulders and sullenly growled, 'That's enough!' Then he turned away and pulled the covers half-way over his face.

His wife reproached him. 'You're being rude. He's made an effort to come and visit you.' But Tsukada would not answer.

Just then, the horse-faced foreigner entered the ward. Like the doctors, he had on a white frock-coat, but he also wore a blue apron.

'Hey, Mr Gaston, you look busy today,' one of the patients in the ward called out. The young foreigner with the peculiar name replied, 'Ye-es. Busy. Much work I have. Two hands, not enough.' He spread his arms flamboyantly.

One of his assigned tasks was to distribute the meals from the kitchen to the patients. Each meal was different, depending upon the condition of the patients.

'Mr Tsuka . . . Tsukada,' Gaston read, glancing at the romanized name on the tray card and stopping in front of Tsukada's bed. 'Mr Tsukada, this for you.' Then, with a truly amiable smile, he handed the tray containing gruel and soup to Tsukada's wife. 'I bringing tea soon.'

As he started out of the ward, a patient yelled out, 'Don't fall down, Mr Gaston. You're so clumsy.'

'I hear you ordered your wife to sneak in some *sake* for you. Of course you know what the doctor said.'

Tsukada had turned his face away at Kiguchi's sermon, and he stubbornly refused to respond.

'If you continue drinking like this, these growths on your blood vessels that they call oesophageal varices will rupture. And they say that will kill you. I know this is hard for you, but you simply must give up drinking.'

Tsukada, who maintained his ill-humoured silence, finally answered in near desperation, 'Leave me alone. . . . I don't care if I die!'

'What are you saying? If that's how you feel, then what was the point of surviving the war?'

'You don't understand anything.'

'You mean, the reason you can't stop drinking? Is there some reason why you've got to have alcohol? If there is, then tell me.'

'Enough.' Tsukada turned back to the wall and said nothing more.

Kiguchi gave up and left the ward to report the conversation to the attending physician.

'He's a stubborn s.o.b. But there seems to be some reason for his drinking that he can't bring himself to talk about.'

'So there is something.'

'How is he doing?'

'Just as I feared, we found oesophageal varices. It's very likely he'll have another massive haemorrhage sometime in the future.'

'If he haemorrhages, will he die?'

'I can't rule out that possibility.'

Kiguchi stared gloomily at the window of the examination-room.

When he thought of his comrades who had died along the Highway of Death and been consumed by maggots, he couldn't help feeling that his own life and that of Tsukada now were nothing more than a bonus tacked on to their span of years. Yet, the reason he had survived was that his wartime friend, Tsukada, had not deserted him when his own strength had sapped. He wanted to do whatever it took to save Tsukada.

He visited Tsukada once or twice every week. Sometimes the volunteer Gaston was there, chatting with Tsukada in his broken Japanese. He learned that Gaston taught at the Berlitz Language School in Shibuya, and that on his days off he came to work at the hospital. There was something engaging about the man, and many patients felt close to him because he was so clumsy that he seemed to have no co-ordination whatever. Even Tsukada reserved his only smiles for Gaston.

'Mr Gaston seems to be the only person at this hospital my husband likes,' Tsukada's wife confided as though she were relaying some dark secret. 'All he does is complain about the other doctors and nurses. Says he can't stand them.'

'The young fellow is fantastic,' Tsukada told Kiguchi. 'He may be a foreigner, but he doesn't turn his nose up at taking care of our bedpans and the like. I thought maybe he did this as a side job to pick up some money, but the nurses tell me he doesn't make a single yen here.'

'He's a volunteer.'

'It's amazing what he does.'

Kiguchi first realized the affection that Tsukada had developed for Gaston one day when he was visiting.

'I asked Gaston if he'd come to Japan because he'd lost his job, and he couldn't come up with an answer. And then the fellow makes this strange gesture before he eats the sweetmeats I offer him.'

'There's nothing unusual about that. It's called crossing yourself, and it's something all the Amen types do.'

'I'm feeling so much better, I think it's about time I returned home.'

'If you just go home and start drinking again, you're better off staying here. I don't think they'll discharge you unless you'll promise to lay off the booze.'

'That's not for somebody else to decide. I'm getting out of here no matter what anyone says.'

'And start drinking again? Even if your old comrade begs you not to?'

Once again Tsukada turned his face to the wall and would not talk. Kiguchi stared at his thinning back for a long while, then muttered, 'I'm going.' A bitter resignation welled up within, and he felt somehow forlorn. He stood up, and just as he was about to go, a muted voice behind him called, 'Wait. Kiguchi, I'm sorry. Don't be angry with me.'

'I'm not angry. But I must keep badgering you because I'm worried about your health.'

'The way I drink... the way I drink... I want to tell you the reason.'

When Kiguchi sat down beside him, tears began to flow from Tsukada's feeble eyes and down his hollow cheeks.

'Tell me.'

'When we... when we were running from the British and Indian troops, and you couldn't go any further, I decided I had to take you back to our unit with me.'

'I've always been grateful for that. I've never forgotten it for a single day. That's why I look on this as an attempt to pay you back.'

'You were so weak, and I wanted to bring you something to eat, but there wasn't anything. Not knowing what else to do, I prized a little rice from the hands of a dying soldier and made some gruel.'

'I remember that. You never abandoned me.'

'On the second day I was starving myself, and I realized I'd end up like you if I couldn't get something to eat. I walked around, kicking over corpses teeming with maggots, to see if I could find something to eat. But... I couldn't find anything. Away in the distance... I heard an explosion, and I hurried on and ran into the jungle. The moment I set foot in there, I heard the wings of flies flapping like a torrent. Half the leg of a soldier, covered with mud and still wrapped in its puttees, was lying there on the ground. You remember that many of the abandoned soldiers killed themselves with grenades, and this leg had flown off by itself.'

For some reason, he avoided the crux of what he felt compelled to relate, and instead slowly jabbered on and on about scenes Kiguchi knew all too well and did not wish to recall. From the corridor they could hear the bright, laughing voices of some nurses. Tsukada stared at the ceiling with hollow eyes, and his mouth seemed to be the only part of his body moving.

'There was a hut.'

Painfully, Kiguchi recalled the scattered huts of Indians and Burmese that they encountered as they escaped along the Highway. In these huts, with their raised floors and staircases of rotting wood, enervated Japanese soldiers leaned against the walls, dropped their heads and squatted in their own excrement as they awaited death.

Kiguchi waited for Tsukada to say what he wanted to say. He could feel the torment in Tsukada's heart as he approached the core of his pain and then quickly retreated from it. He began to have some notion of what it was Tsukada wanted to say but couldn't.

'I heard the flapping of flies' wings again, and the walls plastered with grasses were covered with enormous flies. You remember how much bigger the Burmese flies were than the ones in Japan?'

'It's all right,' Kiguchi finally forced himself to say. 'It's all right. If it's painful for you to tell me, you don't have to say any more.'

'I'll tell you.'

Kiguchi shut his eyes and endured Tsukada's suffering along with him.

'I rested awhile in that hut. I even dozed off for a bit. I woke up when I heard a noise, and two soldiers came in. I'd never seen either of them before. I asked them if they had anything to eat, and they laughed, saying there was nothing left this late in the game. Then one of them mumbled something about being able to buy lizard meat from the Burmese for ten yen. I gave them ten yen, and they went out of the hut.'

Kiguchi vividly recalled what had happened then. The voice of Tsukada shouting 'If you don't eat . . . you'll die!' even came back to him as distinctly as he had expected.

'I was so weak, my stomach wouldn't take it in.'

'You gagged on it and couldn't eat it. You didn't eat it. But I did. I reckoned we'd both die there if I didn't eat it.'

A cloud of anxiety spread through Kiguchi's mind like the black smoke spewing from an erupting volcano.

'The meat I ate . . . it was PFC Minamikawa. . . . You remember him, don't you – Minamikawa?'

The face of the soldier named Minamikawa, who had been in the same company as theirs, surfaced from the depths of Kiguchi's memory. The frames of his glasses were broken, so he had fastened them to his ears with string. He had been drafted out of college and had a young wife he had married just before going into the army. He had shown Tsukada and Kiguchi some of her letters.

'How do you know the meat was . . . from Minamikawa?'

'The paper the meat was wrapped in was one of those letters from his wife that he always carried around.'

'But you ate it thinking it was lizard meat.'

Kiguchi could sense how powerless were his own words of consolation. They merely shrivelled and flapped in the breeze.

'When I got back to Japan, I sent his family that grimy piece of stationery. I thought it would be the least sort of apology I could make. Two months later, his wife came to visit me in Uto with a little child.'

'She came to Uto?'

'Yeah. The child was a boy. His wife said he was born after Minamikawa died.... The kid stared at me with eyes just like Minamikawa's.'

Kiguchi could say nothing.

'You remember, don't you, those mousy eyes of Minamikawa's? He'd look out from behind those glasses strung from his ears, always nervously checking out the looks on the faces of the older soldiers. The kid looked at me with exactly the same eyes.'

Kiguchi remained silent.

'I still can't forget those eyes. It's as if ... as if Minamikawa will go on looking at me with those eyes for the rest of my life. I can never get away from those eyes unless I drink myself blind.'

As he spoke, he stuffed a towel into his mouth and sobbed. The hand that Kiguchi placed on his shoulder trembled. The neighbouring bed was empty, but perhaps some of the other patients could hear Tsukada's weeping. Through tearful eyes Kiguchi could see through the window three crows flying in triangular formation against the grey sky. The crows seemed to Kiguchi to symbolize some profound meaning in life.

Perhaps because his agitation that day had been so severe, that evening Tsukada passed a bloody stool. With blood appearing, it was now clear that he was haemorrhaging from somewhere in his oesophagus or stomach.

He was given an endoscope examination several days later. Tsukada's wife telephoned Kiguchi with the disheartening results. 'They ... they don't know where the haemorrhaging is coming from. The doctors are at a loss.'

The bleeding, though intermittent, continued. Kiguchi felt as though his own demands for a confession from Tsukada had been the cause, and he found as many free moments from work as he could to visit the hospital.

Often the foreign volunteer Gaston would be sitting at Tsukada's bedside.

'Mr Tsukada tell me about rock,' Gaston gleefully announced one day.

'About rock?'

'Mr Tsukada go to river and look for rock. Rock shaped like Fuji-san.'

'I told him about landscape rocks. Although I don't suppose there's any way a foreigner can understand something as cultured as land-scape rocks.'

Kiguchi was relieved at Tsukada's answer, for he seemed not to feel uneasy about his own condition. In any case, at some point in time Tsukada and this horse-faced foreigner had become fast friends.

'But there's one thing about this young fellow I really can't stand.' Tsukada harangued Gaston in his typically haughty tone. 'He says he honestly believes there's a God.'

'Yes.'

'Where is he, then? If he's there, show him to me.'

'Ye-es. Inside Mr Tsukada.'

'In my heart, you mean?'

'Ye-es.'

'I don't get it. How can anybody today claim anything so foolish? Why, we've got rockets flying to the moon!'

Gaston shrugged his shoulders and smiled. He seemed to have real-ized, from the kind of food he was delivering on the trays, that Tsukada's condition was not good. His meals, which had been moving towards normal food for a time, had changed back to a liquid diet again. Kiguchi sensed that Gaston, mocked and made a fool of as he was, brought a meagre sort of comfort to the patients. About the degree of comfort afforded by the wan winter sun trickling through the clouds. Still, each day Gaston brought temporary diversion to the many suf-fering patients here. At this hospital, he performed the role of the pierrot in a circus.

Tsukada finally stopped haemorrhaging and the worried faces around him relaxed. Kiguchi confided only a portion of Tsukada's confession to the doctor in charge. He did not mention Minamikawa's name, and hinted only vaguely that Tsukada had eaten the flesh of an enemy soldier.

'I see. So you were in Burma with Mr Tsukada, were you? It must have been terrible. I was just a child evacuated to the provinces at the time, but even in Japan we had a shortage of food.'

'That doesn't even begin to compare with what we went through!' Kiguchi retorted with unintentional anger. He had heard from family members, and experienced them himself after repatriation, of the desperate shortages of food in Japan, but these bore no comparison to those of the Japanese soldiers who had wandered along the Highway of Death like sleep-walkers, drenched by the rain. Their starvation, after they had eaten tree bark and insects dug from the ground, after they had eaten everything, was of a totally different realm from those who received a ration, however paltry, of rice.

Keenly aware of the difference between his own generation and that of this doctor, Kiguchi concluded that neither this man nor any of the doctors in the psychotherapy ward of this hospital could comprehend Tsukada's suffering.

'I think it would be best if we didn't provoke Tsukada any more.'

'What do you mean, provoke?'

'I don't think it's good to make him talk about the secrets he's buried in his heart. I think it's what caused him to haemorrhage this last time.'

'That may be true. We'll just have to watch him and see how he does for a while.'

'Since he's not drinking while he's here, I think all you have to do is turn that into a good habit for him.'

The doctor, twirling his ballpoint pen between his fingers, nodded as if he understood. Oesophageal varices were, after all, a disease for which there was no treatment.

The event they feared finally occurred. It was Saturday when Tsukada coughed up a huge amount of blood for the second time. When Kiguchi got the urgent message and raced to the hospital, the doctors had stopped his vomiting and moved him from the ward to a private room. Nurses busily scurried in and out of the room, and the atmosphere was taut as a bowstring all the way out into the hallway.

A balloon-like tube had been inserted into his throat, and he moaned in pain. Stains from the blood he had regurgitated still splotched the floor here and there.

'Gaston's the one who picked him up. There was blood all over Gaston's clothes. Gaston. . . .' In her state of distress, Tsukada's wife kept repeating trivial information to Kiguchi.

'He's stabilized for now,' the head doctor, who stood wearily at the door of the room, whispered to Kiguchi. 'But this is the crisis point.'

Five days later the bleeding was finally stanched and the balloon tube was removed from his throat.

Tsukada seemed to sense the approach of death.

'I've really done nothing but cause you one headache after another,' he said with more feeling than he had previously displayed. 'I'm so sorry.'

He said some things privately to his wife. Kiguchi could hear her whimpering as he stood in the hallway. Patients passing Tsukada's room on their way to the bathroom glared uneasily at the hypodermic syringes and the oxygen tank.

'My husband wants you to send for Gaston,' his wife told Kiguchi when she emerged from the room with a tear-stained faced. 'He keeps asking for him.'

'For Gaston?'

'Yes.'

Evidently Gaston was teaching a class at the Berlitz Language School that day, since he had not appeared at the hospital.

'Where's Gaston?' Tsukada repeatedly asked Kiguchi. 'I want to ask Gaston something.'

It was past six, after the patients had finished eating supper, when Gaston finally got the message and appeared. An air of tension still filled the room and the hallway. Gaston got permission from the nurses' station and hesitantly opened the door to Tsukada's room.

'Mr Tsukada. I pray. I pray.'

'Gaston. I ... during the war ... I did something horrible. It hurts me to remember it. Very much.'

'Is OK. OK.'

'No matter how horrible?'

'Ye-es.'

'Gaston. I ... during the war ...' Tsukada gasped for breath, and in a strained voice he continued, ' ... in Burma, I ate the flesh of a dead soldier. There was nothing to eat. I had to do it to stay alive. Someone who's fallen that far into the hell of starvation – would your God forgive even someone like that?'

Tsukada's wife, who had been staring at the floor as she listened to her husband's confession, said softly, 'Darling. Darling ... you've suffered for so long.' She already knew her husband's secret.

Gaston closed his eyes and said nothing. He looked almost like a monk engaged in solitary prayer. When he opened his eyes again, there was a stern look on his comical horse face that Kiguchi had never seen before.

'Mr Tsukada. You are not only one to eat human flesh.'

Kiguchi and Tsukada's wife listened in astonishment to the stumbling Japanese words that came from Gaston's mouth.

'Mr Tsukada. Four years, maybe five years ago, did you hear news that an airplane is broken and falls into Andes mountains? Airplane hit mountain, and many people hurt. Andes mountains is cold. On sixth day before help comes, nothing is left to eat.'

Kiguchi remembered seeing in a newspaper or on television that an Argentine plane had crashed in the Andes four or five years earlier. He had seen a photograph of the search party beside a form that resembled an aircraft but so blurred it looked like a reflection in a pool of water, along with several men and women who had survived the crash.

'A man was in that airplane. Like you, he very much likes to drink, and in plane he only gets drunk and sleeps. When plane has accident in Andes mountains, drunk man hits back and chest, is much badly hurt.'

In his broken Japanese, Gaston related the following story.

The drunken man said to the survivors who had cared for him over the course of three days: 'You have nothing left to eat, do you? After I die, you must eat the flesh of my body. You must eat it whether you want to or not. Help will surely come.'

Kiguchi vaguely remembered this part of the story as well. The survivors, who were rescued on the seventy-second day, openly confessed what they had done. They had miraculously survived because they had consumed the flesh of those who had already died.

'Those who passed away encouraged us to do so,' one of the survivors related. This news had struck Kiguchi, who had roamed and fled through the jungles of Burma, so close at hand and so vividly that it remained in the depths of his consciousness even now.

'When these people come back from Andes alive, everyone very happy. Families of dead people also very happy. No one angry with them for eating people's flesh. The wife of drunk man say, he did a good thing for first time. People from his town always say bad things about him, but they stop saying. They believe he has gone to heaven.'

Gaston exhausted every word he knew in Japanese to comfort Tsukada. He came to Tsukada's room every day after that and held the dying man's hands between his own palms, talked to him and encouraged him. Kiguchi could not tell whether such comfort eased Tsukada's pain. But the figure of Gaston kneeling beside his bed looked like a bent nail, and the bent nail struggled to become one with the contortions of Tsukada's mind, and to suffer along with Tsukada.

Two days later, Tsukada died. His face was more at peace than anyone had imagined it could be, but a look of peace always comes at last to the dying. 'He looks like he's sleeping,' Tsukada's wife mumbled, but Kiguchi couldn't help but feel that this peaceful death-mask had been made possible because Gaston had soaked up all the anguish in Tsukada's heart.

Gaston was nowhere to be found when Tsukada died. The nurses had no idea where he had gone.

SIX

The City by the River

25 October	Arrive Delhi	*City tour*
26 October p.m.	Depart Delhi	
	Arrive Jaipur	
" " evening		*Folk dancing at hotel*
27 October	Arrive Agra	*Sightseeing at Taj*
		Mahal and Agra Fort
28 October	Depart Agra	
	Travel from Allahābād to Vārānasī *	

That evening as they left the Allahābād airport, a humid, lukewarm wind was blowing. The tepid wind was filled with the smell of the earth and the vibrant aroma of trees that cities even in the provinces of Japan had lost. The moment he inhaled that air, Kiguchi remembered a small town in Burma where he had been stationed during the war.

Four or five taxi-drivers appeared from behind trees and came running towards the Japanese tourists. They beleaguered Enami, who spoke Hindi, but once they found out that the Japanese had already reserved

---

* Vārānasī was formerly called Benares

a tour bus, they spat on the ground contemptuously and scattered in every direction.

In their place arrived a band of scrawny children who had been watching the tourists from a distance. They held out their hands and cried 'Bakshish!' The Japanese ignored them, having already had several encounters with identical swarms of children as they shopped in Delhi's old district. Enami had warned his charges that the panting for breath and the pleading expressions and gestures were all for show, and that once you gave money to one child, you would be endlessly thronged by the other children. They turned away and watched out for the arrival of their bus.

'What a wretched country.' A young man named Sanjō, an aspiring cameraman who had come with the group on his honeymoon, grumbled to his bride, who had ill-humouredly covered her mouth with a handkerchief. 'The adults send their children out to beg and then sit back and just watch them do it.'

Oblivious to those around him, he took his wife's hand and began to fondle it. Just then an antiquated bus – the kind that would long since have been put out to pasture in Japan – pulled into the compound, kicking up dust behind it.

'They expect us to ride in a bus like that?' Mrs Sanjōs displeasure showed openly on her face. 'That's why I insisted we should go to Europe.'

'We can go to Europe any time. Don't you remember what Mr Higuchi said – that India was the best, that India was the only place to take pictures?'

Listening to this conversation being conducted behind him, Kiguchi was disgusted with this young couple, who knew nothing of the Japan charred by the flames of war. Even in Japan right after the defeat, everywhere you looked similarly starving children had surrounded the American soldiers and begged for chewing-gum and chocolate. This young couple, who had no knowledge of such hunger and such poverty, had blithely slumped against one another and thrown their arms around each other's shoulders in the aircraft. If any of his wartime comrades who had accompanied him on the miserable retreat through the Burmese jungles had been on board, they would have punched these insolent twits in the mouth.

The seats on the bus were so cracked they looked as if they had contracted elephantiasis. The handle on the door had broken off, and the Indian driver had tied it on again with a piece of string.

'This is why', Mrs Sanjō's half-weepy voice could be heard from the rear seats, 'I said we ought to travel along the Märchen *autobahn* in Germany.'

The other Japanese contemptuously ignored her carping voice, and the bus, bouncing up and down as it went, headed forth.

It was the hour when peasants were herding skinny cows and black sheep back into their pens. Spice huts displayed bottles of variously coloured spices and dried peppers hanging beneath the light of naked electric bulbs suspended from the ceiling. They saw tailors' shops where workers peddled away at old-fashioned sewing-machines. There was an indescribable sadness to the evening in this provincial village, so unlike the city of New Delhi, and the tourists gawked at the scenery like children watching the fair at a village festival.

'Ladies and gentlemen.' Enami, sitting next to the driver, brought the microphone to his mouth. 'This is a typical evening in an Indian village. Cows are sprawled out everywhere. Beside them everyone sits and drinks tea. The milk they pour into their tea is squeezed from those same cows.'

'This is wonderful. I haven't seen anything like this for a long time.' From his seat directly behind Enami, Numada muttered to himself, struck to the depths of his heart. 'In Japan in the old days you could see animals and human beings living side by side.'

'That's right, you came to India to see the animals and birds, didn't you, Mr Numada?' Enami nodded. 'India is packed with bird sanctuaries and animal reserves. There's a small one along this road we're taking.'

'How long does it take to get there? I'd appreciate some information.'

'When we get to the hotel, you should be able to get a map to the animal reserves from the government tourist office. The sanctuaries nearby should be listed in it. There are, after all, over four hundred of them in India.'

'Why did you come to India to study, Mr Enami?'

'In the end, I suppose, because I fell in love with it. Some tourists absolutely despise the place after only one visit, but then there are those who say they want to come back over and over again. I'm one of the latter.'

He stole a glance back at the rear seats where the Sanjōs were sitting, took the microphone from his mouth and whispered, 'And I'm sure Mr and Mrs Sanjō belong to the former.'

The evening sun, red as a winter cherry, was declining into the sky over the village. It was time for the day gradually to give way to twilight, and the breeze that blew in through the open windows of the bus was no longer lukewarm but cool and smelling of trees and soil.

Enami brought the microphone back to his mouth. 'Ladies and gentlemen, when night falls in northern India in this season, it suddenly turns cold. If you brought a jacket or a cardigan with you, please put it on. In a few moments we'll be passing by the spot where the Gangā and Yamunā* rivers meet, so please have a good look. The confluence of two rivers is considered a sacred spot in Hinduism, and during the Magh *melā* festival held between January and February of every year, tens of thousands of pilgrims pitch their tents and sleep along these river banks and bathe in the waters. There, please look out of your windows. It's deserted now, but on festival days the river banks below us are jammed with countless people. Throngs of Hindus push and jostle their way here to bathe in the rivers.'

'Are the rivers clean?' someone asked. It was Sanjō calling in a loud voice, making sure everyone was aware of his presence.

'From the Japanese point of view, they couldn't be called clear-flowing rivers in even the polite sense of the term. The Gangā is yellow, and the Yamunā flows grey, and when the two merge, the water turns the colour of milky tea. But there is a difference in this country between things that are pretty and things that are holy. Rivers are sacred to the Indians. That's why they bathe in them.'

'So it's something like the purification ceremony in Shinto?' Sanjō asked, once again in a shrill voice.

'No. The Shinto purification rites are for cleansing from the pollutions of transgression and the impurities of the body. Bathing in the Ganges, however, while it also has the sense of purification, is at the same time an act of supplication for release from the cycle of transmigration and reincarnation.'

'Do they still believe in transmigration and reincarnation in this day and age?' Sanjō squawked, oblivious to those around him. 'Do you think these Indians really take it seriously?'

'Of course they're serious. Is anything wrong with that?' Enami had ceased for a moment to act as tour guide, and the irritation in his

---

* The Yamunā was formerly known as the Jumma

voice was directed towards tourists like Sanjō who flippantly mock Indian customs. Mitsuko was favourably drawn to the earnestness that this former exchange student suddenly displayed. No doubt it was part of the tour guide job in which Enami worked to make a living to listen to many questions ridiculing the beliefs of Hinduism from Japanese tourists like Sanjō.

'Why would hundreds of thousands of people gather on the banks of this river if they didn't take it seriously? Once we reach Vārānasī, you'll see any number of people soaking their bodies and drinking from the River Ganges, where each day the ashes of cremated bodies are scattered.'

'That's disgusting!' Mrs Sanjō cried out in disbelief.

'There's nothing disgusting about it,' Enami snapped back. 'If you find India disgusting, then you should have chosen a pleasant tour of Europe. But since you're here in India, please make the effort to enter into this unique world, a realm utterly removed from Europe or Japan. No, that's not correct. Let me rephrase that. We're about to enter into a unique world that we once knew but have now forgotten. That's the attitude I'd like you to have as we travel through India. Of course, this is just my personal opinion, but....'

Until then, Enami had displayed no more than occupational affability, but once the zeal of his school-days surfaced on his face, everyone in the bus, the Sanjōs included, lapsed into silence. Enami realized this and apologized: 'I'm sorry. I've said some impertinent things unbecoming of a tour guide.' His charges, absorbed in their own individual thoughts, stared silently through the windows as the bus entered the forest, where twilight was surrendering to night.

Dim lights came on inside the bus. They appeared to be surrounded on both sides by a dense jungle of laurel fig trees and could see no lights or anything else. In the dim lighting the face of each passenger was dimly reflected against the windows of the bus. From Enami's remarks, Isobe sensed that he had at last entered into the land of rebirth. He didn't really believe in anything like rebirth himself. But in the very deepest parts of his ears he could hear his wife's final delirious ravings: 'I... I know for sure... I'll be reborn somewhere in this world. Look for me... find me... promise... promise!'

Isobe shifted his eyes to his own tired, elderly face reflected against the window. The white-streaked head of hair, the splotched cheeks. Like any other Japanese husband, he had been embarrassed to respond gently to her words. He assumed that even if he hadn't answered her, she would understand everything by his travelling here to India. 'After all, that's why I joined this tour,' he muttered to himself, and tapped the pocket of his jacket to reconfirm the presence of the letter from America.

Mitsuko, for her part, stared without moving a muscle at the excessively thick darkness outside the window. A darkness that seemed to consist of several layers of darkness painted over yet other layers of darkness. She thought this must be the realm of spiritual darkness described in Buddhist thought. Had she ever seen such profound darkness before? Enami had said they were 'about to enter into a unique world'. Yes. Thérèse Desqueyroux had muttered much the same thing. The night forest in Les Landes, where she had travelled by herself after leaving her husband in Paris. Thinking of Thérèse, who had journeyed into the darkness in the depths of the human heart, she had set out to explore the impenetrable mind of a woman who had poisoned her own exemplary husband. And in the same way, Mitsuko had....

She thought of Ōtsu. At a class reunion, when everyone else had been talking about their jobs and their children, she overheard a rumour about Ōtsu that someone casually mentioned. A rumour that he was living in Vārānasī.

Kiguchi, watching for half an hour the forest that blocked out the sky, concealing the moon and stars, thought of the jungles in Burma. The jungles through which they had fled in a rout, pursued by soldiers from England and Gurkha troops from India.

'Mr Numada.' Enami turned round in his seat. 'It's right around here – that area designated as a bird sanctuary. As you can see, there is forest to both our right and left.'

They drove a bit further through the tunnel of pitch-black trees until suddenly a single point of light appeared in the distance. Just as those who have had brushes with near-death experiences have claimed to see a dot of light at the end of a black tunnel, at the far end of the darkness a brilliance like the light of a firefly gradually grew larger.

'We're just about there.' Enami shifted in his seat and put the microphone to his mouth. 'I think many of you have been able to see the lights of Vārānasī in the distance.'

They pressed their faces against the windows. Three hours had passed since they had disembarked from their aircraft and climbed aboard this broken-down bus. Each of the passengers was now planting his or her feet in that unique realm Enami had described. Mitsuko superimposed herself on to Thérèse Desqueyroux's journey into the dark night; Kiguchi pondered his flight through the horrid jungles of Burma; and Isobe listened in the depths of his ears to the voice of his wife.

The tiny flicker that had looked like the light of a firefly slowly spread its arms. An expanse of light reflected against the sky. Mitsuko realized that at one of those points of light Ōtsu was living a life completely different from her own. Why was it that thoughts of Ōtsu continued to plague her, just as they had in the past? She couldn't understand it. Ōtsu dangled somewhere inside her heart like an insect carcass caught in a spider's web. *There's no reason to see him,* she kept telling herself. *I'm not going to go looking for him, even if I am here in Vārānasī.*

Seated behind Mitsuko, Isobe suddenly remembered an evening he had spent with his wife. He had come home from work, taken a bath and made himself comfortable before sitting down to a cup of *sake* with some boiled tofu.

'When you eat Japanese food ... you really look like you're enjoying it,' his wife had chuckled as she put a small bowl in front of him. 'It's a miracle you were able to survive alone in America.'

'I was good at English at college. I loved whisky when I was young. But when I got older, I was converted back to Japanese *sake*.'

'You're a Japanese through and through, aren't you?'

'I am. If I die first, pour some *sake* on my grave. And it had better be dry *sake*!'

That long-forgotten conversation was rekindled in his mind, accompanied by a stab of pain.

And now ... at my age, here I am, unable to stand foreign food ... and look at me. I've come all the way to India.

He put his right hand over the pocket of his jacket, almost as though he were confirming the presence of an indispensable passport, and felt the second letter from the University of Virginia which he had read and reread many times. His journey to India was entirely the result of what had been contained in that letter. The letter was signed by John Osis, who had sent him the first courteous reply.

If memory serves me correctly, you asked us to contact you right away if we came across a child who claimed to have been Japanese in a previous life. Unfortunately, here in our research department we haven't been able to come up with any cases other than the young woman from Nathul in central Burma by the name of Ma Tin Aung Myo (who insists that her previous life was as a Japanese soldier who was killed in machine-gun strafing from a Grumman fighter plane). However, we heard a report two months ago of a young woman in a village called Kamloji in northern India who claims to have spent a previous life as a Japanese. We have not included her among our research subjects because she made this admission to her brothers and sisters when she was four years old, and therefore exceeds the age limit of three that we have placed as a condition for those recalling a previous existence. But on the outside chance that this might be of interest to you, I decided to contact you as you requested. Her name in Rajini Puniral, and the village of Kamloji where she was born is near the city of Vārānasī on the banks of the Ganges....

The road was bad, and the bus rocked up and down. Pools of water glistened here and there, as though it had rained. A clamour gradually grew nearer, and rickshaws and cars passed them on the left and right. They saw the scrawny cows that roamed at will through every Indian town. Barrack-like shops. Men sitting and drinking tea under naked light bulbs hung from trees. Instead of heading for the centre of town, the bus detoured to the north of Cantonment Station.

A manor-like building surrounded by thick bushes finally appeared. It was the Hotel de Paris, where the Japanese would be staying the night.

Two durwans dressed in shabby white jackets with wing collars came running from the entrance. The travellers, weary from their long bus ride from Delhi, collapsed into chairs in the lobby, where they craned their necks and yawned while they waited for Enami to complete their check-in at the reception desk.

'I'll be handing out your room keys and passports now. The durwans will bring your bags up to your rooms later.'

As she climbed the stairs alongside Isobe, Mitsuko expressed mild surprise that the hotel appeared seedy and old-fashioned, in sharp contrast to its spacious gardens. 'This hotel is really antiquated, isn't it?'

Even though they had recognized each other in Delhi and on the aircraft, the two had had little opportunity to speak, perhaps because something in Mitsuko wanted to avoid him.

'When the British ruled here,' Isobe replied, 'this was apparently a British club. That's what the guidebook says. Well, it's certainly not fourth- or fifth-rate, but it wouldn't be an A-class hotel these days.'

Then he stopped and peered at her. 'Will you be going straight to bed? After I take a shower, I'd like to cool off in the garden. The garden seems to be this hotel's only selling point.'

'I may join you. But first I want to hop under the shower, too.'

Their rooms were on the same floor, but considerably apart. When Mitsuko opened her door, she realized at once that this was a B-class hotel, just as Isobe had suggested. The bath-tub was black, the chain to the stopper was broken, and there wasn't even a table beside the bed. When she stepped under the shower, the exhaustion of the day seeped from the core of her body. From deep within her trunk she took the bottle of brandy she had bought at Narita Airport and drank down a paper cupful in one gulp.

Carrying the brandy bottle and a couple of paper cups, she went down the stairs and into the garden, where insects buzzed. Several white cane chairs stood in a row, and the scent of the trees was over-powering. Mitsuko took in a full breath of that scent, convinced that this was the aroma of India. She heard the squeak of a swing, and when she turned round to look, Isobe was swinging by himself. It felt somehow forlorn to see this large man swinging back and forth all alone.

'Would you care for a drink?' She held up the bottle of Napoleon brandy.

Isobe looked back at her cheerfully. 'Well now, what have we here?'

'I'll bet you prefer Japanese *sake*, don't you, Mr Isobe?'

'Who told you that?'

'Your wife, of course. The word around the nurses' station was that the days she talked about you were the days she was feeling her best.'

'It must have been miserable for you and the nurses to have to listen to her pointless chatter. But since you've gone to the trouble of bringing it here, I'll have some. I wanted a drink while we were in the bus, but when I asked at the reception desk, they told me the restaurant and bar were already closed for the night.'

He narrowed his eyes to savour the liquid she had poured into a paper cup.

'When you get right down to it, good liquor is good liquor, whether it's *sake* or not. This is delicious,' he mumbled. 'But I have to admit, while she was ill, I never dreamed I'd run into you again in India.

There's really a lot about life that's beyond comprehension.'

She could sense the reality of what he said. There were many things about life that couldn't be anticipated or comprehended. She had no truly firm understanding of why she had decided to come to India. Sometimes she even felt as though her life played itself out not in line with her intentions, but at the whim of some other invisible power.

'Why did you come to India, Miss Naruse?'

'Is there something wrong with choosing India?'

'No, it's just that women usually prefer Italy or Portugal, don't they?'

'I'm not young enough to be attracted to the Appian Way or the *fados*. But what about you? Why did you join this tour?'

Isobe lifted his face from his cup and blushed like a boy.

'Are you making a pilgrimage to the Buddhist holy sites?' Mitsuko asked the question because a majority of their group, including the wife of a Buddhist priest, had come to tour the Buddhist relics.

'No, that's not why....' He hesitated, then made up his mind to be forthright. 'I'm going to admit this to you... because you looked after my wife right up to the end.' He reached into his jacket pocket. The wrinkles on the two envelopes he pulled out were evidence that he had read the letters many times. 'Please read these.'

'Do you mind?'

In the light from the garden lamps, Mitsuko's eyes raced over the pages of the letters. When the two of them stopped talking, the voices of the insects in the garden swelled in volume.

'Your wife,' Mitsuko ventured, 'asked me something peculiar.'

'What was it?'

'"After a person dies,"' she asked, '"are they reborn?"'

'She asked that, did she?'

'It was a Saturday evening, when I was collecting the dinner-trays.'

'And... how did you reply?'

'I pretended not to hear her. I didn't know what I should say.'

That was a lie. She could still remember what had transpired in the hospital room that evening. She realized at once, painfully, why Isobe's wife had asked such a question. The voice asking the question was charged with the yearning to be with her husband once again, even after her death.

Mitsuko had been picking up the food-trays. Keiko's question stimulated the tingling urge to destroy which lurked in the depths of Mitsuko's heart. She despised the sentimental affection a wife felt for her husband.

'Reborn? How should I know?' she had slowly repeated to herself, crisply chopping off every word. 'It's a lot easier to believe that everything ends when you die. It's better than going on to your next life carrying around the burdens of all your many pasts.'

She remembered Isobe's wife's face contorting in pain.

'Could I have another drink?' Isobe held out his cup, shaking off the emotions that surged up inside him.

Mitsuko handed him the bottle of brandy. 'So, then... you're going to go to this village to look for her?'

'Yes.'

'Do you believe in reincarnation, the way these Hindus do?'

'I'm not sure. I'd never cared anything about what happens after death until my wife died. I'd never even thought about death. But something she said to me the day before she died has got stuck in the web of my mind and won't shake loose. It's determined how I live my life. I'm a fool, I suppose. There are things about life I just don't understand.'

The swing continued to sway and creak even after Isobe stood up. Just as the words his wife had spoken continued to sway his life even after she was dead. Even when something comes to an end in our lives, it does not mean that everything has been extinguished.

'It's funny, isn't it, for an old man like me to come to India in search of treasure?'

'No. I think I may have come here in search of something, too.'

'What is it you're searching for?'

'I don't know myself. But a friend from my college days is living here in Vārānasī. I'm not quite sure which part of the city, though. Maybe one of my reasons for coming was to look for him.'

Isobe seemed to believe what Mitsuko was saying.

'Thanks for the drink. It really helped. Tomorrow's another day, so this old man has to go to bed early.'

After he went back into the hotel, Mitsuko remained in the garden where the insects continued to chirp heartily. The swing still faintly creaked. Nights in India were cooler than she had expected – no, not cooler: lonelier.

She took two sleeping-pills, stretched out on the hard bed, and, annoyed by the dimness of the lights, read from a book she had brought with her, *A Student in India*, waiting for sleep to overtake her.

A number of photographs had been reproduced in the book, but the ones that most interested her were those of the goddesses associated with Siva. These goddesses were utterly unlike the European images of the Holy Mother Mary; some rode on water buffaloes and stabbed at the demon gods, while others depicted the savagery of the goddess Kālī, who stuck out her long, snakelike tongue as she trampled on her husband Siva.

Two days earlier, at the New Delhi National Museum, Mitsuko had stared at their collection of photographs depicting the goddess Kālī. Tonight the gardens and the hallway were stone silent; perhaps all the other Japanese tourists had fallen asleep. On a separate page, the goddess Kālī was gazing towards her, her arms outstretched, her eyes brimming with gentleness. Her lips had – or had Mitsuko just imagined it? – curled into a smile. On the next page, that smiling Kālī sucked warm blood from the blood-soaked demon Raktavīja. She held up a freshly severed head, and blood flecked her lips as she poked out her long tongue.

Mitsuko flicked back and forth between the photograph and the painting, and felt that both images were herself. Earlier that evening she had told Isobe: 'I think I may have come here in search of something, too.' Was it the inept Ōtsu she was searching for? Or was she, like Thérèse Desqueyroux, looking for what lay in the depths of her heart?

The sleeping-pills gradually numbed her brain. She stood up and turned off the light switch near the door, then again stretched out on the bed and peered at the thickly painted layers of darkness. In the hospital where she had worked as a volunteer there had always been some light, even if just the faint glow from a small light that the nurses used to examine the faces of their patients. But the darkness here in India was truly a spiritual darkness, the darkness of the soul. Mitsuko had come in contact with a portion of the soul's blackness. As a woman in whom the flame of passion had been extinguished. As a kindred spirit with Thérèse Desqueyroux.

She slept for nearly two hours. In the darkness she could hear a sound like the flapping of a bird's wings. She reached over and groped to turn on the lamp on the bedside table, but she quickly remembered that this dingy room had no such table.

She grew suddenly afraid. She had just finished reading in *A Student in India* that while the author was studying in his room, he had heard a swishing noise outside his window like the sound of a broom sweeping the garden, but when the sound began to come from a corner of his room, he turned round and saw a stark-black cobra poised to strike.

The flapping sound continued incessantly from over by the wall. She would have to walk over to the door in order to turn on the light. If the cobra struck while she was making her way to the door...

Mitsuko leaped from her bed. It was not in her nature to hesitate. She felt along the opposite wall with her hands, searching for the light switch. At last her fingers found it. When the lights came on, she discovered a large hole in the wall of her room. The paper that had been pasted over it to conceal it had come loose and was flapping in the wind. She had to laugh: it seemed so much in keeping with an Indian hotel.

Still smiling wryly, Mitsuko sat down in a rickety, persimmon-coloured chair and reached into her carrier-bag. Once she was awake, it took some time for sleep to pay her another visit. She pulled a brown paper bag from her case and placed it on the table. It contained the several letters that she had exchanged with Ōtsu. It seemed strange even to her that she had taken the trouble to bring them with her.

He had no charm as a man, had nothing in his looks that might appeal to her, and he always aroused her feelings of contempt. Yet, in a realm completely removed from the one where Mitsuko and her friends lived, he had had everything snatched away from him by his Onion. While at the base of her heart she rejected everything Ōtsu stood for, she could not feel indifferent towards him. For whatever reason, even though she tried to obliterate him with an eraser, he would not go away.

And now his letters, written in a clumsy scrawl that looked like the hand of a middle-school boy. It was true that she had dutifully written one or two letters in response, but she couldn't imagine why she had so carefully preserved this correspondence. It made no sense to her. Something transcending herself had made her hold on to it. Perhaps it was fair to say that whatever that something was, it had concocted a quiet little plan and brought her here to Vārānasī where Ōtsu was living. She poured the remaining brown liquid from the brandy bottle down her throat and hazily thought, *You're an idiot.* She muttered the words softly to herself. 'This is so stupid. What does it matter, anyway?'

A copy of Mitsuko's scrawled note
Happy New Year. I'll send this greeting to the address I got when I saw you four years ago in Lyon. Are you still living in Fourvière? For various reasons I have got divorced. I'm living with my family at the moment. The reason for my divorce... at the end of the year I happened to be reading Fukuda Tsuneari's *Horatio Diary* and I ran across the following words, which seem to capture exactly what I am: 'I cannot truly love another person. I have never once loved anyone. How can such a person assert their own existence in this world?' That, ultimately, is the reason for my divorce. Do you still believe that your Onion makes use of any opportunity, even of sin?

Ōtsu's reply to Mitsuko
Your letter was forwarded from Lyon and eventually reached me. As you can see from the return address, I am no longer living in Lyon. I now work every day at a religious training community in Ardèche in the South of France. It's a desolate place surrounded by rocky mountains, but for now I'm working hard at farming and physical labour.

If you were to ask why I came here, I suppose it would be similar to what you wrote in your letter about your divorce. The brotherhood in Lyon concluded that I was not yet qualified to become a priest, and they delayed holding my ordination ceremony. There's something heretical in my nature; you once joked in Lyon that I was lucky I didn't get myself excommunicated. After nearly five years of living in a foreign country, I can't help but be struck by the clarity and logic of the way Europeans think, but it seems to me as an Asian that there's something they have lost sight of with their excessive clarity and their overabundance of logic, and I just can't go along with it. Their lucid logic and their way of explaining everything in such clear-cut terms sometimes even causes me pain.

This is partly because I'm not smart enough and haven't studied enough to be able to understand their magnificent powers of organization, but even more than that, it's because my Japanese sensibilities have made me feel out of harmony with European Christianity. In the final analysis, the faith of the Europeans is conscious and rational, and these people reject anything they cannot slice into categories with their rationality and their conscious minds. For five years in my daily life, in my studies of theology, and even on my trip to the Holy Land in company with my superiors in the priesthood, I have feared that I am mistaken, and I have been all alone. This was the reason I had such a dark look on my face by the River Saône in Lyon. Sorry.

At the seminary they were most critical of what they saw as a pantheistic sentiment lurking in my unconscious mind. As a Japanese, I can't bear those who ignore the great life force that exists in Nature. However lucid and logical it may be, in European Christianity there is a rank ordering of all living things. They'll never be able to understand the import of a verse like Bashō's haiku:

> when I look closely
> beneath the hedge, mother's-heart
> flowers have blossomed

Sometimes, of course, they talk as if they regarded the life force that causes the mother's-heart flowers to bloom as the same force that grants life to human beings, but in no way do they consider them to be identical.

'Then what is God to you?' three of my superiors questioned me at the novitiate, and I was thoughtless enough to answer: 'I don't think God is someone to be looked up to as a being separate from man, the way you regard him. I think he is within man, and that he is a great life force that envelops man, envelops the trees, envelops the flowers and grasses.'

'Isn't that a pantheistic view?'

Then, using the all-too-translucent logic of scholasticism, they ferreted out all the flaws in my slipshod thinking. This is just one small example of what I went through. But an Asian like me just can't make sharp distinctions and pass judgement on everything the way they do.

'God makes use not only of our good acts, but even of our sins in order to save us.' That day, as we leaned against the railing by the Saône where the afternoon sun shimmered on the cargo ships sailing up and down the river, I confessed these honest feelings to you, the same feelings that prompted my comments to my superiors. And then you replied most splendidly: 'Is that really a Christian notion?'

I was scolded for this notion at the novitiate; they told me it was dangerously Jansenistic or Manichaeistic ('heretical', in short). I was told that good and evil are distinct and mutually incompatible.

So, what with this and that, my ordination to the priesthood has been postponed. But I have not lost my faith.

Since my youth, thanks to my mother the one thing I was able to believe in was a mother's warmth. The warmth of her hand as it held mine, the warmth of her body when she cradled me, the warmth of her love, the warmth that kept her from abandoning me even though I was so much more dumbly sincere than my brothers and sisters. My mother told me all about the person you call my Onion, and she taught me that this Onion was a vastly more powerful accumulation of this warmth – in other words, love itself. I lost my mother when I got older, and I realized then that what lay at the source of my mother's warmth was a portion of the love of my Onion. Ultimately what I have sought is nothing more than the love of that Onion, not any of the other innumerable doctrines mouthed by the various churches. (This, of course, was another reason I have been regarded as a heretic.) Love, I think, is the core of this world we live in, and through our long history that is all the Onion has imparted to us. The thing we are most lacking in our modern world is love; love is the thing no one believes in any more; love is what everyone mockingly laughs at – and that is why someone like me wants to follow my Onion with dumb sincerity.

My trust is in the life of the Onion, who endured genuine torment for the sake of love, who exhibited love on our behalf. As time passes, I feel that trust strengthening within me. I haven't been able to adapt myself to the thinking and the theology of Europe, but when I suffer all alone, I can feel the smiling presence of my Onion, who knows all my trials. And just as he told the travellers on the road to Emmaus when he walked beside them, he has said to me, 'Come, follow me.'

Sometimes at night, when I've finished my labours and I look up at the stars glittering above the fields of grapes, I become frightened of where he is leading me.

Mitsuko could remember where she was when she read this letter, scribbled in characters as clumsy as those of a middle-school student.

She was in a hospital room. After her divorce, her father gave her some money to start up a boutique. With some help from her ex-husband as well, she was able to add dresses and accessories from famous Paris couturiers to her stock. Then, once or twice a week she began volunteering at a large private hospital located behind the Tōgō Shrine. It was a spontaneous decision. Around that time, she had concluded that the statement from Fukuda Tsuneari's *Horatio Diary* was an exact reflection of her own heart: 'I cannot truly love another person. I have never once loved anyone. How can such a person assert their own existence in this world?' She had started volunteering at the hospital as a result of these perverse feelings. It was not that love had ceased to smoulder within her; rather she was a woman in whom the spark of love had never been kindled. Many times over she had made a show of passion with a man, but never once had honest flames flickered inside her. Around the time Mitsuko was contemplating her own ridiculousness as she washed out patients' bedpans and fed them their meals, she received the letter from Ōtsu. She didn't feel the least envious of him. Instead, the words of his letter wounded her. She sent him a brief postcard in reply. She remembered that it had been a Munch painting on the postcard. A drawing of the face of a forsaken man. She couldn't remember what she had written on the card, but no doubt she had gone out of her way to select the kind of postcard that would hurt Ōtsu because....

A letter from Ōtsu to Mitsuko

Thank you very much for your card. As I looked over the postcard you sent, I could feel between the lines how lonely you are.

But just as my Onion is always beside me, he is always within you and beside you, too. He is the only one who can understand your pain and your loneliness. One day he will transport you to another realm. We cannot have any idea when that will be, or how it will happen, or what form it will take. He makes use of every means. Like a magician, he will transform your 'charades of passion' and your 'unspeakable nights' (though I have no idea what you mean by these words).

Quinine produces high fevers if you drink it when you are well, but it becomes an indispensable drug for a malaria sufferer. I think sin is very much like quinine.

I expect it will take you by surprise for me to write about

quinine out of the blue. I learned about it from a Jewish doctor here in Israel at the kibbutz by the Sea of Galilee. Even today the Sea of Galilee is more beautiful than I had ever dreamed, but I'm told that in ancient times it was a pestilential land teeming with malaria victims. The Bible describes the miracles that my Onion performed in healing many who had fevers, and it seems likely that these were malaria victims.

I still haven't been able to become a priest. In the opinion of the ecclesiastical leaders at the seminary, I am lacking in the virtue of obedience necessary to become a priest, and I have lost sight of the principles vital for the development of true faith. Their claims that I lack obedience and am wanting in true faith are based on the fact that I continue to write and insist that I do not believe that the European brand of Christianity is absolute.

I now somewhat regret having spoken foolishly in front of the brethren of the Church. But it seems perfectly natural to me that many people select the god in whom they place their faith on the basis of the culture and traditions and climate of the land of their birth. I think that Europeans have chosen Christianity because it was the faith of their forefathers, and because Christian culture dominated their native lands. You can't say that the people of the Middle East chose to become Muslims and many Indians became Hindus after conducting rigorous comparisons of their religions with those of other peoples. In my own case, it was the exceptional circumstances of my mother that led me to my beliefs.

Many years ago, when you asked me 'Why do you believe in God?' I was lost for words because I had not chosen my religion of my own free will. But now the kind of questions I have just mentioned constantly pass through my mind.

'Don't you think it was because of the grace and the love of God that you were born into such a family?' the spiritual director at the seminary asked me.

'I do. But isn't it also the grace of God when those born into other families join another religion?'

I said this with no evil intent, but my response wounded this man, who was set in the standard Christian ways of thinking. I opened myself to the harshest criticism in an oral examination when I said: 'God has many different faces. I don't think God exists exclusively in the churches and chapels of Europe. I think he is also among the Jews and the Buddhists and the Hindus.'

This was an honest declaration of what I had come to believe since my arrival in Europe, but to my teachers it sounded like an outright rejection of the Christian Church.

I was viciously reprimanded: 'These are the notions born of your pantheistic delusions!'

In confusion I blurted out, 'But is there nothing pantheistic within Christianity itself? At the seminary I have been taught that the monotheism of Christianity is in direct opposition to pantheism, but as a Japanese, I believe that Christianity has been able to spread as widely as it has because so many diverse elements exist within it.'

'Tell us what these diverse elements are.'

'When we made a pilgrimage to the cathedral in Chartres, I read in a book that the people of that region had sublimated a belief in their local earth mother goddess to a belief in the Holy Mother. In other words... I think they have fostered a Christianity that has its roots in their faith in the earth mother goddess. In the sixteenth and seventeenth centuries there were many Japanese who converted to Christianity, but their faith was different from that of the people of Europe.'

'How was it different?'

'There were Buddhist elements, and elements of the pantheism you have just belittled, mixed together in their beliefs.'

My teachers were silent, but it seemed to me there was obvious displeasure in their silence.

'Then where do you draw the line between orthodoxy and heresy?'

'We no longer live in the Middle Ages. We live in a time when we must hold dialogues with other religions.'

'Naturally the Vatican recognizes that need.'

'But Christianity does not regard other religions as equal to itself.' By this point, I was half desperate, and decided to let the chips fall where they would. 'A European scholar once remarked that the noble people of other faiths were actually Christians driving without a licence, but you can hardly call this a dialogue among equals. I think the real dialogue takes place when you believe that God has many faces, and that he exists in all religions.'

Silence and chilly expressions. I realized that I had said something incredibly foolish. It was clear that my teachers regarded me as the possessor of highly dangerous thoughts.

'If that is the case,' the rector of the seminary asked, hoping to afford me a path of rescue, 'why don't you go back to being a Buddhist? Wouldn't that be a natural reversion to your way of thinking?'

'No. I wasn't brought up in Japan in a Buddhist household. I was raised in a Christian family, just as you brethren were. So it was natural for me to choose from among God's many faces the same face you chose.'

'Then what are your thoughts on the process of conversion? Of, say, a Buddhist abandoning his Buddhism and becoming a Christian.'

'I think it's possible. In the same way that each individual chooses a suitable member of the opposite sex to marry.'

Along with feeling it was time to let the chips fall, I hoped, if there were some basic flaw in my thinking, that my teachers – those men in whom I trusted – would help to correct me. But I didn't believe that a hypocritical lie would serve any purpose in my life.

As a result – though the outcome was to be expected – I was once again found unqualified to become a priest. Even so, some of the kinder brethren among my superiors in the order did their best on my behalf, and opened up the way for me to work and continue my studies at this novitiate in Galilee.

I know full well that this entire tale will seem boring and distant to you as a Japanese. Forgive me for staying up until the middle of the night tonight to write it to you, knowing all the while how it will affect you. I had to tell it to someone. Just as that man had to express his feelings here in Galilee to the lonely, the sick, and the suffering.

I suppose, in my loneliness, that I wanted to talk to you because you are lonely, too. It's pitiful to have to say it, but I am lonely....

The Sea of Galilee stretches out here in front of the novitiate. From time to time it has been called Kinnaret, the Sea of the Harp, and here where Jesus spoke to the people, and where the fisherman from Capernaum named Peter cast his nets, tonight the light of the moon glitters on the surface of the water. That man – no, since you're a Japanese, Miss Naruse, I suppose you retreat to a respectful distance merely hearing the name of Jesus. If that's the case, then please call Jesus by the name of Love. If the word Love leaves you cold, then you can call him the warmth of life. If you don't like that, then we can go back to our old familiar Onion.

The number of Jews here beside the Sea of Galilee is overpowering, but there are also Christians and Muslims living here. They seem to be curious about me because I'm a Japanese, and sometimes I visit their kibbutzes, and I've been invited into the homes of the Muslims. I have found my Onion dwelling amongst them. So why is it that my brethren have to look down on the followers of other religions and feel a subtle sense of superiority in their hearts? I feel the existence of my Onion within the Jews and the Muslims. He is everywhere.

The entire letter was awash in Ōtsu's syrupy voice. His self-absorbed reminiscences, oblivious to her feelings, scarcely aroused her curiosity. Religion had no part in her life, and she certainly had no interest in Ōtsu's way of life. She had her hands full trying to cope with her own loneliness, let alone his. What she felt within herself was the enervation of love, and to bury the hollowness she experienced after her divorce, she had become involved in relationships with several of her old college friends as well as businessmen she met at hotel bars. But all she found in each of those encounters were men who thrust their heads into the trough to indulge in pleasure, and her own empty eyes studying their movements.

Mitsuko became a volunteer at the hospital. From her own hunger for love, she cultivated the masochistic desire to engage in a make-believe charade of love. It was a simple matter for her to listen to the complaints of the patients, to offer them words of sympathy, to pour spoonfuls of soup down the throats of the immobile, to wash their bedpans, and to hear their words of gratitude. Mitsuko knew that what she performed were not acts of love from her heart, but mere play-acting.

As she watched the unresisting figures of elderly women sleeping in their beds, Mitsuko would suddenly be gripped by a nebulous urge, and at times she would pretend to forget to change their undergarments or to give them the medicines they were supposed to take. On those occasions, she heard another voice identical to hers saying: *This invalid isn't going to get better whether she takes her medicine or not. This old woman isn't doing anybody any good; in fact, she's a burden to her family, and it's a far better thing to put her at ease sooner rather than later.*

None of the nurses or doctors was aware of her two faces. The head nurse watched her playing her role and announced, 'She's fantastic!' Mitsuko plastered on a look of utter modesty and responded, 'No, not at all.' And inwardly she slid into her smile a cold, mocking grin as she thought of the look of blank amazement that would steal across this nurse's face if she knew that the night before, after Mitsuko had left the hospital, she had linked arms with a young man who had spoken to her on the twelfth floor of the Imperial Hotel and accompanied him to his room.

Ōtsu wrote that God has many faces, she suddenly thought as she joined the man in his bed. And so do I.

One evening she attended an annual class reunion. She hadn't attended one for two years, and she couldn't help noticing that Kondō and her other partners in pleasure from college had all now become businessmen wearing midnight-blue suits, while the women had found proper partners in marriage.

Their topics of conversation were the same as those of her ex-husband and his friends: golf and cars, and nothing else. The conversations of the women focused on child-rearing and getting their children ready for elementary school.

'I got a divorce,' Mitsuko abruptly announced to the group.

A nervous silence spread over the crowd for a moment, but finally one of her women friends asked, 'Why? Did something happen?'

'I just couldn't become a good wife like the rest of you.'

'But you'd like a child, wouldn't you?'

'Heavens, no. I can't imagine bringing someone just like myself into this world.'

Everyone laughed, thinking Mitsuko was jesting. Kondō, evidently trying to cover for her, said nostalgically, 'Didn't we call you Moïra back in those days? And at Allo-Allo we had some fun with that guy named Ōtsu.'

'Apparently... he's become a Catholic priest,' someone with access to the information announced. 'I help make up the mailing list for our graduates. When I wrote to his family and asked for his current address, his brother said he'd become a priest and was working at a religious community in India.'

'Where in India?'

'What was it called? It's that place you see in all the pictures of India. The place where everybody bathes in the River Ganges.'

No one, Mitsuko included, knew what the place was called, and no one aside from Mitsuko had any interest in this information. The topic of conversation quickly turned to rumours about a professional baseball player and the décor at a restaurant in Roppongi that one of their classmates had opened.

When Mitsuko returned home, she opened an encyclopedia from her father's library, from which she learned that there were several cities in India that fitted the description of her classmate, but that the most famous was a place called Vārānasī. The encyclopedia included a photograph of several Hindu men and women, their bodies wrapped in saris, submerged in the river.

SEVEN

Goddesses

Isobe had never imagined he would find himself sitting in a hotel room in a foreign country thinking back over his life with his wife. In planning his life, he had assumed that he would die before her, but he had not given much thought to how she would live after he was gone. He supposed she would be able to get by on money from his life insurance and their savings. His vague assumption somewhere below the level of his consciousness was that matters would take care of themselves when the time came. Now that he thought about it, he was an old-fashioned man who had never attached any profound value or meaning to his married life.

Did I love my wife?

He had to ask himself that question, as he endured the unspeakable loneliness and regret in those empty days following her death, each time he looked through her belongings – the chopsticks she had used every day, the linen, the clothes hanging in her cupboard. But, like most Japanese husbands, he had not given any serious thought to the meaning of 'love' during his marriage.

Married life to him was a division of labour between a man and wife who look after one another and tend to one another's needs. They lived together beneath the same roof, and once the feelings of romance had fled swiftly away, what remained was to determine how each could be useful and helpful to the other. It was not particularly important, as it is in foreign countries, for a wife to become active socially in order to promote her husband's rise up the corporate ladder, or to remain ever alluring as a woman. He felt that a wife's most important job was to put up with her husband's tempers and create a place of repose for him when he returned from work each day with frayed nerves.

In that sense, Keiko had certainly been a good wife. She never meddled in his affairs at or away from home, and though she lacked physical appeal, she knew her place and stayed out of his way.

In a speech he gave at the banquet after one of his younger coworkers got married, he had remarked, 'A wife should be just like air to her husband. If you have no air, you're in trouble. But air is invisible to the eye. It never intrudes in your life. If the woman can become like air, they'll never have problems as husband and wife.'

The men sitting at the banquet tables laughed. Some even applauded.

'There's nothing wrong with married life being dull and quiet.'

Isobe couldn't remember the expression on his wife's face as she sat beside him and listened to his speech. But since she never said a word about it that night in the taxi or after they arrived home, Isobe assumed she must have agreed with what he said.

But he had left out something very important in his speech. He had not touched on the fact that the plain, quiet, dull – in short, the 'good' – wife that Isobe had described, grows weary with the passage of time.

In point of fact, around the time they had attended that wedding, the kind of lassitude that develops in every marriage had settled over Isobe and his wife. One reason was that his life with her had become too ordinary and too monotonous. Once they both turned into the airy sorts of existences he had mentioned in his banquet speech, his wife became nothing more than a wife to him, and she ceased to be a woman in his eyes.

By no means did he consider her a bad mate. But at that point in his life, as he attained his prime as a man, his selfish nature sought something other than a good wife; what he wanted was a woman.

He had no wish at all for a divorce. Being no longer wet behind the ears, he knew well enough that wives and women were not necessarily the same thing. In all honesty, two or three times he had played with fire without getting burned.

One of his affairs was with a woman who owned an Italian restaurant in the Ginza where he sometimes hosted business dinners. It was a unique restaurant, offering both native food matched to the tastes of the Japanese as well as Italian dishes, which made it ideal for entertaining clients.

She always decked herself out to look younger than her years in order to attract business. She wore daringly red dresses, tied girlish black ribbons in her hair, and set dishes on the stark-white tables with fingers attractively manicured. She attended to details so diligently that even first-time customers left satisfied.

This businesswoman, who was in every respect the opposite of Keiko, provided Isobe with the things he could not obtain from his wife at that point in their marriage. Their adopted daughter, now married, was in middle school at the time, and Isobe sometimes grumbled to this woman that the girl disliked him for no reason.

'My daughter was like that,' she said, laughing. 'She hated my husband for a while, and she'd hardly talk to him or even go near him.'

'Why?'

'Because her father was drinking health potions. When children are that age, they have an image of an ideal father, and when the gap between that ideal and their actual father gets too wide, they wind up hating him.'

'And just what is the image of an ideal father?'

'Oh, he's a sportsman, tall and thin, and most of all gentle.' She laughed. 'In short, the kind of papa you see in American movies. But her own father always had a weary face, and he'd stand on the train platform guzzling stamina drinks. When a young girl's father won't do anything on Sundays but watch television, she feels betrayed.'

Her laugh was like that of an actress named Taiji Kiwako, who frequently appeared on television in those days. Come to think of it, her face and figure reminded him of the famous performer also.

'So it's bad to be a father who drinks health potions, huh?'

Isobe silently compared his wife with this woman, who volleyed intelligent remarks at him like a tennis-ball. His wife would have answered his question by saying: 'It's because you're too blunt with the child. You talk to her like you're talking to a boy.'

Isobe made the rounds of the bars with this woman, and on one occasion they ended up committing what might well be called an indiscretion together. The clever woman knew full well that Isobe was not reckless enough to cast off his family for her, and nearing fifty himself, Isobe was well aware of how messy a divorce could be.

Isobe had no idea whether his wife knew of the affair. She never said a word about it. Even if she had been aware of it, she would have pretended to know nothing. When the relationship was over, Isobe felt some guilt, but he had very little sense of actually having betrayed his wife. One or two dalliances had nothing to do with the bonds of marriage. Simply put, his wife had come to seem no more like a woman to him than did his own sisters. In exchange, with the passing of the years an invisible link had gradually formed between them in much the same way that dust accumulates.

Did marital love mean this kind of linkage? At the time, not even that thought had crossed his mind, but when she was stricken with cancer and the doctor told him how long she had left to live, he was staggered by the shock and fear of losing his lifelong companion. The sky outside the window was darkly sombre, and he could hear the voice of the potato vendor.

Then came the babblings that ended up being her final words. Until then, Isobe had never known her display such fierce passion. Though they had lived together for many years, he had never considered the possibility that such a yearning could reside within the depths of her heart. He had made her a promise, and that promise slowly took on a weighty, compelling meaning for him . . . and now, he had come to this foreign land.

After washing himself in the rust-coloured water from the shower, Numada put on a new sports shirt and a pair of beige trousers and went downstairs to the dining-room. It was still before 7 a.m., and there was only one guest in the dining-room – their guide Enami, who was reading an English-language newspaper during breakfast.

'Good morning. Anything interesting in the news?' Numada had neither knowledge about nor interest in the political affairs of India, but since the first page of the newspaper lying on the table had a photograph of the prime minister, Indira Gandhi, he dutifully posed the question.

'It looks like there's some real unrest,' Enami answered as he wiped his mouth with a napkin. 'The Sikhs are up to something. It's only the charismatic presence of Indira Gandhi that maintains any sort of order here in India.'

'The Sikhs – are they the bearded Indians with turbans wrapped round their heads?' Numada asked the question, but he had no interest in the subject. He stared at the red, ball-shaped objects on Enami's plate and asked, 'What are those?'

'Onions pickled in vinegar.'

'Nothing but vegetables, huh? Are you a vegetarian, Mr Enami?'

'In the morning I just eat these and a kind of yoghurt called *lassi*. But when I travel with a group, I end up having to take some meat with lunch and dinner. I put on weight easily, I'm afraid. But, tell me, how do you like India so far?'

'I'm content just looking at nature. There are banyan trees everywhere, and it's a simple matter to locate pīpals and udumbaras. This morning when I woke up, the birds were chirping loudly in the garden.... Words fail me.'

'The Hindus plant trees in the places where corpses are cremated.'

'That's true with cherry trees in Japan, too. The cherries at Mount Yoshino were all put there in place of grave-markers. There's a very close connection between death and vegetation.'

'Is that so? I didn't realize that. Would you like to order something for breakfast?'

'Just some hot coffee.'

'You'll be better off on our travels through the day if you put something in your stomach. You might try some of these pickled onions.'

'The Hindus believe that trees bear within them the life force that produces rebirth, don't they?'

'Yes.'

'I'm very struck by that notion.' As he slurped the coffee the khitmutgar brought him, Numada broke into a satisfied smile. 'I write children's stories, you know. Nearly everything I write is about interchanges between children and animals. But coming here to India and seeing those massive banyan trees, I've made up my mind that my next story will be about trees and children.'

'Really?'

'We passed through that thick forest when we were travelling here from Allahābād. The one you told me had the bird sanctuary.... I've never seen such a forest before. What I sensed as we travelled through there was the individual voices of each tree in the forest. They seemed to be saying something to us.'

'When the Indians rose up in rebellion against the British in 1857, the trees of that forest near Allahābād were used in place of a gallows, and Indians were hanged from them. I didn't mention that in the bus.' Enami seemed almost to be tossing water on Numada's enthusiasm.

He had studied Indian philosophy in its native land for four years, but after he returned to Japan he could not find anywhere to apply his hard-earned knowledge. Not a single university department had an opening for him, and discontent over having to work part-time as a tour guide had accumulated in the deepest recesses of his heart. Frankly, he despised the Japanese tourists he had to shuttle around for the Cosmos Tour Company just so that he could put food on the table. The deeply grateful old men and women who made the rounds of the Buddhist relics; the college women who relished the hippie-like homeless; and the men like Numada who searched the natural environment of India for something they had lost. They always took the same souvenirs back to Japan with them: silk saris, sandalwood necklaces, damascene ornaments, gems modelled on the star ruby or emeralds, and silver bracelets. Enami stood in the doorways of stores where once American and European tourists had bought up everything in sight and watched contemptuously as the Japanese roved from showcase to showcase.

Of course Enami never displayed his true feelings. His present maxim for living was 'passive resistance'. He constantly repeated to himself: *In front of your customers, you must always be the affable, accommodating tour guide.*

'You were planning to visit the wildlife sanctuaries, weren't you, Mr Numada?'

'I'm hoping to. I want to see with my own eyes the homeland of birds like the hornbill and the myna that have come from tropical countries.'

'Why?'

'That's a personal secret,' Numada laughed. 'You have some secrets of your own, don't you, Mr Enami?'

'I certainly do. It's strange, you know. Usually when a male Japanese tourist gets me alone this, he acts as though he's telling me some dark personal secret, then asks me in a low voice to take him to a place where he can find women. But you're different, Mr Numada.'

'I really hate that. Here in India at least, I have no interest in such things.'

'Excuse me for saying this, but the natural environment in India is considerably more vulgar than you think.'

'I suppose you mean the contradictory nature that combines the powers of both creation and destruction? It seems as if every book on India I pick up makes that argument, and I'm sick to death of it.'

'Early tomorrow morning we'll be going to watch people bathing in the Ganges. The right bank is jammed with all manner and size of ghāts and buildings, but the opposite bank of the broad river is covered with nothing but trees. To the Hindus, as I understand it, the left bank conjures up images of uncleanliness. I've been to that left bank.'

'And?'

'I've never been anywhere where I've felt more strongly the ghastly vulgarity of nature.'

'You're just saying that to lead me on, aren't you?'

'That's right. You're just too pure a person, that's all there is to it. Ah, everyone else seems to be waking up. Excuse me.'

Tourists dressed for hot weather, each carrying a camera, filtered one after another into the dining-room. Enami quickly got to his feet and translated their breakfast orders to the khitmutgar.

As he studied their tour guide, who had gone through a complete transformation since their conversation, Numada pondered the words Enami had used: 'vulgar nature'. Instinctively, he had a vague idea what that meant, but as a writer of children's stories, nature to him had never seemed cruel or hideous. Nature had to be the medium that facilitated the interaction between man and the life force.

Numada walked down into the garden, stretched his arms wide and took a deep breath. He had heard that India would still be hot at the end of October, but – maybe because it was still before 8 a.m. – the exhilarating air retained the aromas of earth and light that he had not smelled for a long while in the concrete city of Tokyo. Numada sucked in mouthfuls of air and spat out the noxious vapours that had accumulated inside his body.

'Practising your breathing exercises, are you?' Kiguchi, still chewing on the remains of his breakfast, called out familiarly as he came through the door.

'Just my own form of deep breathing.'

'That's wonderful. I never let a morning go by without doing some callisthenics. Even here in India, when I wake up I sit down on the floor and do my exercises.'

'Excuse me,' the young Sanjos called out loudly from behind them. 'Would you mind snapping one for us?'

'Snapping one?'

133

'You just push this button here.' Sanjō foisted his camera on Numada, and he and his wife walked towards a spot where marguerites bloomed madly. With no hesitation he wrapped his arm round his wife's waist, and the new bride rested her head on her husband's shoulder.

'And they call themselves Japanese? Not a scrap of shame about them,' Kiguchi grumbled to himself as he stood next to Numada, who was holding the camera up to his eye.

'Oh, don't be so hard on them. They're newly-weds, after all.'

'You couldn't even imagine such behaviour in our day.'

'In my day, too, a honeymoon overseas was beyond all possibility. But now Japan has prospered, and these young people are no different from the foreigners.'

'Would you mind taking three or four more?' Oblivious to the whisperings passing between Kiguchi and Numada, Sanjō made bold to ask.

From the entrance to the spacious gardens an old man carrying a tattered bag and a basket came shuffling in, accompanied by a young man and a boy. The old man was as thin as a matchstick, and his wiry legs poked out beneath his short trousers.

'Nāmastē,' the boy said with a servile smile. 'Jāpānī? Japānī?'

'Hān,' Numada answered with a Hindi word he had just learned, but nothing else the three said was comprehensible.

Enami appeared from the group of Japanese who had gathered in the doorway, and after he had conversed with the old man he explained: 'He says they're going to show you a fight between a mongoose and a snake. These fellows are snake-charmers known as sāpera. They're outcasts. Their entire village is composed of snake-charmers and their families.'

The old man, wizened like a dead tree, knelt on the ground, and when he began to play a peculiar melody on his flute, the lid of the basket slid off and a cobra shaped like a folded umbrella poked its face out. Mrs Sanjō squealed and clung to her husband.

'It's all right,' Sanjō told his wife. 'They've removed its poisonous fangs. Isn't that right, Mr Enami?'

'Yes. You seem to know all about it.'

'I've seen it on television. The mongoose has had its teeth removed so it won't actually kill the snake.'

'You're spoiling all our fun, Mr Sanjō.' Enami studied the deflated looks on the other tourists' faces. 'When you give away the trick, our whole trip to India loses its fascination.'

When the tour bus sidled up beside the garden entrance, it kicked up a white cloud of dust. Circled by the Japanese, the mongoose adroitly sprang at the cobra and pinned it down. When the group applauded, the old man plunged his twiglike fingers into his bag and pulled out an eerie-looking, grey-coloured snake. Some of the women in the group gasped in fear.

'He says it's a snake with two heads.' Enami had scarcely finished his dutiful explanation when he was suddenly gripped by a feeling of revulsion, wondering how many times he had told tourists about this two-headed snake. He had not pursued his studies in India just so he could describe these inconsequential stunts to others. It wasn't so he could take groups of tourists to the Taj Mahal and repeat the same speeches over and over in the same voice, telling them how it had taken twenty-two years to construct, and how Shah Jahan of the Mogul Empire had built it in memory of his beautiful princess, Mumtaz.

There's no reason to expect that any of them really understand India. And yet, when these religious leaders and men of culture go back to Japan, they talk as though they have understood everything there is to know about India.

He donned his tour-guide smile and cheerful voice in an attempt to wipe away these thoughts of abhorrence. 'Well then, please get in the bus. The temperature will be climbing today, but it'll be cool inside the bus with the air-conditioning on.'

Even inside the bus the smells of the city were obtrusive. The smells of sweat, of the gutters, of foods frying at outdoor stalls; outlandish colours; brass and copper pots glistening even inside darkened shops. Women streamed by, draped in saris of yellow and persimmon and black. Grey cows, so spindly their back and shoulder bones protruded, paraded past. An elephant with firewood piled on its back was herded through the clouds of dust.

'We have finally entered the city of Vārānasī, which might well be called the India within India.' With the microphone to his mouth, Enami fluently enunciated his memorized speech. 'The city lies on the shores of two rivers, the Varanā and the Asi, and the main current of the River Ganges. As I explained to you yesterday, the Hindus regard a place where two rivers flow together as holy ground. The rich in their trains and automobiles, the impoverished on foot – all make their pilgrimages to this city. According to their religious beliefs, all their sins are washed away when they bathe in the sacred waters of the Ganges, and when death comes, if the ashes from their corpses are scattered in this river, they will be released from the cycle of transmigration.'

The tourist bus always drove along the same course. The Bhāratmātā Temple, the campus of Hindu University, and the bathing sites along the River Ganges.

But sometimes Enami, after guiding his tourists to those predetermined locations, would also escort them to a unique Hindu temple of his own choosing. This was a special favour to his clients, as well as an opportunity to take his revenge on them.

The air that had been so refreshing that morning gave way in the afternoon to a quietly pervasive heat laden with humidity.

Enami purposely avoided going to the ghāts on the Ganges in the morning hours. He did not want the Japanese tourists gawking at the holy river, the sacred rituals and the hallowed places of death solely out of curiosity. When the Japanese watched from their boats as the Hindus bathed in the river, they always said the same things:

'Can you believe they actually scatter the ashes from dead bodies in the river?'

'I can't imagine all these Indians don't get sick from it.'

'I can't stand this smell . . .! Doesn't it bother the Indians?'

Once again Enami would have to listen to the scorn and narrow-mindedness of his tourists, but such things did not bother him in the evening.

Instead, Enami led them down the narrow alleys leading to the gateway of the Vishvanātha Temple, which looked particularly 'Indian' to Japanese eyes. The tiny shops, wedged together on both sides of the streets like black-market stalls, were packed with a variety of strange items. There were stores where sugar-cane was washed in a bucket, run through a roller and squeezed to produce juice; shops where coconuts were cracked open with a large knife and straws inserted for the customers to drink. Tobacconists offered rolled leaves filled with betel-nut leaves or spices.

'This is chewing tobacco. It's rather bitter, but it might make a good souvenir.'

The stores where Enami took his charges never varied, and the shopfronts with sleeping dogs where he offered his explanations were always the same. With a smile, he declared in a congenial voice: 'It's called *pān* by the Indians. It turns the inside of your mouth a little red.'

The male tourists inquisitively stuffed the chewing tobacco in their mouths, then contorted their faces at its bitterness. The women watched and laughed. The click of camera shutters. A half-naked man carrying baskets on a pole over his shoulder passed directly beside them.

'That's the yoghurt man.'

'I'd like to buy some Indian silk. Are there any shops around here?'

The sunlight grew increasingly bright. Among the tourists, Enami was mildly interested in Mitsuko. He was drawn to her profile with her broad-brimmed hat and sun-glasses. She had none of the wilfulness or impertinence so common in female tourists, and a smile always garnished her cheeks.

If I slept with her, he imagined to himself as he stared at her profile, *I wonder what kind of look she'd have on her face?*

Enami had slept with two of the women on the tours he led as a side job. Both had been ordinary, middle-aged housewives. There was something in the dank heat of India that stimulated the human libido. That same something could be found in the mysterious aura of Hinduism. As he scrutinized Mitsuko from time to time, he wondered what sorts of relationships she had had with men.

An early lunch. They were finished by one. The bus again took on its passengers and delivered them to the Nakshar Bhagavatī Temple. Most Japanese found this temple boring, and it aroused the curiosity of a meagre few. It was not on the itinerary for the usual tours of India, and only Enami went out of his way to bring sightseers here.

'The name of this temple means "a woman who showers mercy".' Enami gathered his group in an underground chamber smelling of limestone. They were blasted by the sweltering heat the moment they set foot inside. This place, too, teemed with the quietly obscene atmosphere unique to India.

'The "bhaga" in Bhagavatī refers to a woman's genitals,' Enami explained with a deliberately innocent look.

'Bhaga?' A man's voice responded. 'It's hot as a bugger in here, all right. It's like a steam-bath.'

Two or three laughed at his feeble joke, but Mitsuko's expression did not change.

'I brought you here because I wanted you to experience a part of the Hindu religion. Rather than having me explain it, I think the various images of women carved into these walls will help you feel all the groanings and misery and terror of India. Feel free to ask if you want me to explain anything.'

Several of the men and women, unable to bear the moist heat of the interior, would not go any further inside. These were not Buddhist images, so the Japanese displayed no interest in these Hindu deities. These were no more than drab etchings unconnected to their own lives.

The stifling air. The dark subterranean interior. The eerie sculptures floated before their eyes. The hideousness of the images were reminiscent of the feelings of loathing that people experience when they have an unobstructed view of the writhing elements concealed beneath the level of their own conscious minds.

They walked down the abraded stone steps. For an instant Mitsuko had the impression that she was beginning the descent into the depths of her heart. She felt both the anxiety and the pleasure of peering into the interior of her heart with a microscope.

Isobe was breathing roughly behind her. It was, more than anything else, sweltering. Numada and the others followed.

'Watch your step along here, please.'

The dim light from the electric light bulbs made every grimy wall look like a cavern. Black figures, obscenely tangled together like the roots of trees, darted up before their eyes. The Japanese tourists said nothing, and the images did not even tremble.

Their eyes grew accustomed to the darkness. They realized the objects that had appeared to be the intertwined bodies of men and women were in fact multiple arms and legs. Gradually they came to the realization that the hands were holding human skulls and heads. These were goddesses, wearing peculiar crowns and riding on tigers or lions, wild boars or water-buffalo.

'Are these images all of the same goddess?'

When Enami walked up beside her to answer her question, Mitsuko smelled the strong aroma of perspiration coming from the chunky arms protruding through his short-sleeved shirt.

'No, each one is different. Would you like to know their names?'

'I couldn't remember them even if you told them to me. They all look exactly the same to me.'

'Many of the Indian goddesses take on not only gentle forms, but also frightening visages. I suppose that's because they symbolize all the activities of life, both birth and, simultaneously, death.'

'They're very different from the Holy Mother Mary, aren't they, even though she's a goddess too?'

'Very different indeed. Mary is a representation of the Mother, but the goddesses of India are at the same time symbols of the forces of nature that exult in death and blood.'

The men in the group listened silently as Mitsuko conversed with Enami. There was nothing at all about the preposterously irrational, ugly goddesses that caught their fancies. From the word 'goddess' they had been expecting something tender, something maternal. And the sweltering heat of this underground chamber had left their faces and necks stained with sweat.

In a tired voice, Numada muttered to himself, 'There's something about this place that strips away all the joy and hope of being alive.' The Nature he had taken up in his children's stories over the years had been nothing so turbulent and fearful. To him Nature had been a force that gently embraced mankind.

Nor could Isobe find anything compassionate about the images of these goddesses that covered the walls. Even though their bodies boasted voluptuous breasts and full hips symbolic of the earth's fertile harvests, he could not find one with a smile resembling that of his dead wife's.

Kiguchi superimposed the ghosts of the Japanese soldiers who had walked the Highway of Death over this ugly, grimy throng, and as he groped for the beads on the Buddhist rosary he wore round his wrist, he intoned a passage from the Amida Sutra: 'And the entire world, with the gods and evil spirits and every other manner of creature, heard the teachings of the Buddha and, receiving them with gladness, believed.'

'It's just too hot. Can we go back outside?' Numada, unable to bear it any longer, asked.

'Just one more,' Enami said, restraining the group. 'Please have a look at an image of my favourite goddess.' He pointed to an image that resembled a tree sprite no more than a metre tall. 'It's very dark in here, so please come closer. This goddess is called Chāmundā. Chāmundā lives in graveyards. At her feet you can see human corpses that have been pecked by birds and devoured by jackals.'

A large droplet of sweat from Enami's body coursed like a tear to the floor which was dappled with gobs of candle-wax.

'Her breasts droop like those of an old woman. And yet she offers milk from her withered breasts to the children who line up before her. Can you see how her right leg has festered as though afflicted with leprosy? Her belly has caved in from hunger, and scorpions have stung her there. Enduring all these ills and pains, she offers milk from her sagging breasts to mankind.'

Enami, who until an hour before had been joking pleasantly with these tourists, suddenly screwed up his face. The sweat that trickled down his cheeks could have been mistaken for tears. Mitsuko, Numada, Kiguchi and Isobe were taken aback by this, but at the same time they could not help but sense some of the feelings that Enami directed towards these goddesses, whose forms resembled twisted roots.

'I love this image of Chāmundā. I've never come to this city without standing here in front of her statue.'

'I like it too,' Kiguchi unexpectedly announced with deep feeling. 'On the battlefields in Burma, I always felt as though death was close at hand, and when I look at this gaunt statue now, I remember all the soldiers who died in the rain. The war was . . . horrible. And all those soldiers . . . they looked just like this.'

'She . . . she displays all the sufferings of the Indian people. All the suffering and death and starvation that the people of India have had to endure over many long years come out in this statue. She has contracted every illness they have suffered through the years. She has tolerated the poison of cobras and snakes. Despite it all, she . . . as she pants for breath, she offers milk to mankind from her shrivelled breasts. This is India. This is the India I wanted to show each of you.'

As though embarrassed by his own display of emotion, Enami roughly wiped his sweat-soaked face with a large, dirty handkerchief. He had explained this suffering goddess to his tourists with the claim that he was explaining India to them, but in his own mind he was recalling his own mother, who had raised him through many trials of her own after she was abandoned by her husband.

'Then, unlike the other goddesses . . . is this one more like the Holy Mother Mary of India?'

'You could say that. But unlike Mary, she is not pure and refined, and she wears no fine apparel. Rather, she is ugly and worn with age, and she groans under the weight of the suffering she bears. This statue was carved in the twelfth century, but her sufferings have not changed even today. This motherly Chāmundā of India is quite unlike the Holy Mother Mary of Europe.'

Everyone listened in silence to Enami's explanation. Each was caught up in his or her private thoughts.

'Shall we go?' Enami summarily urged the group. 'I'm sure the others are tired of waiting for us.'

140

As he set off walking, Isobe and Kiguchi came up to him.

'Thank you,' Isobe said. 'That was worth seeing.'

Kiguchi added, 'Coming down to this underground chamber... I feel that I understand for the first time why Sakyamuni appeared in this land.'

'Really?' A look of honest delight appeared on Enami's face. 'If that's how you feel, then it will have some meaning tomorrow when I show you the spot where Buddha appeared to his first disciple after completing his spiritual training.'

One step into the open and the bright sunlight slapped their foreheads. Inside the air-conditioned tour bus, the Sanjōs and the other women who had not gone into the cave were drinking chilled Coca-Cola and coconut juice.

'How was it?' Sanjō asked.

'Just as sweaty as you see us looking.' Enami had recovered his earlier affability.

Sanjō laughed. 'That's why I didn't go in. After all, it's just a bunch of dusty Buddhist statues, isn't it?'

'They're not Buddhist statues, they're goddesses.'

'It's all the same to me. Where are we going now?'

'To the sacred River Ganges.'

'I wanted to see the Rhine,' Sanjō's bride guilelessly announced. 'I'll bet it's not as hot there.'

'Here we are at last at the great mother Ganges.' Once he had caught his breath in the air-conditioned vehicle, Enami again took up his microphone.

His words 'great mother' reminded those who had gone down into the cavern of the goddess who endured the bites of poisonous snakes and scorpions and, while afflicted with leprosy and hunger, offered her milk to swarms of children. The mother of India. An image not of a mother's plentitude and gentleness but of an old woman reduced to skin and bones and gasping for breath. Despite it all, she was still a mother.

'What we see today will be something of a prologue to tomorrow. Tomorrow I want to set out just as the sunlight first breaks through the clouds, but I'm bringing you here today for the benefit of those who want to sleep in and not join our tour tomorrow.'

'Is it more interesting early in the morning?' Sanjō inquired loudly.

'It's not "interesting." It's holy. With the golden light of the sun splitting the darkness as their signal, pilgrims who have gathered in the city assemble at the many ghāts. They vie with one another to plunge into the great mother river. The maternal waters accept both the living and the dead. That's what is meant by holy.'

'Is it true that they bathe right next to where the ashes of the dead have been scattered?'

'It's true.'

'Ugh,' Sanjō's young wife said to him. 'I don't want to see anything as filthy as that.'

'Fine, fine, you're welcome to stay behind in the bus. We can't have you feeling ill.' Enami smiled and nodded, as though her feelings were perfectly reasonable.

Sanjō, defending his wife, asked, 'Don't the Indians consider it unclean?'

'Of course not. As I've explained several times, the River Ganges to the Hindu people is a holy, motherly river. For that reason they come to this city, journeying many miles by train or on foot, in order one day to become part of its great current. There, please look out of your windows. An old ascetic with a long withered branch for a stick is crossing at the intersection.'

The skinny old hermit, looking like a white-haired demon, was swallowed up into the swarms of people.

'This is a city where people gather in order to die. There are many roads that make their way here – the Panch Koshi Road, the Raja Motichand Road, the Raja Bazar Road. Many pilgrims journey from every point of the compass in order to die here. Look, you can see buses and cars transporting them. Those who can't ride in the buses and cars take their time walking here like that old hermit. There are no roads like this in a country like Japan.' Enami emphasized the words. 'None at all. None.'

A road travelled in order to die. The words reminded Kiguchi of the Highway of Death in Burma. The sunken-cheeked faces of dead soldiers; the hordes of sick and wounded men collapsed and moaning on the muddy road. The Highway he had walked along like a somnambulist. Along that road he had clung to the faint hope that, if he could merely make it down that highway, he would survive. Did that old hermit maintain the hope that if he could make his way to the Ganges, he would be born again?

In the crowds of people Isobe saw a number of barefoot young girls. One girl wound her way between the cows and sheep and disappeared. Another girl stood in front of a fried food stall and watched with hungry eyes as the proprietor held up a sweet cake with a pair of chopsticks.

'Search for me.' Again he heard his wife's desperate ravings. 'Promise... promise!'

He had decided to speak to Enami and arrange to stay behind in Vārānasī alone. According to the itinerary, the group was setting out tomorrow to tour the Buddhist holy sites, beginning in Sarnāth, where Sakyamuni had delivered his first sermon.

I'll find you. Just be patient. Isobe repeated in his mind the words he had muttered innumerable times.

'Shall we go? Or would you rather not?' He could hear two women whispering behind him.

'I'm going to have a look. I paid a lot of money to come on this trip. It'd be a shame not to see it just so we can tell people about it.'

One after another the Japanese climbed out of the bus when it arrived at the Dashāshvamedha Ghāt, where stairs descended into the river. Only Mrs Sanjō remained in her seat.

In an instant begging girls surrounded them. The writhing children who gestured as though putting something into their mouths, and the leper girl who crawled along the ground and stretched out a fingerless hand tugged at the sympathies of the Japanese tourists. Sanjō handed out a coin and called for everyone to hear, 'Why don't they put these kids into an institution?'

'Every Japanese who comes to India asks that same question,' Enami responded with a smile. 'If these children are institutionalized, their families will starve to death. They're a vital source of income for their families. The crippled children and the girls with leprosy all capitalize on their ailments to become worthy bread-winners.'

'This is an awful country. Who's the leader of this place?'

'You mean you don't know? It's the prime minister, Indira Gandhi – even her name is reminiscent of the great mother Ganges. She's the daughter of Nehru. They call her the mother of India.'

The buildings chaotically arrayed by the river, a jumble of shapes and colours, were lodging-houses for pilgrims and pavilions and temples reserved for royalty. Between the buildings stood flower vendors selling the *gendā* blossoms that were tossed into the river.

After they threaded their way past these buildings, the great river suddenly appeared before them.

Reflecting the rays of the afternoon sun, the broad river cut a gentle curve as it flowed by. The surface of the water was a muddy grey and the level of the water high, making it impossible to see to the bottom. Pilgrims and pedlars still stood on the ghāts. The speed of the current was evident from the movement of a grey object floating on the surface in the distance. When the tiny-looking object drew closer, it turned out to be the bloated corpse of a grey dog. But no one on the ghāts paid it any attention. The holy river took not only humans, but all living things in its embrace as it flowed away.

In the shallows, several men and women beat laundry against rocks and hung it out to dry on ropes stretched along the shore. These were outcasts known as dhobhis, whose lifelong trade was laundering. An old Brahmin priest with a bald head and wearing glasses sat beneath a wide umbrella waiting for the pilgrims on the stone steps leading to the shore of the river. Beside the priest sat a man selling a vermilion powder the colour of blood. The Brahmin priest would paint a small circle on the foreheads of the Hindu worshippers and give them a blessing.

Sanjō seemed to have completely forgotten his earlier anger and scorn, and he scurried around with his prize camera, taking pictures of various scenes.

'Mr Sanjō!' Enami hastily yelled to him. 'As we get closer to the cremation grounds, you will see a number of bodies being carried to the ghāts. Please don't take any pictures of the bodies. You'll make the families very angry.'

'They don't allow pictures of the bodies? I know that. That's why I want to take them. As a photographer.'

'This is no joke. You simply must not do it. You'll make trouble for everyone.'

As Enami had predicted, a group of men in a funeral cortège appeared on the ghāt. They had fashioned a litter from two poles some three metres in length, wrapped with a pale-red cloth. What appeared to be a dead body had been lashed to the litter with gold tape. They laid the stretcher near the river bank. There they waited patiently for their turn to come. First a swarm of flies, smelling death, gathered round, followed soon by a flock of crows which began pacing nearby. But the mourners remained crouched by the river, and made no move to drive the scavengers away.

The river, as always, silently flowed by. The river cared nothing about the corpses that would eventually be burned and scattered into itself, or about the unmoving male mourners who appeared to cradle their heads in their arms. It was evident here that death was simply a part of nature.

At a nearby ghāt, five or six people were bathing in the river. The lower parts of the men's bodies were wrapped in white cloths, while the women wore saris of varied colours. As they soaked in the water, they brought their hands together in prayer, rinsed their mouths and washed their hair, then returned to the ghāt. Some would bathe, then rest on the stone steps, and again return to the river.

The sky grew slightly darker. The sun that had beaten against the stone steps was slowly declining. But the river continued to flow, with no change whatever.

'Those are the cremation grounds,' Enami pointed to the Manikarnikā Ghāt, where a plume of smoke as yellow as sulphur rose into the sky. 'The two- and three-storey buildings to the left are free lodgings for the elderly and the incurably ill who have come to await death. As soon as they die they are taken to the cremation grounds. Those too poor to pay for the kindling are cast as they are into the river.'

'Do you think I could get a picture of the cremation grounds? Would you ask them, Mr Enami, since I can't take any of the bodies?' Sanjō seemed interested in nothing but his photographs, and his plea was insistent, but Enami firmly shook his head.

'No. Absolutely not.'

'How about if I offered them some money?'

'Put yourself in the place of the mourning families who'd be photographed. It's an insult to the Hindu believers and to the deceased.'

Mitsuko and Isobe sat on the stone steps of the ghāt listening to Enami's angry report.

'They're here on their honeymoon, and he leaves his wife in the bus and can think of nothing but his photographs. It's unbelievable,' Isobe remarked as he gazed at the milky surface of the river.

Mitsuko thought of how on her own honeymoon she had left her husband in a Paris hotel and gone off to walk the forest of Les Landes in search of her own private world.

'Couples like you and your wife are a rarity these days. Imagine someone coming to a land like this in search of his dead wife.'

'But, after all, every one of the Indian people who come to dip in the waters of this river believes in reincarnation. And aren't you ... searching for something in this city?'

'In my case it's a friend who's still alive. And it doesn't matter to me whether I see him or not.'

145

'I see. What sort of work does this person do?'

'I hear he's become a Catholic priest.'

'A priest? A Catholic priest living in a city of Hindus?'

As a puzzled look passed over Isobe's face, they heard a conversation behind them between Enami and Numada.

'The ones who aren't cremated are the poor who don't have the money to pay for the kindling, and children under the age of seven. The corpses of the children are placed in reed boats, and the poor are buried beneath the waters.'

'I see some people fishing there, too.'

'Yes. They serve those fish in the hotel restaurants here in town. Of course we try to keep that a secret from the tourists. Well, shall we be going? We'll come here again early tomorrow morning.'

All around them the sunlight had darkened, but the River Ganges alone continued to flow slowly, indifferent to everything. To Numada it seemed like the next world reserved for the dead. He resurrected in his mind a fable he had written many years before.

Shinkichi's grandfather and grandmother had lived in a village by the Yatsushiro Sea. His grandfather had died eight years before, but in his vigorous days he had been known as a master squid-catcher, and he was famed as a fisherman throughout the village. He had, though, been very fond of his liquor, and Shinkichi's father had grumbled that drinking was what had killed him.

Shinkichi lived in Tokyo, and he seldom visited his grandfather's house. Three years before, he had returned to the Ariake Sea for the *obon* festival of the dead. During the day, an elder cousin taught him how to swim in the glimmering Yatsushiro Sea, and at night they took him out fishing. He could not believe how much fun he had every day. When he looked out from the beach, the torches from the squid-catching boats stretched out like a bridge of fire. On the night of the Feast of Lanterns, his grandmother and kinsmen lit lanterns and from their boats set them afloat into the sea.

All around them the candle-lit lanterns floated in the water.

'Your grandpa has become a fish and lives in this sea,' his grandmother told Shinkichi with a serious face. 'This sea is the world where we live after we die. When your grandma dies one day, I'll have them cast my body into this sea, and I'll become a fish and be able to see your grandpa again.'

His grandmother seemed to believe everything she told him. When

Shinkichi asked his cousin, 'Is that true?' the elder boy with a sober look answered, 'Of course it's true. That's what everyone in the village believes. My sister died when she was in elementary school, but she's a fish now, and swims around at the bottom of this sea.'

Numada had written this fable as a tentative study while he was still in college, but it had remained one of his favourites. He had gone on to write that a large factory was built near the village, and that waste from the plant had polluted the sea, afflicted the fish, and made the people of the fishing village ill. But he had cut out that part, feeling it was too painful a story for a fable. The villagers had complained about the factory, not only because it discharged waste that made them ill, but because it had destroyed the next world where their ancestors and their dead parents and relatives and siblings were living as fish, and where they too would one day be reborn. Numada had wanted to include in his fable that journalists, who did not believe in a life to come, had emphasized in their reports of the problem not these ephemeral concerns, but the problems of environmental pollution and sickness.

EIGHT

In Search of What Was Lost

What had sounded like metal scratching against metal was the telephone ringing next to her pillow. The piercing noise seemed like the notification of some mishap. She stretched out her white arm and picked up the receiver.

'Is this Miss Naruse? I'm very sorry. I know I shouldn't be calling you at this hour.' It was the voice of their guide, Enami. 'Mr Kiguchi has a fever. A lot of tourists get diarrhoea in India, so I gave him some antibiotics I brought along, but they don't seem to have had much effect.'

'I'm afraid I'm not a doctor.'

'Yes, I know that. But you worked at a hospital, didn't you? Would you mind helping us?'

'Did you contact the reception desk?'

'The people there are useless. The girl on the night-shift knows absolutely nothing, and all she'll say is that she'll ring a doctor tomorrow. I'm going to ring the university hospital immediately and have them send a doctor here, but could you have a look at Mr Kiguchi before he arrives?'

She dressed quickly and went out into the hallway. It was close to 3 a.m. and pitch-dark. A lizard clung to the wall as if it had been pasted there. The din of insects outside sounded like the roar of a flood. On a well-worn sofa by the reception desk Enami sat with his legs stretched out, exhaustion oozing from his face as he dozed with his eyes open. Huge mosquitoes clung here and there to the walls as though they were part of an insect collection that had been hung there with pins. The girl at the reception desk flicked through the pages of an old magazine and yawned uninhibitedly.

'Ah!' Enami opened his eyes wide and jumped to his feet like a spring-driven doll.

'It's not all that easy being a tour guide, is it?'

'This happens once in a while. But most of the time antibiotics fix them.'

'What are his symptoms?'

'The high fever is the worst of it. I thought it might be food poisoning. A lot of people get sick eating trout from the Ganges.'

With his slippers slapping noisily against his bare feet, Enami led Mitsuko up the stairs. Kiguchi's room was on the second floor, in the hallway directly opposite Mitsuko's.

'Mr Kiguchi, I'm going to run over immediately and get a doctor.' Enami opened the door and turned on the lights. 'While I'm gone, Miss Naruse says she'll stay with you. She's been a volunteer at a hospital before, so that's a relief.'

Kiguchi was clutching both sides of his blanket and had buried his face half beneath it, where he moaned, 'I'm sorry. Sorry for the trouble.'

His fever seemed very high, and his body trembled slightly. Even in the dim lighting of the room, it was evident that his entire face was bathed in sweat.

Enami's footsteps faded away at the end of the hallway, and Kiguchi and Mitsuko were left alone in the room. The towels in the bathroom seemed dirty somehow, so Mitsuko went to her room to bring her own towels and some cologne back with her. When she returned, Kiguchi was still shaking.

'Let me wipe the perspiration off for you.'

The heat of his fever and the smell of his sweat jabbed at Mitsuko's nose. In a rush she remembered the body odours of all the patients she had cared for as a volunteer. She knew just how to move him, and just where to mop his body. The aroma of the cologne helped somewhat to obliterate the body odours and the radiated heat.

'I'm sorry, ma'am.'

'Don't worry.'

'I contracted malaria when I was in the army. They cured it with quinine, but maybe it's got me again.'

As she wiped his bony chest, Mitsuko thought about the disease that Kiguchi had mentioned. Chills and shivers assailed him once again, and his teeth began to chatter even though he was wrapped in a blanket.

'They don't use quinine any more. Now they treat malaria with a much more effective drug called Primaquine. I'm quite sure the Indian doctor will know about Primaquine.'

'Ma'am....' When Kiguchi opened his mouth, she could see that he had removed his dentures. 'Do you think the doctor will come?'

Mitsuko smiled and nodded. This non-committal smile was the look she gave in the hospital as her 'imitation of love'. 'Close your eyes and go to sleep. Everything will be fine. I'm right here beside you.'

She took the ailing man's hand and stroked the back of it. This, too, had been one of her regular 'imitations of love' when she worked as a volunteer. Kiguchi surrendered himself to her ministrations.

About a half an hour later, they heard the faint hum of an automobile at the edge of the garden. Mitsuko listened carefully.

'It's a car. It must be Mr Enami with the doctor. That was faster than I expected.'

Kiguchi wearily closed his eyes. The rays of an automobile's headlights scurried across the window like a revolving lantern.

Mitsuko opened the door to the room and waited for the two men. The doctor who scampered into the room looked to be a young Indian about thirty, wearing rimless glasses like Gandhi's. He pressed his stethoscope against Kiguchi's chest. He apparently mistook Mitsuko for the patient's wife and called her 'Mrs' before asking whether the taking of blood and administering of injections ran contrary to her husband's religious beliefs. He spoke the Queen's English, so Mitsuko supposed that he must have studied in London.

'Is it malaria?' Enami asked.

The doctor shrugged his shoulders, gave Kiguchi a shot to lower his fever, then drew a sample of blood in a small test-tube. Then he signalled Enami with his eyes and walked out into the hallway.

Eventually Enami, blinking eyes that were bloodshot from exhaustion, motioned to Mitsuko to join him in the hall.

'What a mess. If it's some awful contagious disease or malaria, he'll have to be put into the hospital. But tonight I'm supposed to take the group to Buddh-Gaya. Of course I can't just leave Mr Kiguchi like this, and if he ends up in the hospital, I can have a Japanese from one of our contact companies in Calcutta come over to stay with him, but he wouldn't make it here by tonight.'

'But surely you've had unexpected problems like this before?'

'We have, but they've all been people with diarrhoea or stomach cramps, which have been cured with antibiotics. This is my first run-in with malaria.'

After a moment of silence, Mitsuko asked, 'Would you like me to stay here with him?'

'Do you mean it?' Enami eyes widened. But it was clear he had inwardly hoped she would make the offer. 'It would really help me out if you could do that. You can speak the language and everything.'

'My English isn't all that reliable. But I'll manage until a Japanese can get here from Calcutta.'

'I really appreciate this. Thank you. I promise we'll be back by day after tomorrow, so two days is all you'd have to do. Naturally I'll get in touch with my company and have them give you a discount on your expenses in India.'

'You really don't need to worry about that. Pristine places like Buddh-Gaya where Sakyamuni attained enlightenment really don't suit my fancy. I feel much more at home amid the vile smells of this city. I'm actually grateful you'll let me stay on here.'

'I'm going to take you at your word on this.'

She flashed her customary smile. But this was not the smile she used to conceal her true feelings. Since her arrival in India she had gradually developed an interest not in the India where Buddhism was born, but in the India of Hinduism, in which purity and defilement, holiness and obscenity, charity and brutality mingled and coexisted. She was grateful for even one extra day to stay beside the river where all things intermixed rather than having to go see the sites that had been sanctified by the Buddha.

'I'm going back to keep an eye on Mr Kiguchi,' she mumbled. 'You've got to take everyone to the Ganges early this morning, haven't you? You'd better get some sleep.'

'Aren't you coming with us to the Ganges, Miss Naruse?'

'I can't leave Mr Kiguchi in this condition. . . .'

When she was left to herself, she sat down beside Kiguchi, who was sleeping like the dead. She peered down at his toothless, moronic face. It was strange. She was looking into the face of an old man she hadn't even known two weeks before, and passing the night with him. This deathlike Indian night, a night that in Buddhism would be called the darkness of the soul. A night lacquered in a black so absolute it would be unthinkable in Japan.

She suddenly recalled a scene from *Thérèse Desqueyroux*. It was the night Thérèse tended her ailing husband Bernard. It had been a night just like tonight, without even a ray of light shining, without a sound to be heard, a pitch-black night in Argelouse. As she stared at her husband's sleeping face, Thérèse had been gripped by a dark impulse.

It was a scene Mitsuko was fond of. It was the same impulse she had felt not only tonight but on her honeymoon as she had studied her husband's sleeping face. The face of a man who was a paragon of uprightness, a man who cared for nothing but his work, his cars and his game of golf. Every time she stared into that face, she thought of that scene from *Thérèse Desqueyroux*. Those pages she had read over and over again, those pages wherein she had discovered a reflection of something dark within herself.

She had no idea what kind of man this old Kiguchi was. Did he have a wife? What sort of life had he lived in his youth? Why had he come by himself to India? From New Delhi to Vārānasī, nothing about the old man had aroused her interest. But as she looked down at this uninteresting old man's sleeping face, a feeling identical to that of Thérèse flickered across her mind, though for only an instant. Something destructive lurking in the depths of her heart, something she shared in common with the goddess Kālī of Hinduism ...

'Gaston!' Kiguchi moaned in a delirious nightmare. 'Gaston! Gaston!'

Mitsuko had no idea what he was talking about. She wiped the sweat from the old man's head with a towel. She realized that his fever had dropped considerably from two hours before. At the same time, she herself felt the heavy weariness of living come over her, and she sat back in her chair and closed her eyes.

She had no idea how long she slept, but Mitsuko was awakened by the sound of several people scurrying along the hallway. The sun had already come up, and a light redolent of the heat of afternoon was already shining through the window; she could hear the chirping conversations of birds from the hotel garden. The sick man, his mouth open, slept as though in a state of abstraction. She put her hand on his forehead. The fever had almost completely abated, and only the smell of sweat lingered like the aftermath of a storm.

She tiptoed out of the room, and in the hallway ran into Enami coming towards her with two other women.

'We've just come back from the Ganges. Thank you so much. When we set out a couple of hours ago, I peeked into the room, but you seemed to be sleeping, so I didn't invite you along. You've really been a great help.'

Enami's eyes were still blurred with exhaustion, but the two women looked refreshed. 'You've had a rough time of it, haven't you, Miss Naruse?' one of them said in an agitated voice. 'But I think maybe you were better off not coming. The river bank was littered with dog and cow droppings, and the smell of them burning the bodies – there was nothing solemn about it for me, I tell you. I felt sick. These Hindus actually do rinse their mouths and wash their heads right next to where the ashes of the dead are floating.'

'I know I've said this before, but there are people who are drawn to India by seeing that, and those who absolutely hate the place.' Once again Enami played the apologist for India. 'Mr Numada and Mr Isobe were both very moved.'

'We saw a Japanese Hindu there, too,' both women were eager to relate. 'He had that white cloth round his middle just like the other Hindus – didn't he, Mr Enami?'

'It's called a dhoti. What the women wear is called a sari.'

'He was helping carry the bodies of the Hindus to the cremation ground. I was really surprised.'

'I was stunned myself. At first I thought he was some young hippie with an India fixation, but he said he was no mere tourist.'

'You talked to him?'

'Yes, a little. What surprised me even more is he said he's a Catholic priest. When I asked him why a Christian father was dressed up like a Hindu, he said that since he was living in India it felt more natural to wear what the people here wear. He was carrying the body of a pauper who had collapsed in the street.'

Mitsuko shifted her eyes away from the three and was silent for a moment. Finally she asked in a hoarse voice, 'What was this fellow's name?'

'Hmm, he didn't tell us. . . . But he did say that he's living in an āshram here in the city. I've been here any number of times, but that's the first time I've run into a Japanese like that.'

'Āshram?' Mitsuko's voice was still rasping.

'It's the Hindi word for monastery.'

It was Ōtsu. The man had to be Ōtsu. Mitsuko struggled to contain her feelings.

'Do you think you might know him, Miss Naruse?'

She turned her face away and nodded, 'I think . . . he was a class-mate of mine . . . in college.'

Enami was silent for a moment, sensing something unusual, but then he changed the subject and asked whether Mitsuko had eaten breakfast.

'No. I'm going to have something in a while. But I want to take another look at Mr Kiguchi before I go.'

As she walked back to Kiguchi's room, she contemplated the feel-ings stirring inside her.

Wherever he went, Ōtsu had realized nothing but setbacks and fail-ures, and now he was in this place transporting corpses to the funeral pyres. 'If you don't like the word "God", then you can call him On-ion if you wish.' The words Ōtsu had spoken in a throaty, pained voice along the shores of the River Saône crackled in her ears like burning embers. The man was still obstinately living for the sake of his Onion. For something Mitsuko had been unable to find in her own life.

She looked into Kiguchi's room, returned to her own room and washed her face, and went down to the dining-room. The other Japanese tour-ists had finished breakfast and were strolling in the garden or wan-dering the streets during their free time until noon. An Indian man scurried around cleaning up the dirty dishes and barking orders to a young busboy. In the dining-room there was only one other guest, who sat puffing at a cigarette and staring out of the window at the trees that intertwined in a lacy mesh.

'Good morning,' Mitsuko greeted him.

'You're Miss Naruse, aren't you? My name is Numada. I under-stand you're staying behind to look after Mr Kiguchi.'

'Yes, but thanks to that – or maybe I should say I'm doing it *be-cause* I've taken a liking to this city.'

'Is that so? As a matter of fact, I got permission from Mr Enami to remain here too. I made up my mind this morning when we went to see the Ganges. I won't make any trouble for you.' Numada smiled genially. 'I write children's stories, and one of them is set by the Yatsushiro Sea in Kyushu. The villagers believe that when they die, they all become fish in the sea and continue to live there. The sea is

the next world to them, just as the River Ganges is to the Hindus.'
Mitsuko decided she would have nothing to worry about from a
man who could become so absorbed in such a story. 'I'm relieved
you're staying here at the hotel,' she responded as she took a sip of
the Darjeeling tea the khitmutgar had brought.

Happily, no malarial protozoa were found in Kiguchi's blood. The
young doctor telephoned Enami just before noon and reported that the
high fever was probably the result of the heat, the old man's exhaustion and some bacteria, that there was no need for hospitalization, and
that he should be fine after a few days' rest.
Mitsuko was still concerned.
'I wonder if the diagnosis is correct.'
'Of course it is. I killed myself getting them to call the doctor on
duty at the university hospital in Vārānasī. This means you can
rejoin the tour, Miss Naruse.'
'No, I'm going to stay here. I think Mr Kiguchi will feel happier if
I stay with him.'
'This is ridiculous. Mr Isobe and Mr Numada and the Sanjōs are
saying exactly the same thing. Mrs Sanjō says she's seen all she wants
to see of India.'
But Enami concluded that it would be best for Mitsuko to stay, on the
outside chance that something might happen to the old man. That way
he could manage without sending for another Japanese from Calcutta.
At two o'clock the bus arrived to take the tourists to Buddh-Gaya.
Isobe, Numada and Mitsuko came to the lobby to see everyone off. In
the garden of the abruptly emptied hotel only the swing twisted with
a creaking sound in the tepid wind.
'It got lonely here all of a sudden, didn't it?' Isobe muttered as he
listened to the creaking swing. In the deserted garden even the chirp-
ing of insects subsided, and the only noise was a faint bustle from
Cantonment Station far in the distance.
'What's happened to Mr and Mrs Sanjō?'
'Hmm, I don't know.'
'What are you going to do now?'
'I....' Isobe stammered a bit. 'I'm ... going to go out for a while.'
'To the Ganges?' Numada asked innocently. 'Would you mind if I
come with you?'
'No, actually ... I've got a silly little personal matter to attend to,
and I'd rather go by myself.'

Mitsuko, who could guess what this was about, winked at Numada. 'Mr Numada, if Mr Kiguchi s.ems to be doing all right, would you mind accompanying me to the river?'

'I'd be happy to. I've really taken a liking to that river. I could look at it any number of times.'

The three went up to the second floor, where Mitsuko and Numada looked in on Kiguchi.

Isobe unlocked his door, sat down on the hard, still unmade bed, and turned his eyes towards the brightly lit window. A young woman named Rajini Puniral in Kamloji village. The girl he had learned about from the University of Virginia.

Since coming to India, Isobe had started remembering his wife more frequently than he had while still in Japan. Even those recollections were of thoroughly insignificant moments from their daily lives together.

He remembered once when he was putting on his shoes before he set out to work, and his wife had called out from behind him, 'Will you be late tonight?'

'No, I'll be home for dinner.'

'I thought I'd throw some fish and vegetables together for dinner.'

'Whatever you like, it doesn't matter to me.'

His memories were all of such mornings, of such trivial conversations between husband and wife.

Or once when his wife was sewing with nimble hands. With one eye on a *go* magazine, he arranged the stones on the board and then heaved a sigh.

'It's hopeless.'

'What's hopeless?'

'I've been playing *go* for five years now, and I still can't get my first-grade certificate. At lunch today I played a game with Ishikawa, and he whipped me even though he's only been at it three years. I suppose it's pointless trying to learn once you're old.'

'But you enjoy it, don't you?' She stopped working on her point lace and tried to console him with empty phrases. 'It's not a question of whether you're good or bad. It ought to be enough if you're having a good time.'

Hackneyed conversations between husband and wife that he had not once recalled while his wife was alive; moments together that had been neither happy nor unhappy. Why did these incidents come back to him, clutching almost painfully at his chest, as he sat this afternoon in his hotel room in a distant land? His wife had been an ordinary housewife, and he had been a mediocre husband. While she was alive, his wife had suppressed her feelings, but just before her death she had shown him a side he had never seen before.

Isobe changed into his track shoes and left his room with his key, a map and his camera.

While he waited for the taxi, he asked the hotel manager how to get to Kamloji village. The bearded, dark-faced manager had evidently already been notified by Enami, and he flashed Isobe an 'OK' sign and said, 'I'll tell the driver where to go.'

The taxi arrived. When Isobe sat down on the hot seat, a painful throbbing shook his body. While his wife was alive, he had never given reincarnation a thought. But as a result of her screams, the words 'rebirth' and 'reincarnation' had flashed before him as though a large automobile had suddenly darted up before his eyes, changing both the direction and the destination of his life.

And yet Isobe remained sceptical. Even after he got in touch with the University of Virginia and received the letter from the thoughtful scholar, his doubts had still not dissipated, and all that was certain in his mind was the voice of his wife. All he could believe in was the love for his wife that lay buried in his heart. And if someone had suddenly stepped in front of him now and asked him if he would care to marry should there be an afterlife, his wife's name would have surfaced on his lips as his mate of choice without a moment's hesitation.

Mitsuko rang Kiguchi in his room.

'Yes?' his lifeless voice quickly responded.

'How are you feeling?'

'Oh, it's you? Thanks to you my fever has dropped and I'm feeling much better. You've really been a great help.'

'That's wonderful. How's your appetite?'

'Fine. For lunch Mr Enami had room service send up some soup and a sandwich. I haven't touched the sandwich yet, though. I understand the doctor will be coming back to see me tonight.'

'Do you think it would be all right if I went out into the city for a little while? I'll phone you from there, of course.'

'I'm nothing but trouble for you. But I'm just fine, so you go ahead and go out.'

She got ready and went down to the lobby. Numada was waiting there with a sketchbook on his lap.

'Mr Kiguchi seems to be feeling much better.'

'I'm glad to hear it.'

'Would you mind waiting while I make one more phone call?'

Mitsuko had the assistant at the reception desk telephone the Catholic church in Vārānasī. When she took the receiver and put it to her ear, the line rang endlessly and no one answered, until finally the hoarse voice of an old woman responded in Hindi. Mitsuko handed the telephone to the assistant, but the only information she could obtain was that there was no Japanese named Ōtsu at the church, that the English-speaking missionaries were all out for the day, and the location of the church. Mitsuko had to abandon her plan.

After they got into the taxi, Numada, who had been listening behind her, asked, 'Are you looking for someone?'

'This morning, when you went with everyone to see the river, didn't you run into a Japanese man?'

'A tourist?'

'No, a man working at the cremation grounds.'

'Oh, the Japanese fellow who was dressed like the Hindus.'

'I think he was someone I knew when I was at college. He said then he wanted to become a priest.'

'So you're going to the river to search for him?'

'I thought he might still be at the cremation grounds.'

'You were rather close to him, I take it?'

Numada's innocent question made Mitsuko flush. She recalled with vivid clarity how Ōtsu's head had prodded between her breasts.

She abruptly changed the subject. 'It's quite a smell, isn't it?'

'What is?'

'Things that don't even smell in other countries. The smell of humanity.'

'Do you find it disagreeable?'

'Not disagreeable. I like it. It's a smell that doesn't tire me out. On the other hand, if you go to somewhere like Europe ... I don't know much about the place, but that's how France was for me. After three or four days, I was worn out.'

'Really? I wonder why.' Numada studied Mitsuko with a blend of curiosity and delight in his eyes.

'Well, after all, everything in France is so neatly ordered, there's nothing disjointed about the place. There's just not enough chaos. Walking around the place de la Concorde or the gardens of Versailles, I get exhausted by it before I've had a chance to think how beautiful all that systematic orderliness is. Compared with that, I'm much more at home with the confusion here in India, with the way that so many different elements are combined in one scene, with the statues of the Hindu goddesses who mingle good with evil.'

'Westerners hate chaos. You prefer disorder, do you, Miss Naruse?'

'It's not really a matter for debate. It's just a question of like or dislike.' Thanks to the finally cool breeze blowing through the window and the guileless look in Numada's eyes, Mitsuko inadvertently loosened up and joked, 'I'm just a chaotic woman who doesn't understand herself very well.'

'Uh-huh,' Numada responded vaguely.

As they had the previous day, they entered the noisy city beneath the evening sun. The rays of the setting sun bounced off the gilded plates and pots stacked in front of the shops; patrons and rickshaws formed queues before the large marquee at an Indian cinema; a flock of crows perched like notes of music on an electric wire; and sheep and cows, the bells round their necks clanging, brought traffic to a halt.

What he had finally come to understand after his wife's death was the bond uniting a husband and wife. The connection that brought two people together to become lifelong companions from amidst the countless numbers of men and women in the world. Most certainly such encounters were accidental, but Isobe now had the feeling that those ties had existed even before birth.

A row of laurel fig trees planted along one side of the white, dry road shuttled past the window of the taxi. The vehicle kicked up dust. Fields of wheat beyond the line of trees. A pair of vultures perched on the fence of a broken-down farmhouse, and in the fields a large black water-buffalo was slowly led along by a peasant. It was a country scene that could be found anywhere in India.

Isobe was absorbed in memories of his wife.

Their first trip together, to Hokkaido to celebrate their twentieth anniversary. They had decided against flying and booked a sleeper on the train that went through the Tōhoku region. That summer evening as they pulled out of Ueno Station, tree leaves sparkled as they blinked by the train window, and the silhouettes of the mountains against the sky as it turned a madder-red colour were beautiful. When he glanced in her direction, his wife was smiling as she gazed at the distant mountain range. She said nothing, but he was sure she was happy to be able to travel alone with her husband for the first time since their honeymoon. But for Isobe, it was more embarrassing than he could endure, and he stood up and went to the buffet car to get a drink. When he came back, the smile still lit up her face, and he softly yapped at her, 'Hey, go and buy yourself something to drink.' Prosaic memories of this sort bubbled up one after another, then disappeared.

The taxi, rocking fiercely along the bumpy road, passed through several villages. Every village had a communal well, and around each well women with pots or buckets washed their hair or their feet, while in a teetering shanty a man was giving haircuts. Barefoot children scampered around the well.

In a village like this, exposed to the sun, his wife had been reborn – the mere thought made him feel as though his chest were being squeezed with pliers. His wife was among the naked children bounding around the insanitary well. He couldn't believe it. It was all like a dream, and Isobe clenched the hand that held his handkerchief, wondering what foolishness he was engaged in.

'Turn back,' he was about to tell the driver, who stared silently ahead as he drove. But as the words that stuck in his throat tried to press their way past his lips, the driver, as though Isobe's feelings had aroused him, suddenly turned round and shouted 'Kamloji! Kamloji!', pointing ahead through the clouds of dust. They were about to arrive in Kamloji.

The landscape ahead was just the same as every village they had passed through, with rows of laurel figs and crows circling over wheatfields where farmers dragged water-buffalo behind them. The fierce sun before evening held everything under its mighty sway.

He closed his eyes and tried to hear his wife's voice. For some reason, her final words that had sounded so clearly in his ears until that morning would not come back to him.

Spraying dust, the taxi came to a stop beside a well. Naked children had congregated here too, and mothers and their elder daughters, their saris soaked, poured water from pots on to their heads. They watched with uneasy eyes as the driver and Isobe got out of the taxi that had ground to a halt in front of them, and the children began to stretch out their hands to beg for money.

One of the young girls had dark-black eyes and hair. She stood in front of Isobe and motioned as if to put something into her mouth.

'Rajini?' Isobe took out a piece of paper and mouthed the Hindi name Enami had written down for him. 'Rajini?'

The girl vigorously shook her head. But she continued to hold out her hand.

'Rajini! Rajini! Rajini!' The children imitated Isobe and began to chant. But they appeared not to understand anything. A feeling of sorrow spurted up in Isobe's chest, and he felt like one defeated in the battle of life.

'What have you enjoyed most on this trip?'

'Me?' Mitsuko paused for a moment. 'Most of all the Ganges, and then the image of the goddess Chāmundā we saw in that dark, sweltering cave. And I liked what Mr Enami had to say about her. Remember how the sweat covered his whole face and dripped down on to the floor?'

She thought of the dust-laden image of the goddess, whose body was twisted in agony like the tangled roots of trees. In New Delhi, Mitsuko had been moved by the image of the goddess Kālī, who combined mercy with brutality, but what she had enjoyed most about this city was that twenty-minute interval when she had endured the heat and the stifling air of the cavern.

In addition to the children today on the roads near the ghāts, lepers who had lost all their fingers were lined up to beg. Men and women with their stubs of hands and their decaying skin covered with filthy rags called out to Numada and Mitsuko in wailing voices.

'They're all human!' Numada could bear it no longer and cried out. 'These people . . . they're all human like us.'

Mitsuko did not want to reply. In her heart she could hear a voice saying, *Just what is it we tourists can do for them?* The cheap sympathy of Numada and the Sanjōs irritated Mitsuko. She no longer wanted imitations of love. She wanted real love and nothing less.

The scene at the ghāt was the same as yesterday: long-haired Indians, their dhotis dripping with water, received blessings from a monk seated beneath a broad umbrella. As they approached the funeral pyres, they saw a body, swathed head to foot in a black cloth, lying on the ground. Another corpse was just being consumed within the flames. Stray brown dogs and an ominous flock of vultures, on the prowl for any flesh that might survive the fire, peered at the scene from a distance.

'It's the body of an old woman, isn't it?' Numada mumbled as he looked at the gaunt legs and ankles. He could not see the face for the flames. Mitsuko compared this old woman's life with that of the

goddess Chāmundā. Like the goddess, she had suffered and perse-
vered in this life, and after suckling her children with her withered
breasts she had died. And Ōtsu lifted such people on to his back as
though shouldering a cross and brought them here to the river. . . .

'Can you see him?'

'Who?'

'My friend. The Japanese you ran into this morning.'

'Let me look. No, I can't spot him anywhere.'

'I suppose not.'

'He's a priest, isn't he? Why don't you go to that church you phoned
a while ago?'

Suddenly she thought of Isobe. Where was he at this moment? Had
he been able to find the girl in that village described in the letter? Just
as she was searching for Ōtsu here in this city, at the same hour Isobe
was searching for his dead wife.

'Mr Numada, do you believe in reincarnation?'

'Me? I'm sorry to say . . . my real feeling right now is that I have no
idea.'

'That's just how I feel. But there are many things about life we
never understand.'

'What do you mean?'

'I've been thinking about what my friend does here in this city.
From the viewpoint of any ordinary person, my friend has lived a
really pointless existence . . . but since I've come here, I've started to
think maybe it hasn't been so pointless after all.'

No matter how many times she pressed the bell of the church, there
was no response. About the time she decided that to ring the bell any
longer would be the height of discourtesy, she heard a sound like
wooden clogs dragging along the ground, and the door opened. An
old Caucasian priest dressed in a white habit stared back at her with
a stern expression.

'Ōtsu? He's not here.' When he heard the name Ōtsu, a look more of
disapproval than of confusion clouded the old priest's already intran-
sigent-looking face.

'I was a friend of his at college.'

'I know nothing about him.'

'Do you know where he might be?'

'No.'

'He is here in the city, isn't he?'

162

'I think so, but I know nothing more. We take no responsibility for him.'

The headstrong look on the aged priest's face was reminiscent of an old sheriff in a Western movie who strides around defending the law. He spoke in the way a law-enforcing sheriff would speak, bridling his displeasure as he discussed a man who had broken the law. He quickly shut the door.

The setting sun wanly bathed the wall facing the church. Two black mongrels rifled through the garbage at the base of the wall. Mitsuko felt as though she had been cast out. But it wasn't her, it was Ōtsu who had been cast out. It was clear from the old Western-sheriff priest's tone of voice that he harboured no kind feelings towards Ōtsu. Just as he had not been able to fit smoothly into the community of religious at Lyon, he had no doubt committed some blunder here as well.

'Did you find out where he is?' Numada stood waiting for her in front of the taxi.

She shook her head. 'No luck.'

'I've been talking to our taxi-driver while I waited for you. I asked him if he knew of any Japanese who carried corpses to the cremation ground at the Ganges. He said he knew nothing about such a man, but he knows an Indian married to a Japanese woman who runs a boarding-house nearby, and he says we might find something out if we ask there.'

'What's it called?'

'He says it's the Kumiko House. A lot of young Japanese travellers stay there, he says.'

'I wonder if I should contact them.'

'Why don't we have lunch at a hotel around here, and you could ring the Kumiko House from there?'

They asked the driver the name of the closest deluxe hotel, and he answered 'Clark's Hotel' as though he were repeating a memorized speech. As the taxi navigated its way through the swirling mobs of people and cows and rickshaws, ahead of them they suddenly heard an explosion of band music. It was joined by shouting and laughing voices, and cars honked their horns repeatedly.

'Marriage. Marriage.' The driver broke into a smile and explained to Numada and Mitsuko. He told them there was a traffic jam because a large wedding reception was being held at the hotel just ahead of them.

'Can you get through?' Numada asked worriedly.

The response that bounded back to them was the phrase they had heard many times over in India: 'No problem.'

Despite his answer, however, the taxi did not budge an inch after five, then ten minutes.

'What's the name of this hotel?' Numada finally asked impatiently.

With an indifferent look the driver repeated the name of the hotel he had previously given them: 'Clark's Hotel.'

Numada and Mitsuko looked at one another and broke into laughter.

'I never know whether they're serious, or whether they're making a fool of me.'

'That's just another part of India. Anyway, why don't we go and have a look at an Indian wedding?'

They abandoned the taxi and began walking along the street clogged with cars, feeling a bit light-hearted. In front of the hotel, where the trees had been strung with light bulbs that made them look like Christmas trees, the band played, its drum thumping and its trumpets braying. Young men in dinner-jackets and women dressed in lavish silk saris with red marks on their foreheads were swallowed one after another into the hotel.

'This is a wedding for the wealthy class, isn't it?' Numada muttered. 'It's a world apart from the people we saw on the banks of the river.'

Mitsuko turned to a woman beside her dressed in a bright sari and asked, 'What is everyone waiting for?'

'The groom is about to arrive on a white horse.' The young woman, a smile gracing her round, dimpled cheeks, responded in a crisp Queen's English.

'A white horse?'

'Yes. Here the groom comes to his bride riding a white horse. It's one of the beautiful customs of our country.'

After a break the band exploded into sound once again, and young men dressed in suits swarmed in from the street with cheers and applause.

Finally the groom appeared astride a white horse, his head wrapped in a red turban. He dismounted awkwardly from the horse, which was jittery because of the band music, and lifted both his arms into the air like the victor in an athletic contest. The guests who surrounded him took white and red congratulatory flowers from baskets and tossed them at him.

'Are you tourists?' The round-faced, dimpled young woman turned cordial eyes towards Mitsuko. 'You're Japanese, aren't you?'

'Yes.'

'Is this the first time you've seen an Indian wedding? Come inside with me. There's a party in the hotel garden.'

'I haven't been invited. And I'm here with a friend.'

'On happy occasions here in India you can enter without an invitation.'

Mitsuko finally persuaded a shy and hesitant Numada to join her, and they went out into the hotel garden. There too the trees had been decorated with light bulbs, and the whiteness of the tables laden with sweetmeats and fruit stung their eyes. On a hastily constructed stage three girls twisted their arms and legs sensuously as they danced. They were accompanied by four musicians who played on wooden instruments.

After the dimpled woman introduced Numada and Mitsuko to some of her friends, the two were quickly surrounded by friendly young people who asked, 'Do you find this interesting?'

'Yes, very.'

'Because it's so different from a Japanese wedding, I suppose.'

'No, that's not it.' Mitsuko was gripped by her usual urge to be perverse. 'It's because the wedding is so Indian.'

'Aha!'

The young people circling her looked delighted, but Mitsuko proceeded to flip a spitball of sarcasm into their happy faces.

'I'm fascinated because I've just been down by the Ganges, where I met all kinds of children. They lined up and held their hands out to me. And now just three hours later . . .' She groped for the words in English, which she did not speak nearly as fluently as she spoke French. But it would be enough if she got her meaning across. ' . . . I'm here at a splendid, luxurious party with people of a completely different class.'

The socially agreeable smiles disappeared from the faces of the beautifully attired young people. Their faces quivered, and they began to jabber amongst themselves. One young man wearing glasses stepped forward and began to speak in ministerial tones.

'It would seem, madam, that you are critical of our caste system.'

'I'm not critical. I'm simply surprised at the enormous difference between classes.'

'Allow me to explain it to you.' He began to sound even more like a minister. Or perhaps like a young lawyer in an American movie.

'Are you familiar with the name of Dr Ambedkar?'

'No.'

'He helped draft the Constitution of India, and became Minister of Justice for independent India. The constitution he wrote abolishes the religious class distinctions of the past. I think you probably know this, but our beloved Mahatma Gandhi called the outcasts harijan, which means children of God.'

The oratorical English was difficult for Mitsuko, but she understood the gist of what the man was saying. As she watched his mouth move, she suddenly remembered something Enami had let slip: 'The worst thing about Indian intellectuals is that, in spite of their arrogance and the emptiness of their long-winded speeches, they're never lacking in the pride category.'

'Some of the harijan are now serving as government officials. Some are working at universities.'

'I see.'

'We often hear questions like yours from foreign visitors. But India is in the process of moving forward. Have you read the letters exchanged between Nehru and our current prime minister, Indira Gandhi? They became an international best-seller, so I'm sure they were translated into Japanese.'

'I think they were a best-seller in Tokyo, too, but I haven't read them.'

'You must read them. In the book, Nehru writes to his daughter Indira that Asia is presently controlled by Europe, but that originally the civilization of Asia was far more advanced. He said it is the mission of India to restore that former glory.'

The young man's simple-minded loquaciousness was annoying. Her eyes searched for Numada, but he was nowhere to be found among the multicoloured saris and dinner-jackets of the guests.

'What do you think of Indira Gandhi as a woman?'

'I have no knowledge of Indian politics.'

'She is the mother of India. The many conflicts and contradictions between India's various religions and various peoples are held in check by her womanly gentleness and strength.'

'I'm sorry, I have to look for a friend. Thank you for all your helpful explanations.'

'It's a pleasure for us to be able to clear up your misunderstanding.'

Mitsuko did not swallow his reasoning. In the young man's vacuous rhetoric Mitsuko had sniffed out the aroma she found most dis-

distasteful, the spoiled-fish stench of hypocrisy. The goddess Kālī combined mercy and maliciousness, but there was no hypocrisy in her. Suffering and illness and love were intertwined like tree roots in the goddess Chāmundā, but there was nothing hypocritical about her. Mitsuko loved the India she saw in the goddesses Kālī and Chāmundā and in the River Ganges, but she could not bring herself to appreciate this young man's sermon.

Smiles of relief returned to the faces of the young people in the circle with their dark, healthy skins and their socially sanctioned gentility.

'Would you like some punch?' The dimpled young woman returned, like a woman gingerly coming back to search through the ruins of a city ravaged by war.

'Thanks.' Once again Mitsuko took a swipe. 'But I prefer strong liquor to punch. I have to go and look for a friend.'

She went back into the hotel and found Numada staring lifelessly at the show windows along the row of souvenir shops.

'I finally escaped. Let's get out of here.'

'You attracted quite a throng. You were a big hit, Miss Naruse.'

'I had to listen to them going on and on about the Indian Constitution. It was as insipid as the taste of their punch.'

Numada couldn't catch what she meant, but he good-naturedly remarked, 'I phoned the Kumiko House.'

'Really? And?' There was unexpected excitement in her voice. 'Did you find anything out?'

'Yes.' Numada hesitated a moment. 'It seems as though your friend... he frequents some pretty shady parts of the city. They said we'd find him if we went there.'

'Shady parts? What does he do there?'

'I don't know. What do you want to do? Do you want to go there?'

'I'm tired.' Mitsuko gave vent to her irritation as she sighed. This afternoon she felt as though the unseen Ōtsu was leading her about by the nose. And to Numada, who was keeping her company, she said, 'I'm sorry. This is a waste of your time.'

'I don't mind. I'd rather be here in Vārānasī than some other city. How about something to eat?'

'Let's go back to our hotel. I don't want those wedding people getting their claws into me again.'

Some of the beggar children were still standing in front of the hotel. One of the wedding guests came out and scattered a handful of coins over their heads, and they jostled and scrambled about on the ground. As she watched this, Mitsuko recalled the word harijan – 'children of God' – and the smooth, ministerial lecture she had heard.

'If we walk through here, we should come out on a large road,' Numada said, leading the way into an alley that gaped like a cavern.

The alley smelled of animals and urine. Holding her breath, Mitsuko walked along the back street, which reminded her of the inside of a mouth, while the sounds of revelry continued to echo from behind. Something brushed against her leg, and she yelped.

'What is it?'

'I think I stepped on something.'

Numada stooped down and peered at her feet.

'It's a man. Still alive . . .'

'Is he sick?'

'I don't know. He may have collapsed from hunger.'

She heard the sound of Numada dropping coins, just as the man at the wedding had. The sound of the trickling coins echoed only hopelessness and impotence.

NINE

The River

When they returned to their hotel and went into the sole dining-room, located at the rear of the building, the juvenile-looking khitmutgar was sitting half asleep in a chair and Isobe was at a table in the centre drinking, a bottle of whisky propped in front of him. A lizard clung motionless to the wall, looking as though it had been glued there.

'We're back!' Mitsuko called out as she and Numada sat together at a table with ketchup stains on the cloth. They knew without asking, just by looking at Isobe's drunken face and sweaty forehead, that he had spent a futile day.

'How did it go? Did you find your friend?' Isobe was the one to lift his head and call out.

'No. It was a hopeless quest.'

'Oh? The same for me, I'm afraid.'

'She wasn't there?'

'They've moved to the city. The whole family moved, looking for a place to work.'

'Did you get their address?'

'How could I find that out? It was a destitute village. There were no villages like that in Japan even in the old days.' The way Isobe spoke, it sounded as though he were trying to trounce his own despair. The pain in the gentle man's heart was evident in his drunken condition.

Numada and Mitsuko silently ate the scrawny chicken the khitmutgar set before them.

'Miss Naruse. You'll never guess what I did on my way back from the village!' As Isobe half filled his glass with whisky, he sounded almost as though he were trying to pick a quarrel. 'Well, I'll tell you. . . . I went to see a fortune-teller. An Indian fortune-teller.'

'Do you believe in fortune-tellers?'

'Of course not. I don't even believe that business in the letter about my wife being reborn. But people are funny, you know. Maybe I just started feeling cantankerous, or maybe I was grasping at straws. I suppose the taxi-driver I'd hired felt sorry for me, because all of a sudden he says maybe I should go and consult the famous fortune-teller here in town. It seems this fortune-teller, seeing as how we're in India and all, made his fame telling clients who they were in a pre-vious life, and what they'll be in their next life. What a joke! And the joke's on me, because I went to see him!' He gulped the amber liquid down almost desperately. 'This fortune-teller, he was wearing one of those high-collared outfits – that's right, the kind that Nehru always wore. He has a face that looks like a university professor, and he's wearing this ring with a huge stone on his finger . . . and with great confidence he tells me that she's been reborn and that she's very happy now. Then he pulls some big book out of a teakwood box, writes my wife's name out in roman letters, makes some sort of calculation, and then charges me an outrageous amount of money.'

Mitsuko lowered her eyes and wordlessly plied her knife and fork. Isobe chasing his phantoms was oppressive to her. Numada, who knew nothing of the background of this conversation, was dumbfounded by Isobe's behaviour and said nothing.

'Then when I ask him where is she now, he says he'll look into it, and I'm supposed to come back tomorrow. I suppose he'll give me some meaningless address and charge me some more money. . . .'

'Are you going back?'

'Oh yes, I'll go back. Pathetic, isn't it? Just so I can gain some sense of emotional conclusion. Then I'll be able to give the whole thing up. I think, after coming to India and going through everything I've been through, my dead wife'll be able to achieve nirvana. Don't you think she will, Miss Naruse?'

Mitsuko thought of the face of Isobe's wife, who had lain in her hospital bed without uttering a selfish word. And this man, who had come to visit her nearly every day as soon as he had finished work. An ordinary, inconspicuous couple you might find anywhere. Even couples such as they experienced a drama all their own that no one else could see.

'I'm sorry. I'm drunk and I'm all confused.' When he came to himself, Isobe apologized to his two silent compatriots, but his voice was close to tears. He clutched the whisky bottle, which was still about a third full, and stood up. 'To hope for something like rebirth . . . something that cannot be . . . it was a bad mistake.' With a tearful smile, he left the dining-room.

'I wonder what happened to him?' Numada asked in amazement.

'I wonder.' Mitsuko feigned ignorance. But then it occurred to her that she and Isobe were identical in that they were both chasing phantoms. 'I'm more worried about Mr Kiguchi. I'm going to give him a ring.'

The following day was 31 October.

The day of the incident.

That morning, when Mitsuko finished putting on her make-up and went downstairs, the reception desk was deserted, and the ten or so employees of the hotel were clustered round the single television set in the dining-room. Of the Japanese, Numada and Kiguchi, who had barely recovered from his illness, were staring at the television, not bothering with breakfast. The face of the prime minister, Indira Gandhi, dressed in a sari, was frozen on the television screen.

Seeing Mitsuko, Numada announced, 'It's terrible. Indira Gandhi has been murdered.'

'The prime minister? By whom?'

'They're not sure.'

Mitsuko too stared piercingly at the frozen image of the silver-haired premier on the screen. Over and over again the announcer repeated the report from a government spokesman that the premier had been assassinated just after 9 a.m. at her official residence.

'This is terrible.' Numada sank down into his seat at the dining-table, and Kiguchi, following suit, heaved a sigh. Numada nodded his head. 'If we don't watch ourselves as tourists, we may end up being detained here. Mr Enami and the others are supposed to come back tomorrow, but I wonder whether the domestic airlines are even flying. I wouldn't be surprised if they declared martial law.'

171

'I'm sure Mr Enami will contact us,' Mitsuko mumbled. 'Until then, we'd better just lay low.'

The Sanjōs, who had not shown their faces since the previous day, came down to the dining-room with radiant smiles. Sanjō already had his pet camera dangling from his shoulder.

'Good morning! Beautiful weather again today, isn't it? Tell me, has something happened?'

'The prime minister of India has been assassinated. This morning.'

'Really? Is that why everybody's here together? But it's got nothing to do with us....'

'Don't be an idiot. If we aren't careful, our return to Japan could be delayed.' Numada sounded almost angry.

In an instant, the new bride's face twisted up like a child's. 'What will we do? I told you we should have gone to Europe.'

'But think of all the photographs I've been able to take here.' Sanjō was earnest in his excuse-making. 'In the final analysis, it's the subject-matter that makes a photograph. The accolades go to the photographer who can capture moments no one else can.'

The telephone rang piercingly at the reception desk. As though that were some signal, the employees who had been glued to the television suddenly scattered. Someone called from the desk: 'Miss Naruse. Telephone!'

Mitsuko, who had been studying the breakfast menu, stood up at once, certain that it was a call from Enami. It was, in fact, Enami's urgent voice that echoed from the receiver.

'Have you heard about the terrible thing that happened this morning?'

'Yes, we saw it on television. Where are you now?'

'In Patna. Just now things are calm here, but evidently they've called out the troops in Delhi. It's hard to get reliable information. Now listen carefully. We'll be back in Vārānasī tomorrow without fail. I want everyone to keep a close eye on developments and act with caution. The incident this morning seems to be an eruption of dissatisfaction among the Sikhs. Fires may be started in the streets, so please be careful if you go out.'

'I understand.'

'Is Mr Kiguchi all right?'

'He's having breakfast with us in the dining-room this morning.'

Just as Mitsuko hung up, Isobe finally showed his haggard face in the dining-room.

'I'm very sorry for the way I behaved last night.'

'Don't give it a thought.'

When he heard about the assassination, Isobe stared at the television as though he had just recovered from a two-day binge.

Eventually the screen began to show tanks and throngs of soldiers guarding the prime minister's residence, and scenes from New Delhi, where plumes of smoke rose here and there. Once again the employees gathered in the dining-room. The six Japanese were finally able to discern from the heavily accented English of the announcer that the premier had been shot by some Sikhs who were part of her security force as she walked along a path from her residence to the office where she was to be filmed in an interview.

'What's a Sikh?' Sanjō asked, as he shovelled in the food that had finally been brought to his table. But without Enami, none of the Japanese in the group knew anything about the complex relationship of antagonism between the Hindus and Sikhs.

'It says in my travel guide that they wear cloths wrapped round their heads and carry short swords,' Numada responded dolefully.

'At any rate, let's stay here in the hotel until we understand the situation,' Mitsuko proposed.

'It's really all right. Taxis stop right here by the hotel garden, so it isn't a problem.' Sanjō picked up his camera and answered resentfully. 'This really kills me. If I'd been in Delhi, I might have taken a picture worthy of the Pulitzer Prize.'

'You just don't grasp it, do you? That may be fine for you, but you could cause problems for everybody.' Kiguchi took Sanjō to task so forcefully it was hard to believe he had just recovered from an illness.

The tourists loitered in their rooms or in the dining-hall until the afternoon. A curfew was imposed in New Delhi, rioting broke out between the Hindus and the Sikhs, and fires had been started in various locations, but here in Vārānasī it merely grew hotter and birds chirped merrily in the garden as though nothing had happened.

Finally Sanjō asked the man at the reception desk, 'Is it all right to go out?'

'No problem' was the answer.

'I'm going out. You can get wonderful rugs here at cheap prices. My wife's family asked me to pick one up,' he told Numada, who was still watching the television. 'I can't waste this whole trip just because something stupid has happened. My wife's had enough of visiting old relics, but she says she's all for shopping for silk and rugs.'

With the curtains to his room shut to ward off the afternoon sun, Isobe poured what little whisky was left in the bottle into his glass and began to drink. He had the feeling he could hear the voice of that potato vendor calling from somewhere.

Yaki imo-o-o. Yaki imo.

The room, like his heart, was empty. A beam of white light spilled between a crack in the curtains, and a single cockroach crawled nimbly through a rip in the carpet.

'It's your fault.' Isobe began making excuses to his wife. 'I looked for you . . . but you were nowhere to be found.' He thought of the game of hide-and-seek he had played as a child with his younger sister. 'I looked for you.'

I'm here.

'My last resort is that phoney fortune-teller.'

Isobe poured the hot liquor down his throat, trying to drown his wife's voice. The unexpected incident in New Delhi today had roused him from his act of folly. Otherwise he would at this very moment be visiting the fortune-teller in the Nehru jacket. The antique fan on the fortune-teller's ceiling twirled with a rasping noise. With solemn movements he had picked up the large, impressive-looking book and placed it on his desk. A large-stoned ring decorated his finger. No doubt he had fleeced some wealthy American or European woman of her money with that very finger.

'She liked fortune-telling.' He suddenly remembered making the obligatory New Year's shrine pilgrimages with his wife, and how she had never neglected to draw a divination slip from the box. She would smile to herself each time the man at the shrine office studied the number on her slip and handed her a piece of paper with the words 'Good Fortune' written on it. And now, in a hot, distant land he was recalling these trivial actions that had meant nothing to him at the time.

Intoxication looped through his body, and he stared at the white afternoon sunlight trickling on to the floor. This was the afternoon light of India.

Mitsuko was sitting on the orange sofa in her room, staring at the same white light. A faint hum buzzed constantly in her room, perhaps because the air-conditioner was so old. Even though she had travelled all this way to India, the entire day was slipping by without meaning. Why had she come all the way to India? No, a more important question was why she had stayed behind in this city instead of making the circuit of the old ruins and holy places with the other Japanese tourists. She had virtually no interest in the Taj Mahal or in the Indian dance shows that delighted other sightseers. It was the River Ganges and the image of the goddess Chāmundā that Enami had explained to them: the goddess festering with leprosy, encoiled by poisonous vipers, gaunt, yet nursing children from her drooping breasts – these were what had pierced Mitsuko's heart. In them she had discovered the Asian mother who groans beneath the weight of the torments of this life. She was utterly different from the lofty, dignified Holy Mother of Europe.

The white light filtering through her window unexpectedly reminded her of the Kultur Heim chapel after classes. That day, she had waited in the chapel for Ōtsu with evil intent in her heart. At the bottom of the stairs, the chimes of the large clock had rung out with solemnity, and a Bible with a loose cover was spread open before her eyes.

. . . he hath no form nor comeliness; and when we shall see him, there is no beauty that we should desire him.

He is despised and rejected of men; a man of sorrows, and acquainted with grief: and we hid as it were our faces from him. . . .

Surely he hath borne our griefs, and carried our sorrows.

Why am I searching for this man?
The image of the goddess Chāmundā was superimposed upon that of this man, and the wretched figure of Ōtsu as she had seen him in Lyon overlapped them both. As she thought about it now, it seemed as though she had unconsciously been following in Ōtsu's wake, chasing after something she could not define. This fellow they had nicknamed Pierrot, who had 'no form nor comeliness', whom she had despised and rejected. Though she had made him a plaything of her pride, he had deeply wounded that same pride.

With a knock at her door Numada shattered her reverie.

'Everything seems calm in the city. The Sanjōs and Mr Isobe have all gone out. I thought I might go look at the city myself. Would you like to join me?'

The same as yesterday, the badly oiled fan creaked as it spun near the ceiling. Leather-bound books were crammed into the bookcase against the wall to create a sense of majesty, and the fortune-teller in the Nehru jacket sat down behind the large desk and declared, 'No problem.'

He wrote something on a piece of paper with a thick silver Parker fountain-pen, then thrust it towards Isobe with the ringed hand. It was the address Isobe had requested. As Isobe carefully studied the man's face, a faintly cunning smile puffed across his cheeks like vapour and vanished. In that moment Isobe understood, but resignation rather than anger swelled in his heart. The fortune-teller quickly announced: 'One hundred rupees.'

When he went outside, an oppressive heat still enfolded the road even though it was near sundown, and there was no wind. The driver of the the taxi he had hired to bring him here was patiently waiting for him in the heat. Here, too, a pair of young siblings hounded Isobe, their hands extended like those of the fortune-teller to beg for money.

As Isobe watched the younger girl, who appeared to be four or five, feigning hunger, fear suddenly welled up inside him. What if this were his wife? The thought that this could be his reincarnated wife swiped past him, leaving an open wound in his heart like the stab of a knife. He hurriedly gave the girl some coins and fled into the taxi.

The driver glanced at the piece of paper on which the fortune-teller had written the address, nodded, and slammed his foot on the accelerator. A motor-driven rickshaw noisily whizzed past them, and a cow had stretched out to sleep in front of a stall selling sugar-cane juice. As he vacantly watched these scenes whirl by, Isobe felt as though he were in the midst of a dream. He did not believe he would find his resurrected wife at the address he had given the driver. But he bore up against the same kind of futility felt by a terminal cancer patient who clings to a slender thread of hope even after the doctor has proclaimed the day of his death. *After this, I can give it up*, he told himself. *After this, I'll be able to give the whole thing up.*

At the small compound lined with rows of dilapidated huts, two or three rickshaws waited for fares. At a repair shop for bicycles and rickshaws men were busily assembling some vehicle, while at a roadside stall a woman crouched on her haunches beside brightly coloured statues of Śiva and fruits arrayed on the ground.

'Here.' The driver stopped his taxi.

'Where? Which house?' Isobe asked, but the driver shook his head and handed back the piece of paper from the fortune-teller. Only the name of the road had been written on the coarse paper; the house number had been omitted. Although he had already resigned himself to failure, remorse still stirred within him.

Even so, he got out of the taxi and went into the rickshaw repair shop.

'Do you know a young girl named Rajini?'

'Rajini?'

'Rajini. A young girl.'

The men peered with baffled looks into Isobe's face, then began to jabber amongst themselves in a Hindi that sounded to Isobe as if they were spitting on the ground. Then a toothless old man pointed to the end of the road, and in a nasal voice said: 'Ra-ji-ni.'

A faint breath of coolness finally insinuated its way into the stuffy heat of sundown. The smells of Vārānasī to which Numada and Mitsuko had by now grown accustomed – the blended smells of sweat and animals and the earth – grew even stronger when they entered the city.

'A bird shop! A bird shop,' Numada muttered to himself.

'What?'

'Would you mind if we stopped off at a bird shop on our way?'

'Of course not. You've given me a good deal of your time. What are you going to buy at a bird shop?'

'A myna.'

'They sell mynas in Tokyo, don't they?'

'They've all had their tails cut. I want to get my hands on a myna from the wild.'

Mitsuko gave Numada a dubious look, but she asked nothing else. She had her own secrets she wished to reveal to no one. When she had done volunteer work and one of her patients – usually a middle-aged or elderly woman – had started to confess some secret to her, the moment the words first crossed their lips, she would turn away and pretend not to listen. Turning her back on them was a display of rejection, letting them know there was nothing she could do for them even if she heard their confessions. She always told them, 'The head nurse won't allow it. She's forbidden us volunteers from getting involved in patients' private affairs.'

Numada seemed displeased that Mitsuko had not asked him his reason for buying a myna. When Mitsuko pointed to a barracks-like shop and said, 'I wonder if that's a bird shop?', he headed quickly off in that direction.

A monkey was tied to a pole. Parakeets squawked in lantern-shaped cages stacked one atop another, and chickens noisily scratched about in boxes.

Standing in the doorway of the shop, Numada asked, 'Do you have any great hill mynas?' Mitsuko, who hadn't known the English word for myna, realized that this was no sudden impulse of Numada's, but that he had been planning to get such a bird even before they set out on this trip. His conversation with the shop-owner continued briefly, after which Numada gave the man his name and the name of their hotel and rejoined Mitsuko.

'He says they'll deliver it to the hotel.'

'Are you taking the myna back to Japan?'

'Oh no.' Numada smiled meaningfully. 'Just the opposite.... Many years ago, a myna helped save my life. Now I'm going to pay him back. A pretty sentimental thing to do, when you think about it....'

From the outside the building looked the same as every other one in the vicinity. The stucco walls of each house had peeled as though from some skin disease. One of them was the whorehouse to which the reception-desk assistant had directed Numada.

'Even if this isn't the place your friend frequents... we may be able to get some clue to his whereabouts.'

'I'm sorry to make you come to a place like this.'

'It's all right. To tell the truth, I've taken quite a fancy to this treasure-hunt of yours. Why is it you're so determined to track down this priest?'

Mitsuko answered Numada's intemperate question brusquely. 'The same reason you were searching for your myna bird.'

'I see.'

He may have spoken the words 'I see' with his lips, but there was no possibility that Numada could have comprehended the reason for Mitsuko's curtness.

'What shall we do? Would you like me to go in by myself and ask for you?'

'No, please take me with you. It'd be even more peculiar for a woman to be standing by herself in front of a place like this.'

'That's true.'

As the two started up the flaking stucco steps, a man who had been standing in the street watching them began waving his hands and shouting, 'No lady. No!'

Numada turned back and answered, 'No problem!'

Murky water had puddled here and there on the stairs, and dingy laundry had been hung to dry in the courtyard, which more closely resembled a junkyard. There was a wooden door at the top of the stairs, with a round peephole that glared back at them like the eye of a monster. When Numada rang the doorbell, someone peered at them through the peephole.

'You are welcome,' a voice said, and they heard the sound of a lock being turned. The face of a man with a fake smile and only two teeth in the front of his mouth snaked out, but the moment he saw Mitsuko, he repeated what the man in the street had said: 'Lady, no!'

'We're looking for a Japanese man,' Numada explained. 'Is he here?'

'No.'

The man started to close the door, but when Numada took a dollar bill from his pocket, the door remained open a crack. Through the opening Mitsuko caught a glimpse of lattice bars like animal cages. From behind the bars women wrapped in raglike saris peered back at her, their eyes strangely flashing. They were eyes like a wild cat's. Among the women was one young woman who might still be called a girl, stretched out prone on a tattered bed.

When yet another dollar bill crossed the man's palm, a vulgar smile lit up his face, changing it into the face of a corruptible traitor.

'He hasn't come yet.'

'When will he be here?'

'I don't know.' The man's dull-witted reply erupted from between his missing teeth.

'Where is he?'

'I don't know.'

'If he comes here, please tell him to call this number.'

When Numada handed him another dollar bill, the man smiled contemptuously, but the moment he heard footsteps at the base of the stairs, he waved his hand as though chasing a dog away, signalling them to leave. A young man, dressed in the same kind of suit as the youth who had delivered the splendid speech to Mitsuko at the previous evening's wedding celebration, stopped in his tracks when he saw Mitsuko and hesitated as he was about to enter the house.

Following behind Numada and supporting herself with a hand against the peeling wall, Mitsuko stepped from one puddle of filthy water to another.

'Now what?'

'I'm giving the whole thing up. I've already caused you enough trouble, Mr Numada.'

An evening mist had engulfed the city, and Mitsuko suddenly felt as though everything in her life had been meaningless and futile. Not just this trip to India, but everything about her up to the present day: her years at school, her brief marriage, her hypocritical imitation of volunteer work. Even walking around this unfamiliar city in search of Ōtsu. Yet, at the core of her senseless actions, she vaguely perceived that she yearned for *something*. A something that would provide her with a sure sense of fulfilment. But she could not fathom what that something might be.

Suddenly an explosion of sound, identical to the blaring of the band they had heard the previous day, echoed from the distance and seemed to be heading towards them.

'Another wedding?' Numada stopped walking and peered in the direction of the noise. Drums were banging, and a large number of people had formed a line and were walking in rhythm to the beat. 'It's a demonstration!'

But the band was playing a sombre funeral march. Phrases in Hindi and in English had been blackly inscribed on the white banners carried by the men who walked in measured step to the music: WE WILL NOT FORGET INDIRA. INDIRA IS OUR MOTHER.

Genteel Hindus, like those they had seen at the wedding, marched solemnly beneath the banners. Behind them followed beggar children and multitudes of the poor.

'Indira is our mother,' they loudly chanted together. Helmeted police kept mute watch over the procession.

'Indira is our mother.' Numada read aloud the words from a banner. 'Our mother is dead. Our mother is dead.'

'Miss Na-ru-se!' Mitsuko's name was called out in Japanese. A familiar voice. A voice she had heard in college. His peculiar way of saying 'Miss Na-ru-se.' She discovered Ōtsu, dressed in a dirty, long-sleeved *achkan* jacket and a pair of threadbare jeans.

'I heard you ... were looking for me. *Nāmastē*.'

'*Nāmastē*.' Mitsuko felt the huskiness in her own voice, and forced a smile. 'I've looked everywhere for you. I even asked at the church.'

'Sorry.' Ōtsu's quick habit of apologizing had not been cured over the many long years. 'I'm no longer at the church. I've been taken in by one of the Hindu āshrams.'

'Āshram?'

'It's like a seminary.'

'Have you converted to Hinduism?'

'No, I'm ... I'm just like I've always been. Even what you see here now is a Christian priest. But the Hindu sādhus have welcomed me warmly.'

'Let's go somewhere and talk. Will you come to our hotel?'

'Dressed like this ... they wouldn't like having me at the hotel.'

'Because of their beautiful gardens, I suppose. But there are benches in the garden.'

'You're staying at the Hotel de Paris, aren't you?'

'You know a great deal.'

'The outcast who does their laundry is a friend of mine. Their gardens are famous.'

Mitsuko introduced Ōtsu to Numada, who was watching all of this with eyes shot through with curiosity.

'Thank you very much. A friend and I will come over to your hotel right away.'

'INDIRA IS OUR MOTHER. WE WILL NOT FORGET INDIRA.' The procession marched past the three Japanese, continuing their *Sprechchor*. 'OUR MOTHER IS DEAD. OUR MOTHER IS DEAD.'

TEN

The Case of Ōtsu

With a display of tact, Numada deposited the two in a taxi and announced he was going to drop in at the bird shop once more, then disappeared into the crowd of demonstrators. They were silent inside the taxi for a few moments, until Ōtsu said haltingly, 'You've come to India at a frightening time.'

'Yes, but I don't understand anything that's going on.'

'A number of riots seem to have broken out in New Delhi.'

'It's strangely peaceful here, isn't it?'

'That's because . . . to the Indians this is a holy place.'

'Will Indira's body be floated down the Ganges too?'

'Yes. Just like the impoverished outcasts, she'll be sent down the River Ganges. They say the funeral will be on the third of November.'

When the long day ended in Vārānasī, it suddenly turned cold. In the garden, various kinds of insects began singing as though they had been restored to life, and the swing, though no hand had touched it, creaked and swayed on its own. Ōtsu sat on the bench, his legs deferentially pressed together. His diffident posture reminded Mitsuko of the way he had sat on the campus bench many years ago, putting up with her taunts.

'Would you like a sandwich? Something to drink?' She even talked just as she had in their school-days. 'So you're living with some Hindus, are you?'

'Yes. Here in India, when a Hindu grows old, he turns his house over to his children and sets out on a wandering journey of spiritual training. Such people are called sādhus. It was some sādhus who took me in.'

'Like an abandoned dog, it sounds.'

'Yes, I was just like an abandoned dog by then.' Ōtsu spoke as though his nose was clogged up. 'I was really at my wit's end.'

'Moving in with a group of Hindus... weren't you condemned by your church?'

'My whole life I've been reprimanded by the Church.'

After a few moments of silence, Mitsuko said, 'I don't quite follow. You're still a priest?'

'Yes. But a straggler....'

The assistant from the reception desk, who brought them some sandwiches and black tea, directed a look of open contempt at Ōtsu.

'I'm often mistaken for an outcast. Dressing like this allows me to carry the bodies. If I dressed as a missionary, they wouldn't let me touch the corpses. The Hindus forbid those of other faiths from setting foot in the cremation grounds.'

'I had heard some people saw you at the cremation grounds,' Mitsuko said with surprise. 'But you... you actually carry bodies?'

'Yes. Here in the city many people who have finally made their way to the Ganges to die there collapse in the streets. A truck from the city makes its rounds once a day, but they overlook some.'

'I saw someone like that.'

'Those who are still alive I take to a facility on the banks of the river. The dead I deliver to the funeral pyres on the ghāts.'

Mitsuko recalled the lapping of the flames she had seen two days before at the Manikarnikā Ghāt. The mummy-like corpse of an old woman, wrapped in red and black cloth and placed on a bamboo bed. If someone had peeled away the wrappings, no doubt what would have emerged would have been the crumbling form of the goddess Chāmundā. The diverse torments of life and the stains from many tears lingered on each of those corpses.

'And so you... you take them to the Hindu cremation grounds?'

'That's right. The wealthy are taken by their families on a litter. There are few to carry the poor, solitary outcasts. But even such people come dragging their legs to this city with the hope of having their ashes scattered in the River Ganges.'

'But you're no Hindu Brahmin....'

'Is that distinction so important? If that man were here in this city now...'

'That man? Oh, your Onion?'

'Yes. If the Onion came to this city, he of all people would carry the fallen on his back and take them to the cremation grounds. Just as he bore the cross on his back while he was alive.'

'But the Onion's church isn't very pleased with what you're doing, are they?' By reflex Mitsuko hurled the thorned words at her old schoolmate, but even as she spoke them she found her own audacity odious.

'No one has been very pleased with me. At college and at the seminary, at the novitiate ... and at the church here too. But it doesn't matter any more.'

'Don't you think that's just your own...'

'Yes, I know. But, in the end, I've decided that my Onion doesn't live only within European Christianity. He can be found in Hinduism and in Buddhism as well. This is no longer just an idea in my head, it's a way of life I've chosen for myself.'

Through the open window they could hear a performance of Indian music that was being presented for a group of American tourists who had just arrived that day. Snatches of music from a harmonium, an instrument resembling a harmonica, flowed towards them.

'But you've pulled the rug out from under your own life.'

'I have no regrets.'

'Do the Hindus know that you're a Catholic priest?'

'Those who have fallen by the roadside? I seriously doubt it. But when all life has been drained from them and their bodies are enshrouded in flames, I say a prayer to my Onion. "This person I'm handing over to you," I pray, "please accept and enfold him in your arms."'

'In the end aren't you believing in reincarnation the same as the Buddhists and the Hindus? You're a Christian priest, after all.'

With the little pride she had left in her heart, she was driven to pose the question by a feeling that she had lost out to Ōtsu's way of life.

'When the Onion was killed,' Ōtsu muttered, staring at the ground, as though speaking only to himself, 'the disciples who remained finally understood his love and what it meant. Every one of them had stayed alive by abandoning him and running away. He continued to love them even though they had betrayed him. As a result, he was etched into each of their guilty hearts, and they were never able to forget him. The disciples set out for distant lands to tell others the story of his life.' Ōtsu spoke as though he had opened up a picture-book and was reading a story to the impoverished children of India. 'After that, he continued to live in the hearts of his disciples. He died, but he was restored to life in their hearts.'

'I just don't get it.' Mitsuko loudly dissented. 'It all sounds like a story from some other planet.'

'It's not from another planet. Look at me – he's alive even inside a man like me.'

It was true that Ōtsu's words were substantiated by the life of mis-fortune he had led. His words were different from the fluid, punch-flavoured rhetoric of the young man at the wedding, whose convictions had gone no further than his lips.

The lights were turned on in the garden lanterns, illuminating the profile of Ōtsu's ulcerated face.

'Every time I look at the River Ganges, I think of my Onion. The Ganges swallows up the ashes of every person as it flows along, re-jecting neither the beggar woman who stretches out her fingerless hands nor the murdered prime minister, Gandhi. The river of love that is my Onion flows past, accepting all, rejecting neither the ugliest of men nor the filthiest.'

Mitsuko no longer protested, but she sensed the distance separating herself from Ōtsu. Ōtsu's way of life and the things he said were quite literally of a 'different planet' from her own. She knew nothing about his Onion, but it was clear to her that the Onion had irrevoca-bly snatched Ōtsu from her grasp.

'Mr Ōtsu, you've got some sort of eruptions on your face.'

'I know. It's because I spend so much time at the whorehouse.'

'I can't believe . . . you haven't touched any of those women, have you?'

'Oh, I've touched them, all right. But only after those pathetic women who have worked themselves to the bone for their men have died, and I carry their raglike corpses away.'

It was the first time Mitsuko had ever heard Ōtsu make a joke. It suggested that a certain span of tranquillity had opened up in his heart.

When the Indian music show concluded, the laughter and conver-sation of the Americans buzzed like a swarm of mosquitoes. As if that were his signal, Ōtsu got up from the bench and said, 'Well, I've got to be going. . . . I have to start early again tomorrow.' He gave a sad smile. 'I suppose I may never see you again, Miss Naruse.'

'Why do you say such things? Where are you going tomorrow?'

'I don't know. Every day the fallen and the dead can be found somewhere in this city. One will collapse and die behind someone's house, or a sick whore will be tossed out on the ground where the sewer flows. So tomorrow morning when they begin the cremations at the Ganges, I may well be roaming around near the Manikarnikā Ghāt.'

Isobe searched out a bar. He felt, as he had the previous evening, that he must have a drink. He no longer bore any resentment towards the fortune-teller with his professorial face. Having come to India and witnessed the poverty of the people, he had seen that they were not simply beggars, but that they had learned to earn they daily bread by turning their physical infirmities and afflicted limbs to their advantage. That fortune-teller was merely one more of their number, a man, Isobe had learned, who profited from the 'incomprehensible mystery of India' to make his living. But a feeling of unendurable pain that he could not put into words surged through his chest.

That unendurable pain drove him in search of liquor. He had roamed the alleyways, which were as filthy as he had imagined them to be, and he had discovered any number of young girls named Rajini. They had each looked up at Isobe with fear in their eyes, and then held out their hands to beg for food, chanting, '*Bābūji, bakshish!*'

He wandered, walking on and on with no destination in mind. Finally in a back street he located a bar that would never have dared hang its sign on the main road. The shop mainly sold grain and strange-looking tinned goods covered with dust, but when he asked for a whisky, the proprietor shook his head and brought out a bottle of what he said was Indian liquor. He pointed to the bottle and called it 'Chhān. Chhān.'

Isobe brought the bottle to his mouth and swigged on it as he continued to wander along the street, oblivious to direction. His only wish was for intoxication speedily to numb his mind and blot out his intolerable pain.

Several Indians were arguing in the street. They dragged a healthy-looking man from his house and began beating him. When the man called for help, his face covered with blood that gushed from his nose, a policeman finally came, and the attackers fled like the wind.

One young man who had observed the scene offered an apologetic explanation to Isobe, though he had not requested it. 'He's one of the leaders of the Sikhs. Are you aware that some Sikhs assassinated Prime Minister Gandhi this morning?' He exaggeratedly covered his face with his hands. 'There is no reason why the Sikhs should kill our mother. The prime minister appointed one of the Sikhs, Zail Singh, to be president of India.'

In an attempt to flee this young man's explanation, Isobe pretended not to understand English. As he began to walk away, the young man called out to him.

'You had better get back to your hotel quickly. A night-time curfew has been proclaimed in several cities. If trouble starts up here as it has in Delhi, foreigners will be in danger.'

By now Isobe had no interest in these religious disputations. As a Japanese he knew nothing whatever about the background or circumstances of the strife between Hindus and Sikhs in this land. The bottom line was that, even in religions, people hated one another, rose up in opposition and killed one another. He could not place his trust in such things. To Isobe now, the most valuable thing in all the world seemed to be merely his memories of his wife. And he realized that he had come to an understanding of his wife's value, and of what she had meant to him, only once he had lost her. He had lived firm in the belief that his work and his accomplishments were everything, but he had been wrong. He understood how much of an egotist he had been, and he felt profound guilt towards his wife.

Intoxication circled his body and he lost his way, moving his feet along merely in an effort to wear himself out. He wanted to tire out and fall into a drunken stupor. 'Sir!' 'Sir!' Rickshaw-drivers called out to him from left and right. To his left Isobe noticed a flower shop and a stall selling copper pots, and he realized that he had walked all the way to the river.

Several beggars still slept on the stone stairs leading to the ghāt. Seeing Isobe, they called out to him. He flung a handful of coins at them, scurried up the ghāt and hid behind a few pieces of laundry that had been hung out on the river bank to dry.

The enormous river opened up before his eyes. Moonlight reflected on the surface of the water like silver foil. There were no bathers to be seen, and the clamour of the daytime had subsided. Not a single boat had put out.

He sat down on one of the rocks where laundry was pounded and watched the tin-coloured river as it silently flowed from south to north. An occasional dark floating object bobbed on the surface of the water. The river, oblivious to all, departed along with its flotsam.

He hurled the liquor bottle into the river. Countless Hindus believed that this great river purified them and formed their link to a better life to come. Had his wife been transported by some means to such a place?

'Darling!' he cried out. 'Where have you gone?'

He had never called to his wife with such raw feeling while she had been alive. Like many men, he had been absorbed in his work, and had often ignored his household until the time of her death. It wasn't that he had not loved her. He had long felt that being alive meant first of all work, and working diligently, and that women were happy to have such husbands. Not once had he wondered what depths of affection for him were buried in his wife's heart. And he had no notion of how strong were the bonds linking him to her in the midst of his complacency.

But after hearing the words his wife babbled at the moment of her death, Isobe came to understand the meaning of irreplaceable bonds in a human being's life.

Every once in a while the sound of tumult echoed from the city. Perhaps the Hindus had launched another attack against the Sikhs. Each party believed themselves in the right, and hated those different from themselves.

Revenge and hatred were not limited to the world of politics, but were the same in the realm of religion. When a group is formed in this world, oppositions emerge, dissension is created and strategies are concocted to belittle the opponent. Isobe, who had lived through the war and post-war periods in Japan, had seen so many people and groups of that inclination that he was sick of it all. He had heard the word 'right' so often that he had wearied of it. At some point the vague feeling that he could never believe in anything had come to rest permanently at the bottom of his heart. He had ultimately got along well with everyone in his company, but he had not been able to believe sincerely in any of them. He had learned through experience that egoism resided in the hearts of every individual, and that a man's insistence on his own good intentions and the propriety of his actions was merely an attempt to gloss over his egoism. He had tried to live an unassuming life himself, tempered by his understanding of human nature.

But now that he was all alone, he had finally come to understand that there is a fundamental difference between being alive and truly living. And though he had associated with many other people during his life, he had to admit that the only two people he had truly formed a bond with were his mother and his wife.

'Darling!' Once again he called out towards the river. 'Where have you gone?'

The river took in his cry and silently flowed away. But he felt a power of some kind in that silvery silence. Just as the river had embraced the deaths of countless people over the centuries and carried them into the next world, so too it picked up and carried away the cry of life from this man sitting on a rock on its bank.

ELEVEN

Surely He Hath Borne Our Griefs

In the courtyard, two or three stray dogs rummaged through the garbage. When Ōtsu returned, their eyes flashed and they snarled at him, but they did not attack. Inside the smelly stone house it was pitch-black. The five sādhus living in this āshram had to rise early, so they had already gone to sleep. A space in the furthest corner of the main floor – it could scarcely be called a room – had been given to Ōtsu as his spot to sleep. He opened the door that was loose on its hinges and went in to where it still smelled of sweat and the heat of the day, and switched on the bare bulb. The light illuminated the indentations in his dank bed and the several volumes of books that had been flung on top of them. A prayer-book; the Upanishad; a book by Mother Teresa. Mosquitoes buzzed. He lit a mosquito-coil he had had sent from Japan, removed his *āchal* and the chappals he wore, then dipped a rag into a bucket of water and meticulously wiped his body.

He knelt and prayed briefly. He then picked up a book of sayings by Mahatma Gandhi and stretched out on the bed still damp from the previous night's sweat. As he waited for sleep to come, his eyes scanned the words he had read so many times before as he had waited for sleep to come: 'As a Hindu, I believe instinctively that there are varying degrees of truth in all religions. All religions spring forth from the same God. But every religion is imperfect. That is because they have all been transmitted to us by imperfect human beings.'

A tiny mouse darted like a bullet across the floor. This was nothing unusual in this building; sometimes large rats leaped over Ōtsu's bed as they scurried across the room.

'There are many different religions, but they are merely various paths leading to the same place. What difference does it make which of those separate paths we walk, so long as they all arrive at the identical destination?'

Ōtsu was fond of these words. Because he had felt like this himself before he ever encountered these sayings, he had been frowned on by his superiors at the seminary and the novitiate, and had aroused the antipathy and scorn of his compatriots in France.

'If that's how you feel, then why do you remain in our community?' one of his upper classmen at the novitiate had said, denouncing him. 'If you dislike Europe so much, why don't you leave the Church immediately? It is the Christian Church in the Christian world that we are set to defend.'

'I can't leave the Church,' Ōtsu said almost tearfully. 'Jesus has me in his grasp.'

The book of sayings tumbled to the floor from between his grimy fingers. As he snored, he had a dream. Even in his dreams he saw the pallid face of Jacques Monge, the brilliant upper classman who had berated him incessantly in the religious community at Lyon.

'God was fostered in this world of ours. In this Europe you detest so.'

'I don't believe that. After he was crucified in Jerusalem, he began to wander through many lands. Even today he roams through various countries. Through India and Vietnam, through China, Korea, Taiwan.'

'Enough! If our teachers knew you were such a heretic...!'

'Am I... am I really a heretic? Was any religion truly heretical to him? He accepted and loved the Samaritan.'

Only in his dreams could he defy Jacques Monge and his superiors, plead his case and refute their arguments; in reality his face turned tearful and he lapsed into silence. He was, in sum, no more than a loser, a coward. He lacked the power to stand up and fight for what he believed even in word alone.

Three-thirty. The hour when a subtle coolness finally infiltrates the dormant heat of the air. In the dark courtyard a stray cow slept. Three sādhus dipped water from the well and purified their bodies.

Four o'clock. Ōtsu arose, similarly washed his body and face with the well water, and then in his own room held a private mass. 'Ite Missa est.' He remained on his knees, even after he had muttered the final prayer. In his days at the novitiate, too, the time he spent in conversation with his Lord was the only time he could recapture the peace and tranquillity that lay beyond words. At all other times he was constantly afraid he might hurt someone else, or invoke their wrath.

Already a faint light had begun to appear outside. When he closed the door and went out into the courtyard, the scrawny cow woke up, stared at him with expressionless eyes, stood up and sluggishly hobbled away. The streets, which by day would be filled with the voices of the Muslims chanting from their minarets, with rickshaws, and with people thronging past like swirling eddies, were still hushed, the doors of the shops with their peeling paint were still tightly shut, and the city seemed like a deserted film studio backlot. The only movement came from packs of stray dogs and cows slowly rising to their feet in the middle of the streets. A feeble coolness still lingered in the air. Ōtsu walked the streets that would eventually be awash in dazzling light, turning to the right, then cutting to the left along roads paved with humidity and squalor. He searched after the fallen, hunched like piles of rags in deserted corners, panting for breath as they awaited the coming of death. These were they who, though taking human form, had not spent a moment of their lives able to live like human beings; they who had made their way to this city, their final hope being to die at the River Ganges.

Like one who knows where cockroaches lurk, Ōtsu instinctively knew where in the city they would fall. It was always along slender byways, guarded from the eyes of men, places where the light of the outside world seeped wanly through cracks in a wall.

Until they breathe their last, people always seek out such trickles of light, as though these are their final hope.

Ōtsu's chappals slapped along the stone pavement soiled with filthy water and dog droppings, then came to a stop. At his feet, an old woman leaning against a wall peered up at Ōtsu. Hers were eyes bereft of feeling, like the eyes of the cow that had looked at him and then sauntered away. Her shoulders heaved as she panted for breath. Crouching down, Ōtsu took from the bag on his shoulder an aluminium cup and a bottle filled with water.

'*Pāni. Pāni.*' He gently encouraged the woman. '*Āp mērē dost hain.*' Water. Water. I am your friend.

He placed the aluminium cup to her tiny mouth and slowly poured the water in, but it merely moistened her chin and soaked the tattered clothing that wrapped her body. In a faint voice she muttered: '*Gangā.*' The Ganges.

When she spoke the word Gangā, a look of entreaty flickered in her eyes, and finally a tear flowed down.

Ōtsu nodded, and in a loud voice asked, '*Tabiyat kharāb hai?*' Do you feel ill? '*Koyi bat nahin.*' There is no need to fear.

From his bag he took an Indian-style sling he had woven from rope, wrapped her frail body in it, and lifted her on to his back.

'*Gangā.*' With her body resting on his shoulders, the old woman repeated the word over and over in a weeping voice.

'*Pāni chahiye?*' Do you want to drink of the waters? Ōtsu responded as he began to walk.

By now the morning light had begun to trickle into the city, as if to suggest that God had finally noticed the sufferings of man. Shops opened their doors, and flocks of cows and sheep, the bells around their necks tinkling, crossed the streets. Unlike Japan, here no one gave Ōtsu a strange look as he passed by with the old woman on his back.

How many people, how much human agony had he taken on his shoulders and brought to the River Ganges? Ōtsu wiped away the sweat with a soiled cloth and tried to steady his breathing. Having only a fleeting connection with these people, Ōtsu could have no idea what their past lives had been like. All he knew about them was that each was an outcast in this land, a member of an abandoned caste of humanity.

He could tell how high the sun had climbed from the intensity of the light that struck his neck and back.

O Lord, Ōtsu offered up a prayer. *You carried the cross upon your back and climbed the hill to Golgotha. I now imitate that act.* A single thread of smoke already was rising from the funeral pyres at the Manikarnikā Ghāt. *You carried the sorrows of all men on your back and climbed the hill to Golgotha. I now imitate that act.*

TWELVE
Rebirth

Although it was still dark outside the hotel, the voices of early-rising birds could be heard singing throughout the garden. The commotion at the reception desk was caused by a group of some thirty American tourists who had arrived the previous day from Calcutta and were now assembling in the lobby in preparation for their early morning sightseeing of the river bathing.

Mitsuko, who would be riding in the same bus as Kiguchi, was forced into the role of conversation partner for a large, loquacious American woman with a beaming smile who sat beside her in the lobby.

'I've been to Japan. It was three years ago, in the summer, and it was blisteringly hot. We went to the hot springs in Beppu. But the towels in those Japanese hotels are so small, they hardly covered anything, I'll tell you!'

The woman seemed to have confused the wash-cloths at the bath for a bath towel.

Unable to escape conversation, Mitsuko asked, 'When did you arrive in Calcutta?'

'Yesterday. There were just as many people there as in Japan, and it was just as hot, too!' She smiled artlessly.

'Was the situation dangerous there?'

'Not really. The strategic points were guarded by soldiers and tanks, but nothing out of the ordinary happened.'

Then it was likely that Enami and the other Japanese tourists would return safely to Vārānasī this evening. The two days without them had seemed endless.

'Ladies and gentlemen.' In a theatrical voice, the man at the reception desk called out to the group of tourists, who were chirping as loudly as the birds in the garden. 'Now we shall start.'

Their bus had arrived. Following behind the Americans, Kiguchi and Mitsuko found seats. Kiguchi turned round and looked at the pleasant smiles of the Americans and haltingly muttered, 'This is unbelievable. Forty years ago, we Japanese and these people were murdering each other.... It seems like just yesterday. Of course it was the British and the Indians I was fighting myself.'

Antagonism and hatred characterized not just the relationship between one nation and another; they persisted between one religion and another as well. A difference in religion had yesterday resulted in the death of the woman who had been prime minister of India. People were linked together more by enmity than by love. It was not love but the formation of mutual enemies that made a bonding between human beings possible. By such means had every nation and every religion survived over the long span of years. In the midst of all that strife, a pierrot like Ōtsu had aped the behaviour of his Onion and in the end been discarded.

'How many times have you been to the Ganges, Miss Naruse?' Kiguchi asked.

'Twice.'

'Thanks to you, I feel at last that there's been some purpose in my coming to India. I wanted to have a memorial service performed for my dead war comrades by the river, or at some Indian temple, but I didn't know there were so few Buddhists in this country. This is the land where Sakyamuni was born, but it's turned into a Hindu nation now.'

'There's still the river.' Mitsuko shifted her eyes towards the gradually brightening landscape and bared her true feelings. 'It's a deep river, so deep I feel as though it's not just for the Hindus but for everyone.'

It was dirty and drowsy along the street, where few stores had yet opened for business, and though there were no signs of human life, cows continued to wander slowly along, without destination.

The bus stopped beside the Dashāshvamedha Ghāt. Mingling with the cheerfully laughing Americans, Mitsuko and Kiguchi stepped down on to the dirty road. A swarm of beggars, poised like waiting flies, thrust out their hands to the tourists.

Following behind the affable American woman who distributed coins to the children, Mitsuko climbed the ghāt. She was surprised to see that many more Indian men and women than she had imagined had already started bathing.

'Each year, over a million Hindus come to this river to pray.' The voice of the guide spilled from the circle of American tourists.

'A million!' someone exclaimed in surprise.

'Yes, a million. The Hindus believe that once you enter this river, all of your past sins are washed away and you can be born into better circumstances in the next world.'

'Born in this world again? I've had enough of it myself!' A smiling American woman winked at Mitsuko. 'Are you a Buddhist?'

'Me?' Mitsuko answered. 'I have no religion.'

'You're a member of a wicked, wicked generation. I believe in God myself.' She seemed to be jesting with Mitsuko. 'You're going to miss your sightseeing boat.' She pointed to the boats into which her compatriots had started piling. The tourists had been divided into groups, and they were about to observe the funeral pyres from a point near the cremation grounds in boats paddled by four or five Indian men.

'No, but thank you. We're going to walk.'

'OK!' Once again the American woman winked. 'Let's have a beer at the hotel tonight.'

At the dock, where the sun had not yet fully risen, the waves beating against the shore sounded like a dog lapping water. As their boat slowly pulled away, Kiguchi and Mitsuko set out for the Manikarnikā Ghāt, where a vast crowd of men and women were milling about. Many of the buildings on the ghāt were temples or cheap lodgings for the pilgrims, and the narrow streets were littered with the droppings of dogs and sheep. Mitsuko, tottering as her feet slipped each time she took a step, asked, 'Mr Kiguchi, are you all right?'

'I'm fine. This is easy compared with the roads I once fled along in the jungle.' Kiguchi repeated the same phrases over and over, as though they lent meaning to his life. 'Those roads were nothing like this. Besides the filth, everywhere you looked there were scattered corpses of decomposing soldiers.'

Mitsuko nodded broadly. Within the heart of this man, who looked for all the world like a middling industrialist, there resided a past that had compelled him to come to this river. Each of the people who came to the river had a past like the goddess Chāmundā, and each had been stung by scorpions and bitten by cobras.

They walked past several ghāts and, at each, pilgrims who had finished their ablutions were shaking the water from the saris and loin-cloths or rags they had wrapped round their bodies to bathe, wiped themselves dry, and were changing into fresh clothing. Beneath a large parasol a Brahmin dressed in a yellow robe raised his hand over those who came to beg a blessing and made a mark on the foreheads of the faithful. A group of itinerant ascetics had painted their faces white: these were Hindus who, in the later stages of life, had abandoned their homes, bid farewell to their family members, and would end their lives as ascetics, making pilgrimages from one holy place to another. Mitsuko, who had learned about these pilgrims from Enami, explained them to Kiguchi.

'Well, then.' Tired, perhaps, Kiguchi sat on the stairs of the ghāt and watched the dark scene before him. 'I suppose this trip to India is an itinerant pilgrimage for me, too, isn't it? My one hope as I've lived out my life has been to go one day to Burma or to India in my later years and hold services for my dead comrades. And, Miss Naruse, it was just last year that I finally found some time in my busy work schedule. But after all that, I come to India and contract some ridiculous illness . . .'

'Your illness can serve as one memento of your pilgrimage.'

'Miss Naruse, when I had my fever, I babbled something, didn't I? The name Gaston.'

'I don't remember. It doesn't concern me.'

'No, Miss Naruse, I didn't bring it up because I'm embarrassed about it. Gaston is the name of a foreigner I knew many years ago. He was a foreigner who took care of my closest friend just before he died.'

The sky gradually cracked open to reveal a rosy tint. When the sun appeared, the river suddenly sparkled gold, and cries of joy echoed from the ghāts on either side of them. A row of men wearing only loin-cloths charged down the stairs and dived into the river, tossing up a spray of water.

'My war comrade, he ate human flesh in the Burmese jungle. He did it so he could help save me, since I'd collapsed with malaria. . . .'

Abruptly, as though he could no longer suppress the surge of emotion, he asked, 'Miss Naruse, have you ever experienced starvation? I don't think you can begin to imagine what real starvation is like. In Burma during the rainy season, we Japanese soldiers had thrown away our weapons, we had nothing to eat, and all we could do was run beneath the pounding rain. We were surrounded by a jungle, and everywhere along the road, from between the ferns and between the trees, we could hear the weeping and moaning of sick soldiers who couldn't move any further. There wasn't anything we could do to help them. We staggered on ahead, hearing behind us the wailing voices pleading, "Help me!" "Take me with you!" ... The most painful to hear were the young soldiers who yelled out "Mo-o-other!" Maggots oozed from their wounds. . . . I was saved from all that by my friend.'

Directly beneath the two of them, naked men and women stood in array, their bodies exposed to the rosy light of the morning sun as they filled their mouths with the water of the Ganges and joined their hands together in prayer. Each had their separate lives, the secrets they could relate to no one else, secrets which they carried as heavy burdens upon their backs as they lived out their existences. Each had something that needed cleansing in the River Ganges.

'We couldn't help it. The way things were, even if we had to eat the flesh of the dead . . .'

'Well, to one degree or other, we all live by eating others.'

'No, no, that's not it at all. Miss Naruse, you don't understand. My friend suffered his entire life because of it. When he came back from the war, he . . . he . . . he met the wife and child of the soldier whose flesh he had consumed. The innocent eyes of the child who knew nothing of what had happened . . . they pierced his heart and tormented him for the rest of his life. He endured those eyes all by himself. He couldn't even tell me, his best friend . . . all he could do was drink. He tried to forget by drinking. At the very end, he spat out blood over and over again, and ended up in the hospital, where he met the volunteer Gaston.'

Mitsuko kept her eyes on the Manikarnikā Ghāt as she listened to Kiguchi's monologue, directed mostly, it seemed, at himself. There comes a place and a time when people want to reveal the secrets they have kept hidden away in their hearts. For Kiguchi, the time was now, and the place the banks of the River Ganges. At the Manikarnikā Ghāt, white smoke trailed over the surface of the river, a white smoke that consumed those whose lives had ended.

'That Gaston I was babbling about listened to my friend's confession, and then he said that when a plane crashed in the Andes mountains, the passengers survived by eating human flesh.'

'What?'

'As they waited in the snow-covered mountains to be rescued, they ran out of food. The critically injured asked the others to eat their flesh after they had died. Stay alive by eating my flesh, they asked.... My friend wept as he listened to that story. I wonder if he felt some slight release from his own torment after he had heard it. When he breathed his last, his face seemed unusually at peace.'

'Why are you telling me this all of a sudden?'

'I'm sorry. I don't know myself why I'm jabbering on about something I should never have revealed.'

'Maybe it's because of the Ganges. This river embraces everything about mankind.... Maybe it just makes us feel like talking about such things.'

Mitsuko had begun to believe earnestly in what she said. There was no city in Japan even remotely resembling Vārānasī. This place was different from the little she knew about Paris and Lyon as well. A river where people from afar gathered so they could be cast into it when they were dead. A city to which people came on a pilgrimage in order to breathe their last. And the deep river bore up all the dead and silently carried them away.

With wrinkled hands, as though he were scraping the scales from his own eyes, Kiguchi rubbed his face, which displayed the splotches characteristic of old age.

'Miss Naruse, since that experience, I've been thinking about a lot of different things. I've started reading books on Buddhism, even though I don't really understand them.'

'Is this Gaston fellow still in Japan?'

'I don't know. I understand that after my friend died, he stopped turning up at the hospital. Sometimes I have the feeling he came there to help my friend, and after my friend died, he left. When my friend was about to die in his despair, having done a thing no human should ever do, that fellow came to be with him. He ... for my friend, at least, that fellow was another pilgrim who walked with him along the same paths.'

As she listened, it was Ōtsu that Mitsuko was thinking of, but Kiguchi muttered something completely unrelated to her thoughts.

'What I've been thinking ... is what in Buddhism is described as

"Good and evil are as one", that there's nothing a human being does that can be called absolutely right. To put it the opposite way, the seeds of salvation are buried in every act of evil. In all things, good and evil are back to back with each other, and they can't be separated the way you can cut things apart with a knife. My friend surrendered to an unbearable hunger and put the flesh of another human being into his mouth, and that act destroyed him, but Gaston said that you can find the love of God even in the midst of such an awful hell. It may sound self-important of me to say this, but ever since my friend died, I've kept myself going by mulling over what Gaston said time and time again.'

Standing just beside the two, a wealthy-looking young girl in a pretty orange sari stared at them with large black eyes and listened curiously to their Japanese conversation. On the rose-coloured surface of the river the heads of the bathers bobbed like the now-extinguished lanterns cast adrift on the waters to transport the souls of the departed dead.

'Miss Naruse, I've heard that Indians believe that when they enter this river, they can come back to a better life in the world to come.'

'The Hindus apparently call the Ganges the river of rebirth.'

'Rebirth? I have to tell you, the night I was delirious with fever, I had a vivid dream. I can still remember it. In this dream, my war comrade appeared before me, looking as if he were in great pain, and Gaston was there holding my suffering comrade in his arms. And I thought how similar Gaston and my friend were. My friend ate human flesh in order to save me. And in the dream Gaston said that it was a frightening thing to eat the flesh of another, but that my friend would be forgiven because he had done it out of compassion.'

Mitsuko did not respond.

'I wonder if that isn't what rebirth really means.'

This man – the sort of man who could well be the president of a mid-level industrial firm to be found anywhere in Tokyo – this man had lived a life that Mitsuko could not begin to imagine. There were individual dramas of the soul to be found in every one of the people cupping their hands and praying down by the river. And in the corpses that were carried to this spot. And the river that engulfed them all, the river that Ōtsu had called the river of the love of his Onion. Kiguchi untied the knot on the *furoshiki* parcel he had brought with him and took out a book of Buddhist sutras.

'Miss Naruse, excuse me, but would you mind if I chanted a sutra

for my friend and my other comrades who died in the war?'
'Please, go ahead. I'll walk around for a little while.'
Staring into the river, Kiguchi began to intone a passage from the
Amida Sutra that he had committed to memory.
The river flowed by. The River Ganges moved from north to south,
describing a gentle curve as it went along. Before his eyes Kiguchi
saw the faces of the dead soldiers on the Highway of Death, those
lying prone on the ground, and those with their faces turned to the
sky.

In the land of the Buddha may always be found
Rare and multicoloured birds of all varieties:
White swans, peacocks, parrots, kalavinkas and curlews.
Three times each day and three times each night
These myriad varieties of birds join together in songs
of harmony.

Standing beside Kiguchi as he chanted the Amida Sutra, the young
girl kept her large black eyes fixed on him and did not move a
muscle. Each time he intoned this passage from the Amida Sutra,
Kiguchi thought of the countless birds he had heard singing in the
jungles of Burma.

In that land of the Buddha
A gentle breeze stirs
Through the rows of palm trees and strings of bells
And a sweet, enrapturing sound proceeds from them.

The rains that poured throughout the day would sometimes let up
for a spell, and suddenly in the jungle birds that must have been
hidden away during the downpour began to sing cheerfully here and
there. Although the moans and cries of the wounded soldiers sprawled
upon the ground were audible, the birds seemed to care nothing for
them, and chirped noisily back and forth. Then from somewhere far
in the distant sky came the faint hum of an enemy plane searching
for the whereabouts of the Japanese Army. Those had been cruel days,
when the groans of the soldiers had seemed more filled with pain the
brighter and more cheerfully the birds sang forth....

At places along the route from Vārānasī west to Allahābād the paved road was cracked, and the already ancient taxi shook violently, while the driver held on with one hand to his door, which was about to lose its handle. At each tremour Numada had to grab hold of the birdcage beside him. The myna bird he had brought back from the bird shop that morning fretted at each bump.

'It's all right, it's all right,' he repeated over and over, trying to calm the bird. 'It's all right, it's all right.'

The driver turned round in his seat, flashed a toothless smile, and mimicked the Japanese: 'It's all right, it's all right.' Then in strikingly poor English he asked, 'This bird, it's belong to you?'

'Yes.'

'You eat this bird?' He pretended to be eating with one hand.

'No!'

'You are Japanese? Chinese?'

'Japanese.'

'You take this bird to Japan?'

'No, I'm going to set the bird free.'

It seemed, however, that the driver could not understand this last remark, and after that he clutched his steering-wheel and said nothing.

When the myna finally settled down, Numada steadied the cage between his knees and peered inside. The bird was poised with both feet on its perch, and it cawed in a phlegm-choked voice. It was the same voice he had heard many years before in the hospital.

There was little difference in size and shape between this bird and the bird Numada had tended in the past. The way it cocked its head as the taxi sped along the road was identical, too.

'Do you remember those nights?' Numada asked softly.

Once again the driver turned round. 'You want something?'

'No.'

The driver turned the knob of his radio and what must have been a popular Indian song, with a woman's high voice and the thumping of a *mridangam* drum, came blaring out.

A thick forest walled both sides of the road. Fan-shaped coconut and banyan trees grew in profusion, the white limbs of the banyans so tightly twined and interlocked that they looked like couples making love. Numada pressed his face against the window, searching for a sign that they were approaching the wildlife sanctuary. The areas around Sarshaka and Bharatpur near Agra were expansive and home to famous wildlife preserves, but Numada had learned from Enami that there was a small area near Allahābād where hunting was prohibited.

When he opened up his map and began searching it, the driver, who seemed to have already got directions at the hotel desk, said, 'I know. I know. No problem!'

The taxi turned on to a dirt road where once again it shimmied wildly, and inside its cage the myna bird, with fear in its eyes, flapped its wings. They drove ahead a short distance, and the taxi finally slowed down.

'Here.'

'Wait for me.' Numada held out his watch and pointed to a time thirty minutes later.

The makeshift office was deserted. He called out two or three times, but no one answered. From every direction he heard the same chirping of birds that one would hear in a zoo after closing-hours. The forest land had been prepared with unusual care, the trees had been meticulously thinned, and ponds had been dug in various spots to provide drinking water for the birds.

He sat down beside one of the ponds and placed the birdcage on the ground.

'Do you remember those nights?' he asked the myna. As he spoke, memories of those late nights in the hospital came back to him with a painful stab to his chest. After nearly two years in the hospital and two failed surgeries, in his exhaustion the only one to whom he could open his heart was that myna bird. Late at night, after everyone else had gone to sleep, he would turn on the small light at his bedtable and mutter to the bird, as though to himself, a confession of his anxiety and loneliness, not wanting to cause his wife any further concern. The myna was jet-black, the colour of a woman's wet hair. It planted its screw-hook claws on its perch, tilted its head and squawked: 'Ha ha ha!' At times its voice sounded as though it were mocking Numada's lack of nerve and cowardice, while at other times it seemed to be offering consolation. 'Am I going to die?' 'Ha ha ha!' 'What should I do?' 'Ha ha ha!' Then, on a snowy day in February, his third operation was performed. When haemorrhaging from his fused pleurae caused the needle on the electrocardiograph to cease its undulations, the myna bird died, as though in his stead.

He slid out the stick of wood that kept the door to the birdcage shut. It was a crude cage made of bamboo and wire.

'All right, come on out.'

He tapped the outside of the cage lightly with his fingers. The myna bird came hopping out, as though in confusion, scurried along the grass, spread its wings and hesitated for a moment, then raced across the ground again. Watching its laughable movements from behind, Numada felt as though a heavy burden he had carried on his back for many years had been removed. He felt as though he had been able to make a faint gesture of gratitude towards the myna that had died for him that snowy day.

The heat fried his face and neck, but when he stepped beneath the shade of a large betel-nut palm tree, he was able to hear the songs of the many birds echoing back and forth, from close at hand to far off in the forest. Assuming various shapes and colours, they nimbly and cheerily hopped from branch to branch. Where had the myna bird gone?

He heard the rustle of leaves on a linden tree. The flapping of insect wings near his ear. Those sounds served to deepen the silence of the forest. Something quickly swung from one coconut tree to another, and when he turned his eyes in that direction, he saw a long-tailed monkey. Numada closed his eyes and inhaled the sultry, unripened aroma, like the fermented smell of *sake* brewing, that emerged from the earth and the trees. The unadorned aroma of life. That life flowed back and forth between the trees and the chirping of the birds and the wind that slowly set the leaves fluttering.

He suddenly took note of his own foolishness. The feelings he had just absorbed were of no marketable value in the world of human affairs. What foolishness to give himself over to these feelings despite that knowledge. The smell of death was thick in the city of Vārānasī. And in Tokyo as well. And yet the birds blissfully sang their songs. To escape from that contradiction, he had created a world of children's fables, and when he returned home, he would most certainly write stories with birds and animals as their heroes once again.

THIRTEEN

He Hath No Form Nor Comeliness

In endless repetition, the television at the hotel reported on the assassination of the prime minister, Indira Gandhi.

According to the news, the premier had followed her usual custom and left her official residence at 9:15 a.m., walking the distance of about 180 metres to her office. At the office, the British actor Peter Ustinov was waiting to interview the prime minister. Just then, Ustinov heard a sound like the exploding of fireworks outside the window. This was followed by shouting voices. Assistant police inspector Beant Singh, who was one of the prime minister's bodyguards, and officer Satwant Singh, another of her security force, had opened fire on her with automatic weapons. The stricken prime minister was rushed to a hospital, but she was already dead. Fifty bullet wounds were found in her body.

A photograph of Ustinov appeared on the screen. His voice was commenting: 'All the preparations had been completed, and they were just pouring some tea in my cup when suddenly we heard three shots. Someone said it must be fireworks.'

The hotel employees and Isobe were staring at the screen in the dining-room when Sanjō appeared, carrying a travel bag.

'Good morning! Are you here by yourself, Mr Isobe? Where's everybody else?'

Sanjō's voice was shrill. Isobe kept his eyes off Sanjō as he replied, 'They've gone by bus with an American tour group to see the river.'

'What, the River Ganges? I wish I'd gone with them. I went dancing with my wife last night at the Hotel Taj Ganges, and I overslept. That's a wonderful hotel. Why do you think Mr Enami puts us up in a second-rate dive like this? There are hotels in this city that could rival the Ōkura in Tokyo.'

'Where's your wife?'

'Still asleep. I don't know what to do with her. She's such a child, and she doesn't understand why her husband wants to become a first-rate photographer.'

'I suppose you've got your camera in that bag?'

'Not a bad guess. It looks like my wife'll sleep till noon, so I'm going to have a cup of coffee and head for the Ganges this morning.'

'You do remember that Mr Enami said that photographing funeral pyres along the Ganges is strictly prohibited? Particularly because the Hindus have worked themselves up into a frenzy over the past two days. Last night I saw them beat a Sikh man until he was bloody. Don't you think it'd be better if you left your camera behind today?'

'Robert Capa says a photographer who doesn't risk danger can never shoot a masterpiece. As the Indians themselves would say: "No problem." It's fine, don't worry. I won't take any pictures of the cremation grounds.'

When Sanjō finished slurping his coffee, he ordered a taxi at the reception desk and then returned to his room. His wife, in a sky-blue négligé, slept with her arms flung wide, but with her body curled into a ball like a basket worm. When he touched her white arm, she languidly opened her eyes a crack. 'Let me sleep.'

'I'm going out. I've got work to do. Otherwise there's no point in coming here. Would you like me to get you something from room service?'

'Nothing.'

'Fine, fine, you're going to snooze away when they've just assassinated the prime minister?'

'It's got nothing to do with us. Let me sleep. Please!'

That was how Sanjō preferred things anyway. In all honesty, Sanjō was at his wit's end with his wife. Her eyes sparkled in high-class hotels or in stores selling Indian silks or cashmere shawls, but in New Delhi and here in Vārānasī all she had to offer was a volley of complaints: 'It's filthy!' 'I can't stand it!' 'I wanted to drive along the Märchen *autobahn!*'

Watching Sanjō scurry into a taxi and head off by himself, Isobe suddenly felt uneasy. Every company had to put up with a generation of workers who were pleasant enough on the surface but never gave a thought to the trouble they made for others. Isobe knew from experience that Sanjō was not a bad fellow, but that in his youthfulness he lacked sensitivity.

'The Dashāshvamedha Ghāt.' With a certain degree of pride, Sanjō announced his destination to the driver who clutched the steering-wheel.

'Yes, sir!' The Indian driver instinctively responded with respect to Sanjō's high-handed tone. Sanjō stroked the camera in his bag. This solid object. The source of a life worth living. His partner.

When he got out of the taxi, he was surrounded by beggars like a swarm of locusts. 'No!' Sanjō sounded as though he were scolding a dog. 'No!' He was no longer plagued by the pity and empathy he had originally felt towards these fingerless girls and children feigning hunger. If he gave just one of them a paltry amount of loose change, their numbers would merely increase.

No doubt as a result of the assassination, two soldiers had been posted at a four-way crossing lined with stores selling tourist flowers and bottles to capture the water of the holy river. He might be interrogated if the soldiers could see what he had in his travel bag.

He whistled the 'Starlight Blues' as he made his way along a back street by the river. *Everything's going well*, he thought with pride. *Everything on schedule, right on schedule.* After graduating from the fine arts department of a private university, he had become assistant to a famous photographer, and everything was going his way. As his bride he had chosen a young woman from a family that could guarantee his future. Once he passed the observatory, he began to encounter two, then three processions of men walking along, carrying corpses wrapped in cloths of various colours. These were the bodies of pilgrims who had died in lodgings along the river bank. His travel guide had explained that the corpses of women were sheathed in cloths of red or orange.

He touched his camera through the bag.

He wanted to take a surreptitious picture precisely because it was forbidden. Even a greenhorn like Sanjō knew that no Japanese photographer had ever taken a picture of this ceremony. If he were successful, a mainstream photography magazine would be likely to reproduce his picture with his name attached.

Photographs did not concern themselves with philosophies but with subject-matter. That is why he had chosen India for his honeymoon. Even Robert Capa would not have become famous throughout the world without the dramatic backdrop of the battlefield.

With the corpse suspended over poles about three metres long, several men heaved it on their shoulders and passed down a narrow alley. After he let one group pass by, Sanjō swiftly unzipped his bag and pulled out his cherished camera. When he brought the camera up to his face, a man at the back of the litter suddenly turned round, and in clearly enunciated Japanese shouted, 'Stop it! Photographs are prohibited!'

Sanjō stared vacantly at the man, forgetting even to press the shutter button.

Then he remembered. Several days before, when Enami had brought them to see the river, they had run into this Japanese man near the cremation grounds. Enami had tried speaking to him, but the man, ashamed perhaps by the shoddiness of his attire, had given only a vague reply and then fled away with the other Indians.

Following behind the corpse and its carriers, Sanjō decided in fact that it was fortunate he had run into the Japanese man.

'It's going well, it's going well.' In his customary way, he took everything as working to his advantage. *I wonder if I could have a word with that fellow and have him help me take a picture? I'm sure he wouldn't refuse if I gave him some money.*

As they approached the *shmashāan*, the characteristic odour of death filled his nostrils. The deceased's family sat nearby with crossed legs, waiting for the litter to be placed above the firewood and the flames to be lit.

Hatred was spreading everywhere, blood was being spilled everywhere, wars were breaking out everywhere. Seated on the steps of the ghāt, Mitsuko spread open the *The Times of India* and scanned the pages of the newspaper she had bought along with some postcards at a relatively tidy shop along the pilgrim's route. She couldn't locate a single article concerning Japan. It did appear, however, that the prime minister, Nakasone, would be joining many other heads of state to attend the funeral for Indira Gandhi in two more days. It was not just in India that hatred smouldered and blood flowed – Iran and Iraq were bogged down in war, and fighting continued in Afghanistan. In such a world, the love of the Onion that Ōtsu worshipped was impotent and pathetic. Even if that Onion were alive today, Mitsuko thought, he was of no use in this world of enmity.

... he hath no form nor comeliness; and when we shall see him, there is no beauty that we should desire him.
He is despised and rejected of men; a man of sorrows, and acquainted with grief: and we hid as it were our faces from him....
Surely he hath borne our griefs, and carried our sorrows.

Silly Ōtsu. Silly Onion. Mitsuko searched for Ōtsu among the white-robed silhouettes moving near the cremation grounds. Why did she care about him, why did she keep searching for him even as she went on mocking him? There were a number people dressed in white robes. And there were the several red dogs waiting to consume the flesh that survived the flames. Vultures also spread their wings near the mountain of firewood, waiting for an opportunity to peck at the flesh left by the dogs. On the rear of her eyelids Mitsuko sketched a picture of the goddess Chāmundā, who had endured the snapping of cobras and the stinging of scorpions. When she opened her eyes, she noticed one skinny cow standing on a stone step nearby, watching the same scene with moist eyes.

'Mr Kiguchi!'
At first Kiguchi, who was chanting a sutra, did not recognize Mitsuko dressed in a sari.
'Eh?' He stared at her suspiciously. 'Oh, is that you? I didn't recognize you in the sari.'
'I bought it on a back street. The shop-owner showed me how to put it on.'
'What's happened to your other clothes?'
'The store is holding on to them for me. They do that for foreigners who want to go swimming.'
'You're going swimming?'
Kiguchi followed with his eyes as Mitsuko, wrapped in her sari, slowly descended the stone steps. She brought one foot near the water, which was the colour of milky tea. The water was lukewarm. A large Indian man who was soaking in the river waved his hands and animatedly called something to her.

'What did you say?' she asked, and in a loud voice he responded: 'Come in! The river feels wonderful!'

Mitsuko nodded and put one leg into the river, then submerged the other. Like death itself, she hesitated just before taking the leap, but once her entire body was submerged, the unpleasant feeling disappeared.

To her right two, to her left four Hindu men and women were washing their faces, pouring water into their mouths and clasping their hands in prayer. No one gave Mitsuko a strange look. On close inspection, it appeared that the men had naturally gathered in one spot, while the women had congregated together separately.

Swaying back and forth, Mitsuko approached the sari-clad women. The women were placing flower petals they had bought at a stall on top of leaves and setting them afloat in the water. On the stone steps the yellow-robed Brahmin beneath his large parasol was blessing a newly-wed couple. Far away on the southern shore, the ashes of the body that had just been cremated were being shovelled into the river by three men dressed in white. Even though the waters bearing the ashes of the dead came flowing towards the bathers, no one thought it peculiar or distressing. Life and death coexisted in harmony in this river.

Yellow and pink flowers that had been blessed also came drifting by. The flowers collided with an object that looked like a floating plank of white wood and clustered there. It turned out to be the carcass of a dead puppy. Utterly oblivious to it, the people continued to float and submerge their bodies and pray. Mitsuko sought out the cremation grounds with her eyes. There, a new corpse wrapped in a persimmon-coloured cloth had been suspended above the firewood. The men who had carried the litter left to bring another body. She could not find Ōtsu anywhere.

Mitsuko turned her body in the direction of the river's flow.

'This is not a real prayer. I'm just pretending to pray,' she rationalized, embarrassed at herself. 'Like my fabrications of love, this is just a fabricated prayer.'

At the end of her range of vision, the river gently bent, and there the light sparkled, as though it were eternity itself.

I have learned, though, that there is a river of humanity. Though I still don't know what lies at the end of that flowing river. But I feel as though I've started to understand what I was yearning for through all the many mistakes of my past.

She clutched her fist tightly and searched for the figure of Ōtsu beside the funeral pyres.

What I can believe in now is the sight of all these people, each carrying his or her own individual burdens, praying at this deep river. At some point, the words Mitsuko muttered to herself were transmuted into the words of a prayer. *I believe that the river embraces these people and carries them away. A river of humanity. The sorrows of this deep river of humanity. And I am a part of it.*

She did not know to whom she directed this manufactured prayer. Perhaps it was towards the Onion that Ōtsu pursued. Or perhaps it was towards something great and eternal that could not be limited to the Onion.

At that moment, a cry erupted near the steps descending to the cremation grounds. The Hindus who had been on their knees rose as one and began to run and shout. They were charging towards an Asian man, who quickly ran away. It was Sanjō. Unquestionably Sanjō. Then, from among the group of men who had carried the body and were now resting, one man sprang forward, planted himself in the path of the mourners, and tried to pacify them. The angry crowd surrounded this man and began to beat and kick him from every side. While they were thus diverted, Sanjō slipped away down a labyrinthine road across from the river bank. The Hindus, stirred up by the assassination of their prime minister, directed their rage at the man who had tried to subdue them. Like baggage hurled down from a freight carrier, the man tumbled down the stairs of the ghāt and finally stopped, unmoving.

Those who had been bathing gathered about, forming a circle around the fallen man. In a gap between the wet bodies, Mitsuko saw the blood-splattered body of Ōtsu.

'Mr Ōtsu!'

When she screamed, the people in their dripping dhotis and saris turned round and opened a path for her.

'He's not the one!' Mitsuko crouched beside him. 'He hasn't done anything!'

Ōtsu opened his eyes a crack and forced a smile, but his neck was twisted to the right like the branch of a *bonsai* tree.

'I think ... maybe ... my neck's broken ...' he gasped hoarsely. 'Damn.'

'Hold on, we'll call an ambulance.'

'I told him he couldn't photograph the dead. I told him ... as forcefully as I could.'

'He's one of the Japanese tourists in my group. I'll call the ambulance.'

'My outcast friends ... will carry me.' His face twitched into a smile. 'I'm still alive, but they'll carry me on a litter used for the dead.'

Ōtsu seemed to be trying to make a joke to provoke a smile from Mitsuko. Still on her knees, she used the towel she had brought to wipe the grimy blood from Ōtsu's mouth and chin. His bloodied round face looked just like a pierrot's. As Ōtsu had supposed, the men who carried the dead brought along a bamboo litter used for corpses. Seeing this, the group of onlookers fled. When they lifted him on to the litter, Ōtsu gave a cry of pain that sounded like the bleating of a lamb.

'Where will you take him?' Mitsuko asked the men carrying the litter. They said nothing. Mitsuko persisted, and finally one man said, 'To a hospital.'

'Which hospital? Please take him to the university hospital here.'

'Goodbye.' From the litter, Ōtsu seemed to be muttering to himself. 'This ... this is how it should be. My life ... this is how it should be.'

'You're a fool. You're really a fool!' Mitsuko shouted as she watched them carry the litter away. 'Really a fool! You've thrown away your whole life for some Onion! Just because you've tried to imitate your Onion doesn't mean that this world full of hatred and egotism is going to change! You've been chased out of every place you've been, and now in the end you break your neck and get carried away on a dead man's litter. When it comes down to it, you've been completely powerless!'

Crouched to the ground, she pounded her fists futilely on the stone steps.

Awful crowds of people, awful heat. The shouting voices of taxi-drivers, scrambling for passengers. Announcements in Indian English, enunciated as though in anger.

'Please keep an eye on your luggage. In Calcutta if you don't pay attention, someone will just walk away with it.'

Once he had assembled his Japanese tour group in one location and given them instructions, Enami went off to search for the airport bus he had chartered, but he returned without success.

'After all the trouble I went to to make sure it would be here, it hasn't arrived yet. This is what maddens me about India.'

'Will we be on time for our flight?'

'That's not a problem. We still have three hours.'

'This is just like a steam-bath. And all this noise – it hurts all the way down inside my ears.'

'That's Calcutta for you. The city's got a population of nine million, and it's just a mess of people of every nationality.'

Enami never forgot to provide an explanation worthy of a tour guide. It was probably a habit with him by now.

'Miss Naruse, I have to apologize to you. You came all the way to India and didn't get to see a single one of the Buddhist relics.'

'It's all right. Instead of the Buddhist relics, I got to see the river.'

'When we get back to Japan, I'll talk to my company and get them to give you a rebate on your tour costs.'

The television was blaring in the waiting-room, heightening the confusion. People were eager to see the live broadcast of the funeral of the prime minister, Indira Gandhi, which was being conducted that afternoon. The body, decorated with flowers, was placed on a gun-carriage, which set out for the cremation grounds on the banks of the Yamunā River. The route of the funeral cortège and every strategic spot along the way were guarded by throngs of soldiers. From the crowds lining the streets some waved the national flag. Women wiped away tears with the sleeves of their saris.

'And she worked so diligently,' Enami muttered as he turned his face towards the tiny screen.

'Why was she murdered?' Numada asked. 'Was it the religious animosity of the Sikhs?'

'That was the direct cause, yes. But ultimately it was the contradictions inherent in a nation populated by seven hundred million people with different languages and faiths, and the poverty you have all witnessed. And the caste system. She tried to bring some kind of harmony to it all, but in the end she failed.'

The Japanese nodded their heads as Enami exhaled the words in a sigh, but no one listened with real interest. Even Numada, who had asked the question, was thinking of the skies over the forest near Allahābād, the whispering of the wind, the sparkling leaves, and the myna bird he had set free. The women on the tour were jabbering amongst themselves, wondering if the souvenirs they had yet to buy could be purchased at the airport, while Kiguchi was rewrapping the tiny Buddhist image he had finally located in Vārānasī.

'That woman – she's foaming at the mouth.' One of the women jabbed Kiguchi. An old woman was leaning against a wall, her face upturned, her shoulders heaving. A yellow foamy liquid spewed from her mouth. But the Indians walking by her showed no particular surprise and scrambled away.

'She's dying!' the tourist reported to Enami, but after casting a glance towards the old woman, Enami replied, 'People are collapsing everywhere you go in India. You saw them in Delhi and in Vārānasī. One or two hundred people die in the streets each day here in Calcutta.'

'But this is the first time I've seen it happen so close at hand. Can't anyone do something for her?'

'What would you like us to do?' Enami asked angrily. 'This old woman isn't the only one dying in this country!'

His voice was so intense that the Japanese tourists, overwhelmed, shifted their gaze from the old woman and wordlessly turned their faces towards the distant television. The cremation platform, with bricks stacked in three levels; the prime minister's corpse decorated with green eucalyptus leaves, her face covered by a pink scarf. A military band played a solemn funeral march. The premier's son stepped forward, preparing to set fire to the wood. The faces of those in attendance appeared one by one on the screen. The British prime minister, Thatcher, Imelda Marcos, and the profile of Prime Minister Nakasone. The flames shot up. Just as the cloth-shrouded corpses, and the lives they had led, had been consumed in the flames of the pyres along the River Ganges. And yet the survivors in this world would continue to detest one another and contend with one another. The war between Iran and Iraq continued unchecked, civil war raged in Lebanon, and in Brighton terrorists had blown up the hotel where the prime minister was staying, wounding and killing over thirty.

'It's unbearably hot, isn't it?' commented Mitsuko, stepping over beside Isobe. 'You must be worn out.'

'No, not at all. I'm glad I came.' Isobe gave an embarrassed grin.

'At the very least, I'm sure your wife has come back to life inside your heart,' Mitsuko said by way of consolation.

Isobe blinked and lowered his eyes to the ground. As he stood hunched over, it looked as though he was bearing the full weight of his mounting sorrow with his entire body – no, with his entire life.

'What the hell is the bus doing?' Sanjō asked Enami. His exhausted bride was sitting on their trunk. Sanjō seemed not to give a thought to the problems his actions had caused.

'How many hours are we going to have to wait in this heat?'

'What does it matter? This is a part of India, too,' Kiguchi interjected. 'It'll be one of your memories of the place.'

Sanjō looked disgruntled, but he pulled himself together, brought his camera up to his eyes and searched for a photographic subject. He turned the camera towards the old woman leaning against the wall with yellow foam spurting from her mouth, and the shutter clicked over and over again. At that very moment, the crowd suddenly opened a pathway. Two young nuns in grey frocks, a white woman and an Indian woman, approached the old lady, leading two men who carried a litter. They whispered something in Hindi to the old woman, then wiped her vacant face with wet gauze.

'Those nuns work with Mother Teresa,' Enami informed the Japanese. 'I think you must have heard of them. These are the nuns who created the Home for the Dying here. They search out the fallen in Calcutta and care for them until they die.'

'That's pointless,' Sanjō jeered. 'That's not going to get rid of the poor and the beggars throughout India. Seems futile and stupid to me.'

The word 'stupid' reminded Mitsuko of Ōtsu's pathetic life. It was just as Sanjō said: even if Ōtsu carried dying old men and women to the free lodging-houses or to the cremation grounds beside the river, how much good did it really do? But still, these nuns and Ōtsu ...

'I'm a Japanese,' Mitsuko spoke to the Caucasian nun. 'Can I ask why you're doing this?'

'What?' With a look of surprise, the nun opened her blue eyes wide and stared at Mitsuko.

'Why are you doing this?'

Her eyes still brimming with surprise, the nun slowly answered. 'Because, except for this ... there is nothing in this world we can believe in.'

Mitsuko had a hard time hearing whether the nun had said 'except for this' or 'except for him'. If she had said 'except for him', she would be talking about Ōtsu's Onion. The Onion had died many long years ago, but he had been reborn in the lives of other people. Even after nearly two thousand years had passed, he had been reborn in these nuns, and had been reborn in Ōtsu. And just as Ōtsu had been taken off to a hospital on a litter, the nuns likewise disappeared into the river of people.

'Mr Enami!' Mitsuko ran over to Enami and asked, 'Is there any way you can get in touch with that doctor at the university hospital in Vārānasī?'

'What?' Enami was taken aback. 'Is something wrong?'

'A friend of mine was injured day before yesterday and taken to the hospital. The Japanese man you met at the cremation grounds. I'd like to find out how he's doing.'

'Oh, is that all? I can find that out easily. If the bus comes, have them wait just a minute.'

Enami generously made his way through the crowds of people towards a pay-phone. He chattered away for three or four minutes, then hung up the receiver and returned to the group of Japanese tourists, who were tired of waiting for the bus. He gave Mitsuko a sober look and said, 'He was your friend? That Japanese fellow who was hurt?' He swallowed and continued, 'He's in a critical condition. About an hour ago he took a sudden turn for the worse.'

New Directions Paperbooks — A Partial Listing

Walter Abish, *How German Is It*. NDP508.
Ilangô Adigal, *Shilappadikaram*. NDP162
César Aira, *How I Became A Nun*. NDP1043.
Ahmed Ali, *Twilight in Delhi*. NDP782
John Allman, *Curve Away from Stillness*. NDP667.
Alfred Andersch, *Efraim's Book*. NDP779.
Sherwood Anderson, *Poor White*. NDP763
Eugénio de Andrade, *Forbidden Words*.† NDP948.
Wayne Andrews, *The Surrealist Parade*. NDP689.
Guillaume Apollinaire, *Selected Writings*.† NDP310.
Homero Aridjis, *Eyes to See Otherwise*.† NDP942.
Paul Auster, *The Red Notebook*. NDP924.
Gennady Aygi, *Field-Russia*. NDP1085.
Jimmy Santiago Baca, *Martín and Meditations*. NDP648.
Honoré de Balzac, *Colonel Chabert*. NDP847.
Djuna Barnes, *Nightwood*. NDP1049.
Charles Baudelaire, *Flowers of Evil*.† NDP684.
  Paris Spleen. NDP294.
Bei Dao, *At the Sky's Edge*.† NDP934.
  Unlock.† NDP901.
Gottfried Benn, *Primal Vision*.† NDP322.
Nina Berberova, *The Accompanist*. NDP953
  The Book of Happiness. NDP935.
Adolfo Bioy Casares, *A Russian Doll*. NDP745.
Carmel Bird, *The Bluebird Café*. NDP707.
R.P. Blackmur, *Studies in Henry James*. NDP552.
Roberto Bolaño, *By Night in Chile*. NDP975.
  Distant Star. NDP993.
  Last Evenings on Earth. NDP1062.
Wolfgang Borchert, *The Man Outside*. NDP319.
Jorge Luis Borges, *Everything and Nothing*. NDP872.
  Labyrinths. NDP1066.
  Seven Nights. NDP576.
Kay Boyle, *The Crazy Hunter*, NDP769.
  Death of a Man. NDP670.
Kamau Brathwaite, *Ancestors*. NDP902.
  Black + Blues. NDP815.
William Bronk, *Selected Poems*. NDP816.
uddha, *The Dhammapada*. NDP188.
Mikhail Bulgakov, *The Life of Monsieur de Molière*. NDP601.
Basil Bunting, *Complete Poems*. NDP976.
Frederick Busch, *War Babies*. NDP917.
Can Xue, *Blue Light in the Sky*. NDP1039.
Veza Canetti, *The Tortoises*. NDP1074.
Hayden Carruth, *Tell Me Again How ...* NDP677.
Anne Carson, *Glass, Irony and God*. NDP808.
Mircea Cartarescu, *Nostalgia*. NDP1018.
Joyce Cary, *Mister Johnson*. NDP657.
Camilo José Cela, *Mazurka for Two Dead Men*. NDP789.
Louis-Ferdinand Céline, *Journey to the End of Night*. NDP1036.
  Death on the Installment Plan. NDP330.
René Char, *Selected Poems*.† NDP734.
Inger Christensen, *alphabet*. NDP920.
  it. NDP1052.
Chuang Hua, *Crossings*. NDP1076.
Jean Cocteau, *The Holy Terrors*. NDP212.
  The Infernal Machine. NDP235.
Maurice Collis, *Cortes and Montezuma*. NDP884.
Cid Corman, *Nothing/Doing: Selected Poems*. NDP886.
Gregory Corso, *The Happy Birthday of Death*. NDP86.
Julio Cortázar, *Cronopios and Famas*. NDP873.
  62: A Model Kit. NDP894.
Robert Creeley, *Life & Death*. NDP903.
  Just in Time: Poems 1984-1994. NDP927.
Edward Dahlberg, *Because I Was Flesh*. NDP227.
Alain Daniélou, *The Way to the Labyrinth*. NDP634.
Guy Davenport, *DaVinci's Bicycle*. NDP842.
  7 Greeks. NDP799.
Osamu Dazai, *No Longer Human*. NDP357.
  The Setting Sun. NDP258.
Madame De Lafayette, *The Princess of Cleves*. NDP660.
Tibor Déry, *Love & Other Stories*. NDP1013.
H.D., *Collected Poems*. NDP611.
  Hippolytus Temporizes & Ion. NDP967.
  Trilogy. NDP866.
Robert Duncan, *Bending the Bow*. NDP255.
  Ground Work. NDP1030.
Richard Eberhart, *The Long Reach*. NDP565.
Eça de Queirós, *The Crime of Father Amaro*. NDP961.
  The Maias. NDP1080.
William Empson, *Seven Types of Ambiguity*. NDP204.
Shusaku Endo, *Deep River*. NDP820.
  The Samurai. NDP839.
Jenny Erpenbeck, *The Old Child*. NDP1017.
  The Book of Words. NDP1092.

Caradoc Evans, *Nothing to Pay*. NDP800.
Gavin Ewart, *Selected Poems*. NDP655.
Hans Faverey, *Against the Forgetting*. NDP969.
Lawrence Ferlinghetti, *A Coney Island of the Mind*. NDP74.
  A Far Rockaway of the Heart. NDP871.
  Americus, Book One. NDP1024.
Thalia Field, *Point and Line*. NDP899.
  Incarnate. NDP996.
Ronald Firbank, *Caprice*. NDP764.
F. Scott Fitzgerald, *The Crack-Up*. NDP757.
  The Jazz Age. NDP830.
Gustave Flaubert, *Dictionary of Accepted Ideas*. NDP230.
  A Simple Heart. NDP819.
Forrest Gander, *Eye Against Eye*. NDP1026.
  Torn Awake. NDP926.
John Gardner, *Nickel Mountain*. NDP1086
  October Light. NDP1019
  The Sunlight Dialogues. NDP1051
Romain Gary, *The Life Before Us*. NDP604.
William Gerhardie, *Futility*. NDP722.
Goethe, *Faust (Part I)*. NDP70.
Henry Green, *Pack My Bag*. NDP984.
Allen Grossman, *Sweet Youth*. NDP947.
Martin Grzimek, *Heartstop*. NDP583.
Lars Gustafsson, *The Tale of a Dog*. NDP868.
Sam Hamill, *The Infinite Moment*. NDP586.
John Hawkes, *The Beetle Leg*. NDP239.
  The Blood Oranges. NDP338.
  Second Skin. NDP1027.
Robert E. Helbling, *Heinrich von Kleist*. NDP390.
William Herrick, *That's Life*. NDP596.
Hermann Hesse, *Siddhartha*. NDP65.
Yoel Hoffmann, *Katschen & The Book of Joseph*. NDP875.
Gert Hofmann, *Lichtenberg &the Little Flower Girl*. NDP1075.
Susan Howe, *The Midnight*. NDP956.
  My Emily Dickinson. NDP1088.
Hsieh Ling-Yün, *The Mountain Poems*. NDP928.
Bohumil Hrabal, *I Served the King of England*. NDP1067.
Vicente Huidobro, *The Selected Poetry*. NDP520.
Qurratulain Hyder, *River of Fire*. NDP952.
Christopher Isherwood, *The Berlin Stories*. NDP134
Fleur Jaeggy, *SS Proleterka*. NDP758.
  Sweet Days of Discipline. NDP758.
Henry James, *The Sacred Fount*. NDP790.
Gustav Janouch, *Conversations with Kafka*. NDP313.
Alfred Jarry, *Ubu Roi*. NDP105.
Robinson Jeffers, *Cawdor and Medea*. NDP293.
B.S. Johnson, *Albert Angelo*. NDP628.
  House Mother Normal. NDP617.
Gabriel Josipovici, *In a Hotel Garden*. NDP801.
James Joyce, *Finnegans Wake: A Symposium*. NDP331.
  Stephen Hero. NDP133.
Franz Kafka, *Amerika: The Man Who Disappeared*. NDP981.
Bilge Karasu, *The Garden of the Departed Cats*. NDP965.
Mary Karr, *The Devil's Tour*. NDP768.
Bob Kaufman, *The Ancient Rain*. NDP514.
John Keene, *Annotations*. NDP809.
Alexander Kluge, *Cinema Stories*. NDP1098.
  The Devil's Blind Spot. NDP1099.
Heinrich von Kleist, *Prince Friedrich of Homburg*. NDP462.
Kono Taeko, *Toddler-Hunting*. NDP867.
Deszö Kosztolányi, *Anna Édes*. NDP772.
László Krasznahorkai, *The Melancholy of Resistance*. NDP936.
  War and War. NDP1031.
Rüdiger Kremer, *The Color of the Snow*. NDP743.
Miroslav Krleža, *On the Edge of Reason*. NDP810.
Shimpei Kusano, *Asking Myself/Answering Myself*. NDP566.
P. Lal, ed., *Great Sanskrit Plays*. NDP142.
Tommaso Landolfi, *Gogol's Wife*. NDP155.
James Laughlin, *Poems New and Selected*. NDP857.
  The Way It Wasn't. NDP1047.
Comte de Lautréamont, *Maldoror*. NDP207.
D.H. Lawrence, *Quetzalcoatl*. NDP864.
Irving Layton, *Selected Poems*. NDP431.
Christine Lehner, *Expecting*. NDP572.
Siegfried Lenz, *The German Lesson*. NDP618.
Denise Levertov, *The Life Around Us*. NDP843.
  Making Peace. NDP1023.
  Selected Poems. NDP968.
Li Ch'ing Chao, *Complete Poems*. NDP492.
Li Po, *The Selected Poems*. NDP823.
Clarice Lispector, *The Hour of the Star*. NDP733.
  Soulstorm. NDP671.
Luljeta Lleshanaku, *Fresco*. NDP941.
Federico García Lorca, *The Cricket Sings*.† NDP506.

For a complete listing request a free catalog from New Directions, 80 Eighth Avenue,
New York, NY 10011; or visit our website, www.ndpublishing.com

†Bilingual

Five Plays. NDP506.
In Search of Duende.† NDP858.
Selected Poems.† NDP1010.
Nathaniel Mackey, Splay Anthem. NDP1032.
Xavier de Maistre,Voyage Around My Room. NDP791.
Stéphane Mallarmé, Mallarmé in Prose. NDP904.
Selected Poetry and Prose.† NDP529.
A Tomb for Anatole. NDP1014.
Oscar Mandel, The Book of Elaborations. NDP643.
Abby Mann, Judgment at Nuremberg. NDP950.
Javier Marías, All Souls. NDP905.
A Heart So White. NDP937.
Tomorrow in the Battle Think On Me. NDP923.
Your Face Tomorrow. NDP1081.
Written Lives. NDP1068.
Carole Maso, The Art Lover. NDP1040.
Enrique Vila-Matas, Bartleby & Co. NDP1063.
Montano's Malady. NDP1064.
Bernadette Mayer, A Bernadette Mayer Reader. NDP739.
Michael McClure, Rain Mirror. NDP887.
Carson McCullers, The Member of the Wedding. NDP1038.
Thomas Merton, Bread in the Wilderness. NDP840.
Gandhi on Non-Violence. NDP1090.
New Seeds of Contemplation. NDP1091
Thoughts on the East. NDP802.
Henri Michaux, Ideograms in China. NDP929.
Selected Writings.† NDP263.
Dunya Mikhail, The War Works Hard. NDP1006.
Henry Miller, The Air-Conditioned Nightmare. NDP587.
The Henry Miller Reader. NDP269.
Into the Heart of Life. NDP728.
Yukio Mishima, Confessions of a Mask. NDP253.
Death in Midsummer. NDP215.
Frédéric Mistral, The Memoirs. NDP632.
Teru Miyamoto, Kinshu: Autumn Brocade. NDP1055.
Eugenio Montale, Selected Poems.† NDP193.
Paul Morand, Fancy Goods (tr. by Ezra Pound). NDP567.
Vladimir Nabokov, Laughter in the Dark. NDP1045.
The Real Life of Sebastian Knight. NDP432.
Pablo Neruda, The Captain's Verses.† NDP991.
Love Poems. NDP1094.
Residence on Earth.† NDP992.
Spain in Our Hearts. NDP1025.
New Directions Anthol. Classical Chinese Poetry. NDP1001.
Robert Nichols, Arrival. NDP437.
Griselda Ohannessian, Once: As It Was. NDPi054.
Charles Olson, Selected Writings. NDP231.
Toby Olson, Human Nature. NDP897.
George Oppen, Selected Poems. NDP970.
Wilfred Owen, Collected Poems. NDP210.
José Pacheco, Battles in the Desert. NDP637.
Michael Palmer, The Company of Moths. NDP1003.
The Promises of Glass. NDP922.
Nicanor Parra, Antipoems: New and Selected. NDP603.
Boris Pasternak, Safe Conduct. NDP77.
Kenneth Patchen, Collected Poems. NDP284.
Memoirs of a Shy Pornographer. NDP879.
Octavio Paz, The Collected Poems.† NDP719.
Sunstone.† NDP735.
A Tale of Two Gardens: Poems from India. NDP841.
Victor Pelevin, Omon Ra. NDP851.
A Werewolf Problem in Central Russia. NDP959.
Saint-John Perse, Selected Poems.† NDP547.
Po Chü-i, The Selected Poems. NDP880.
Ezra Pound, ABC of Reading. NDP89.
The Cantos. NDP824.
Confucius to Cummings. NDP126.
A Draft of XXX Cantos. NDP690.
Personae. NDP697.
The Pisan Cantos. NDP977.
The Spirit of Romance. NDP1028.
Caradog Prichard, One Moonlit Night. NDP835.
Qian Zhongshu, Fortress Besieged. NDP966.
Raymond Queneau, The Blue Flowers. NDP595.
Exercises in Style. NDP513.
Gregory Rabassa, If This Be Treason. NDP1044.
Mary de Rachewiltz, Ezra Pound, Father and Teacher.
NDP1029.
Margaret Randall, Part of the Solution. NDP350.
Raja Rao, Kanthapura. NDP224.
Herbert Read, The Green Child. NDP208.
Kenneth Rexroth, 100 Poems from the Chinese. NDP192.
Selected Poems. NDP581.
Rainer Maria Rilke, Poems from the Book of Hours.† NDP408.
Possibility of Being. NDP436.
Where Silence Reigns. NDP464.
Arthur Rimbaud, Illuminations.† NDP56.

A Season in Hell & The Drunken Boat.† NDP97.
Edouard Roditi, The Delights of Turkey. NDP487.
Jerome Rothenberg, Pre-faces & Other Writings. NDP511.
Triptych. NDP1077.
Ralf Rothmann, Knife Edge. NDP744.
Nayantara Sahgal, Mistaken Identity. NDP742.
Ihara Saikaku, The Life of an Amorous Woman. NDP270.
St. John of the Cross, The Poems of St. John ... † NDP341.
William Saroyan, The Daring Young Man ... NDP852.
Jean-Paul Sartre, Baudelaire. NDP233.
Nausea. NDP1073.
The Wall (Intimacy). NDP272.
Delmore Schwartz, In Dreams Begin Responsibilities. NDP454.
Screeno: Stories and Poems. NDP985.
Peter Dale Scott, Coming to Jakarta. NDP672.
W.G. Sebald, The Emigrants. NDP853.
The Rings of Saturn. NDP881.
Vertigo. NDP925.
Aharon Shabtai, J'Accuse. NDP957.
Hasan Shah, The Dancing Girl. NDP777.
Merchant-Prince Shattan, Manimekhalaï. NDP674.
Kazuko Shiraishi, Let Those Who Appear. NDP940.
C.H. Sisson, Selected Poems. NDP826.
Stevie Smith, Collected Poems. NDP562.
Novel on Yellow Paper. NDP778.
Gary Snyder, Look Out. NDP949.
The Real Work: Interviews & Talks. NDP499.
Turtle Island. NDP306.
Gustaf Sobin, Breaths' Burials. NDP781.
Voyaging Portraits. NFP651.
Muriel Spark, All the Stories of Muriel Spark. NDP933.
The Ghost Stories of Muriel Spark. NDP963.
Loitering With Intent. NDP918.
Symposium. NDP1053.
Enid Starkie, Arthur Rimbaud. NDP254.
Stendhal, Three Italian Chronicles. NDP704.
Richard Swartz, A House in Istria. NDP1078.
Antonio Tabucchi, It's Getting Later All the Time. NDP1042.
Pereira Declares. NDP848.
Requiem: A Hallucination. NDP944.
Nathaniel Tarn, Lyrics for the Bride of God. NDP391.
Yoko Tawada, Facing the Bridge. NDP1079.
Where Europe Begins. NDP1079.
Emma Tennant, Strangers: A Family Romance. NDP960.
Terrestrial Intelligence: International Fiction Now . NDP1034.
Dylan Thomas, A Child's Christmas in Wales. NDP1096
Selected Poems 1934-1952. NDP958.
Tian Wen: A Chinese Book of Origins.† NDP624.
Uwe Timm, The Invention of Curried Sausage. NDP854.
Morenga. NDP1016.
Charles Tomlinson, Selected Poems. NDP855.
Federico Tozzi, Love in Vain. NDP921.
Tomas Tranströmer, The Great Enigma. NDP1050.
Yuko Tsushima, The Shooting Gallery. NDP846.
Leonid Tsypkin, Summer in Baden-Baden. NDP962.
Tu Fu, The Selected Poems. NDP675.
Niccolò Tucci, The Rain Came Last. NDP688.
Frederic Tuten, Adventures of Mao on Long March. NDP1022.
Dubravka Ugrešić, The Museum of Unconditional Surrender.
NDP932.
Paul Valéry, Selected Writings.† NDP184.
Luis F. Verissimo, Borges & the Eternal Orangutans. NDP1012.
Elio Vittorini, Conversations in Sicily. NDP907.
Rosmarie Waldrop, Blindsight. NDP971.
Curves to the Apple. NDP1046.
Robert Walser, The Assistant. NDP1071.
Robert Penn Warren, At Heaven's Gate. NDP588.
Wang Wei, The Selected Poems. NDP1041.
Eliot Weinberger, An Elemental Thing. NDP1072.
What Happened Here. NDP1020.
Nathanael West, Miss Lonelyhearts. NDP125.
Paul West, A Fifth of November. NDP1002.
Tennessee Williams, The Glass Menagerie. NDP874.
Memoirs. NDP1048.
Mister Paradise and Other One Act Plays. NDP1007.
Selected Letters: Volumes I & II. NDP951 & NDP1083.
A Streetcar Named Desire. NDP998.
William Carlos Williams, Asphodel ... NDP794.
Collected Poems: Volumes I & II. NDP730 & NDP731.
In the American Grain. NDP53.
Paterson: Revised Edition. NDP806.
Wisdom Books:
The Wisdom of St. Francis. NDP477.
The Wisdom of the Taoists. NDP509.
The Wisdom of the Zen Masters. NDP415.
World Beat: International Poetry Now From New Directions.
NDP1033.

For a complete listing request a free catalog from New Directions, 80 Eighth Avenue
New York, NY 10011; or visit our website, www.ndpublishing.com

†Bilingual